THE QUIET YOU CARRY

Nikki Barthelmess

THE QUIET YOU CARRY

Nikki Barthelmess

Mendota Heights, Minnesota

First Edition
First Printing, 2019

Book design by Jake Nordby
Cover design by Jake Nordby
Cover images by Pixabay
Interior images by phyZick/Shutterstock

Flux, an imprint of North Star Editions, Inc.

Library of Congress Cataloging-in-Publication Data (pending)
ISBN 978-1-63583-028-6

Flux
North Star Editions, Inc.
2297 Waters Drive
Mendota Heights, MN 55120
www.fluxnow.com

Printed in the United States of America

For Robby. Thank you for loving me, not despite what I've gone through, but because of who it's made me.

BEFORE

*D*ad's door slams. He locks it, too, by the sound of it. He shuts himself in his room with his wife—leaving me in the dark hallway with this woman, this stranger. Her shape blurs before me, and I reach out to the nearby wall to steady myself.

"I'm with Child Protective Services," the woman tells me. "It's going to be okay, Victoria, but you have to come with me."

I stare at the back of my dad's closed bedroom door and wipe my tear-soaked face. "I don't understand," I plead. "I didn't do anything. I didn't—"

"Shh." The woman reaches out to put a hand on my shoulder but drops it when I flinch. Dad touched my shoulder. Just minutes before, Dad touched my shoulder and my hair. He came close, too close, and I froze.

My stepsister Sarah is asleep in her bedroom at the end of the dim hallway, completely unaware of everything happening outside her door.

The woman clears her throat. "My name is Fran." She wears a puffy black jacket and jeans. Her gray hair is tied back in a loose bun, and strands slip onto her face. She doesn't look tired, even though it's so late. I glance into the kitchen and see the microwave clock reading 3:08 a.m.

"I didn't do anything," I say again.

"I understand that's what you told the police officer, but your father is telling a different story. I want to hear your side. You can tell us what happened, what's been happening. And you can press charges—"

"Press charges?" I interrupt. "No. Nothing happened. I already told *him* that." I wave maniacally toward the police officer sitting on our couch, who's probably writing notes about his conversations with me and my dad. "I'm not going to press charges, because whatever you think happened, didn't. My dad and I had a misunderstanding." I let out a breath and close my eyes. I have to think clearly. I have to make sense of this.

It happened so fast, after Dad left the room, and I closed and locked the door. Tiffany banged on it moments later, saying my father was ready to talk to me. Instead, when I opened the door, Dad pushed Tiffany aside, grabbed me by the arm and dragged me outside. No jacket, no shoes. Locked me out in the cold. A few minutes later, blue-and-red police lights shone through the dark residential street.

Sitting on the curb, shivering, I watched as the police officer got out of his squad car and sat next to me.

"My name is Officer McDonnell. I'm with the Reno P.D." He reached a hand out to shake and I grasped it, wiping tears off my face with my other hand. "Are you hurt?"

I shook my head no.

The man's voice was deep and he spoke slowly as he asked me more questions. I could focus on his voice, but not the words he was saying.

I shook my head again. Told him my dad and I had a misunderstanding.

"Did he touch you? Did your father try to make you do anything you didn't want to?"

"No, no, no. Nothing happened!" I was yelling. Beyond the officer, the door creaked open to reveal Dad and Tiffany. Dad gave her a meaningful look, like the fact that I was shouting proved this was my fault.

Officer McDonnell stood, seemingly sizing my dad up. He told him it was pretty cold outside, being December, for me to be locked out there. And late, too. He ushered me in, past Dad and Tiffany, and told me to stay in my bedroom. I waited until the sound of his footsteps became softer before cracking my door open to peer outside. Officer McDonnell was in the living room, pulling a small notepad from his pocket. Dad, dressed now with his hair combed, stood by the couch. He started talking quietly, calmly. I couldn't make out his words. He didn't seem as angry as before. Maybe he would talk to me. Maybe he would look at me.

Maybe he would stop whatever was happening.

Stop everything.

But instead another stranger stormed through the front door—this woman with messy gray hair and deep lines on her face, brandishing a Child Protective Services badge for my dad to see. *Fran.* Officer McDonnell thanked her for coming and motioned for Dad to give them some space. Dad scowled and obeyed, waiting in the kitchen as Fran and the officer spoke in hushed voices in the dining room. I blew on my hands, still numb from outside, as I strained to hear what was going on.

Eventually, after seemingly having made some kind

of decision, Officer McDonnell met Dad in the kitchen. I watched them whisper before Dad stormed to his bedroom, not bothering to look at me as he went.

Officer McDonnell shook his head in Dad's direction with a look of disgust and hung back by the door, seemingly keeping an eye on all of us.

I sat in silence, watching Fran write in a notebook. Time stretched on as my world fell apart around me.

Now, a few moments or a century later, the lights are still on in Dad's bedroom, but I can't hear him and Tiffany talking.

"I need you to gather your things." Fran says, her no-nonsense tone yanking me back to the present. "Nothing valuable, nothing that could be stolen. Just enough clothes to get you by for a week."

"What do you mean I can't bring anything valuable? Where are we going?"

My breathing quickens, faster and faster. I suck in all the air I can, and it's not enough. I stop suddenly. Close my eyes. I can't breathe. I can't think. I can't anything. "I'm sorry—what if I just say I'm sorry?"

I raise a hand, ready to bang on Dad's door. I can apologize. Tell him that I misunderstood. That he doesn't have to make me go. Couldn't we pretend it never happened? Couldn't we forget?

Fran shakes her head slightly, casts her eyes down for a moment.

I stumble back from the door.

Everything's a blur. I don't know what Dad told his wife.

What he told the police. I don't know *anything*. Except Fran's saying I can't stay here.

I wipe away a fresh batch of tears. "I don't have a suitcase. My dad keeps the luggage in his closet."

Fran produces a black garbage bag from her purse. She hands it to me. I inhale deeply and walk into my room, passing a photo collage of my best friend Jess and me. Fran follows.

"Where are we going?" I ask again, suddenly realizing it might be too far to walk to school. My dad never let me get my license. He liked driving me around.

She sighs, seeing my confusion. "There aren't a lot of options at this hour, unfortunately. Your father said you don't have any other family, is that right?"

I nod. My grandparents are dead; both of my parents were the only children in their families. All the family I have is in this house.

"What about friends? A teacher who you're close with, who might consider taking you in while we figure this out?"

I shake my head vigorously. I'm not telling anyone I know about this. No matter where this woman wants to take me. There's no way.

Fran frowns, looking like she's sorry for me.

"Well, then we'll head to my office, you can sleep on the couch, and then by mid-morning I hope to have secured a placement for you."

"Why can't I stay here?"

"Your parents don't want you staying, and even if they

did, at this point we couldn't really allow you to stay until after some kind of investigation."

I let it slide that Fran called Tiffany and Dad my "parents." My stepmom, Tiffany, wouldn't dream of treating me like I was actually her daughter.

Fran pauses, her eyes narrowing as she seems to think over what she wants to say next.

"Your father is very upset, deeply agitated. He's accusing you of"—Fran hesitates, the many wrinkles around her mouth deepening as she frowns—"well, we can talk about that later. The point is, in his anger he locked you, a minor, out of the house in the middle of the night. With no coat. That's unacceptable. We can't allow you to stay here."

"Winter break ends in two weeks. How will I get to school?" The words tumble out of me. "I'm a senior. I have to keep my grades up. I just got early acceptance to UNR. I can't miss any school."

Fran exhales. She looks at the time on her phone, and then back up at me. "Don't worry about it now; we don't know that you'll miss any school. A lot's up in the air until I can find you a foster home."

Cold dread creeps its way down my chest to the pit of my stomach. *Foster home.* I don't realize I've echoed the words aloud until Fran nods.

"We can talk about it in the car," she says, firmly this time. "Come on, pack some clothes. Hurry."

I reach for my cell phone, plugged into its charger on the top of my dresser.

"Nothing valuable," Fran tells me. "I'm sorry. You have to leave it."

I drop the phone, letting it smack back down on the dresser loudly. I open drawers and grab as much as I can stuff in the garbage bag. I wish I had done laundry earlier. I thought I'd have time tomorrow. I didn't think I'd be leaving in the middle of the night. I didn't think my own father would kick me out. I head to my nightstand and take out my mother's letter, the one she wrote me before she died years ago, and put it in my pocket.

Back in the hallway, I hesitate outside Sarah's room. "Can I say goodbye?" I ask Fran. "My stepsister, she's in there, asleep. Can I tell her where I'm going?"

A touch of sympathy flashes in Fran's eyes. Hers are green, I realize when the light catches them, like mine and Dad's.

"Your father won't allow it," she says. "We have to go."

I stand with my hand on Sarah's doorknob, stunned.

I open my mouth, but no words come out. Fran leans forward, like she might try putting her hand on my shoulder. Instinctively, I back away.

Fran looks at the time on her cell phone again. Like this is just another night for her, like my world isn't falling apart in front of her eyes.

Fran clears her throat. "This is frightening and awful, I know, but we have to go, and you can't say goodbye. We can talk more in the car."

But this is my home.

Without meaning to, I head toward the living room. I

watch TV on that couch, with my dad. Even the documentaries he rages at for being unrealistic, he sometimes puts up with—for me. I stare into the dining room. I eat dinner at that table, with my family. The constant arguments, the silent treatment, Tiffany's disgusting meatloaf—none of it is great, but it's mine.

I stumble back to my room, my eyes landing on the bed with the covers strewn off. I'm trapped again, feeling what I felt earlier. Dad pinning me down, me crying, trying to claw my way out from under him.

The space around my heart and lungs gets tighter, my bedroom walls seem like they are closing me in.

This can't be happening.

Wildly I look around, seeing but not seeing.

The pictures on the walls. My cell phone. My book collection. Everything I own. My whole life.

This isn't real. It's a nightmare, and I just need to wake up. I blink rapidly, pinch the inside of my wrist. *Snap out of this.* Please don't be real. *Please.*

But instead of my pillows and the light streaming from my window to warm my closed eyelids and the assurance that I'm safe in my bed, waking up, all I have is Fran. Clicking her tongue, waiting for me.

In a daze, I follow Fran back into the hallway, through the living room and out the door.

CHAPTER
ONE

Two weeks later

Silver Valley High School is definitely nothing like my old school in Reno.

For starters, everyone here just kind of moseys from place to place, like they can't be bothered to show up on time. At home, kids packed tightly on the right side, rushing in one direction so everyone on the other side could do the same. Here, they all walk wherever they like, their footsteps a constant thud on the linoleum floor, stopping only at the most inconvenient of times—like when I'm about to smack into someone's back.

Stepping around and out of the way, I stop to glance at the paper in my hands. My class schedule for the second semester of senior year. I've got history, AP English, physics, and calculus. If I stay here, that is. Maybe my new social worker, Mindy, will grace me with her presence again. Maybe she'll find me *a more suitable placement* back in civilization, at least until I graduate in five months.

Trophy cases holding 4-H awards and plaques for state championship-winning basketball teams line the blue walls of the only hallway in the entire school. And yet the walk to my locker is a long one. Because all the students are staring—every Wrangler-and-cowboy-boot-wearing one of them stands at their blue lockers watching me.

"Who is she?" I hear whispered as I walk by. A pretty brunette who looks like the kind of girl you'd see in a shampoo commercial giggles into her friend's ear as I pass by. I swat my unruly auburn hair out of my face, stuff my schedule in the pocket of my skinny jeans—not Wranglers—and pull the straps of my tattered backpack, the one my new foster mother Connie got me with the "measly stipend" the state pays her for taking me in. What a joke to call her any type of mother, rather than someone who takes money from the government for letting foster kids live with her. Not to mention the house rules. We have to let her search our bags whenever we enter or leave the house and ask permission before we so much as go to the bathroom.

The bell rings. I stop at locker one hundred and ninety-nine, as in I'm the one hundred and ninety-ninth student who goes here. I open it and in goes everything but a binder, with a notebook and a couple pencils. A guy with floppy blond hair, really white teeth, and a letterman's jacket smiles at me from the locker next door. "Hey, New Girl."

I nod at him but don't say anything, and instead rush to room four for history.

At the front of the room, behind a tattered wooden desk, a balding man with a white beard and round gut smiles widely as I slip into his classroom. "Victoria!" he says. "Welcome, welcome! The name's Mr. Gordon, but you can call me Santa. Everyone else does."

My face goes hot as students begin to shuffle in around me. There are only about fifteen of them, and again, they're all looking at me.

"You know, because I look like Saint Nick," puffy-cheeked and smiling Mr. Gordon continues with a belly laugh.

"I get it." I look back down at my books. "Uh, where should I sit?"

"Here's a seat for you, right up here in the front," Mr. Gordon says, indicating the empty seat next to the door. I move there quickly.

Mr. Gordon laughs. "Now that's the kind of excitement for learning we like to see here, Ms. Parker!"

I look back at him, my notebook suspended over my desk. He knows my first and last name before even meeting me.

I sit down slowly, hoping Mr. Gordon doesn't see the panic in my eyes. The fear that he knows more than my full name. That he somehow knows why I moved here. A few more students walk through the open door to their seats. Mr. Gordon clears his throat and smiles, but it doesn't reach his eyes.

"Well," he says, still looking at me, "I'm sure you'll find Silver Valley High different from your old school in the big city, but just as good. And we do have our own charms."

Reno, the big city? On what planet? I nod.

There's a window on the left, behind Floppy Hair,

Shampoo Commercial, and a few more jocks. On the other side of the parking lot, in an open grassy area, the janitor, driving a humongous green tractor, moves stacks of hay.

Mr. Gordon clears his throat again and speaks up so the whole class can hear him. "Speaking of charm, how many of you lovely ladies have asked a young man to the Valentine's Day dance?" Mr. Gordon, standing, picks up a dry eraser from the whiteboard ledge and tosses it from one of his hands to the other. He looks at me, as he explains. "It's not Sadie Hawkins, per se, but we teachers thought it would be fun to use that little twist for good ol' V-Day." He looks up, back to addressing the rest of the class. "Now you know what we guys have to go through all the time!"

The girl sitting at my left snorts. "Isn't Sadie Hawkins sexist?" she asks without raising her hand. She flips a long, black curl off her shoulder before adjusting her letterman's jacket. "That was rhetorical, because the answer is 'Of course it is.'"

Mr. Gordon smiles at her. "Well, Ms. Martinez, what could possibly be sexist about empowering young women to choose a date for themselves? For a dance that we—"

"Well, *Santa*, I'm glad you asked." She grins right back at him. "First off, who says girls need a stupid dance to give us permission to ask a guy on a date? We're not in the stone age." The girl leans forward over her desk. "I can ask a guy to a dance anytime I want," she says matter-of-factly. "Second, wasn't Sadie Hawkins something created in the thirties as a joke or comic strip or something where unmarried women chased the bachelors in town and married the one they caught?"

From a few seats to the left in the row behind us, Floppy Hair joins in. "And where'd you hear that, Christina, *Ms.* magazine?" He scrunches up his nose and smiles at Christina when she turns to face him, but she rolls her eyes and looks away. The burly guy sitting next to Floppy Hair guffaws, and Shampoo Commercial and her friend from earlier giggle.

"No, Wikipedia." Christina smirks and turns back to face forward. "Although I'm impressed a Neanderthal like yourself, Alex, knows what *Ms.* magazin*e* is."

Mr. Gordon chuckles. "Okay, okay, kids. That'll teach the school to try to incorporate some girl power. In any case, you have about a month to figure out your dates before the dance, if you choose to go. Let's get to today's lesson, the opening of a new section on slavery and abolitionism." Mr. Gordon sets the eraser back on the whiteboard. "A new semester, a new text book. When I call your name, come pick up your copy." He sweeps his arm toward three piles of what looks like the biggest book I've ever seen stacked on his desk.

The class groans collectively. Except me. I like history. It's nice to read about awful things that have happened in the past and know that people keep living.

"Mr. Jackson," Mr. Gordon calls. Alex stands and walks over, drumming his fingertips on Christina's desk as he passes. She makes a point to not look at him as she turns toward me.

"Pssst," Christina whispers. "I'm Christina."

"I know," I say. "I'm Victoria."

"I know." She smiles.

"Ms. Parker," Mr. Gordon calls. I nod at Christina and stand to get my book.

After class, Christina smiles at me as she puts her book in her bag. I grab my stuff, heading for the door. She follows me into the hallway. "Hey, Victoria!"

I turn to acknowledge her, and we both keep walking. "Do you want to sit with me and my friends at lunch?" she asks.

An image of me sitting with the pretty, confident, and definitely *chatty* Christina flashes in my mind. She leans over the lunch table and smiles at me like we're best friends. *Where are you from? Why did you move here?*

I tug a wayward curl out of my face and tuck it behind my ear, looking away. "You know, I think I have some paperwork I have to do in the office. Some stuff my mom and I didn't get to when she dropped me off. But maybe some other time."

The lie slips off my lips the second the thought comes. I stop breathing for a second but see in Christina's expression that she believes me. Good. The lie is easier than telling the truth.

Dad's face pops into my head. His lie.

The hallway around me is replaced with the four walls in my bedroom and Dad in between me and the door, coming closer, trapping me.

My jaw tenses. I don't know why he did what he did; he

probably doesn't either. It was a misunderstanding. It had to have been. But I can't think about it because I feel my face reddening, my palms sweating. I don't know. Maybe I don't want to.

From across the hall, Alex calls out. "Chris!" He and some other guy—he's tall, slim, and has light brown hair—try to wave Christina over.

I exhale, thankful for the distraction. I look at them and then back at Christina, saying nothing. She misreads my expression.

"Okay, I give Alex a hard time, but he's not all that bad." Christina's big, dark eyes dart away as she smiles sheepishly. "And mostly I only hang out with him because he's friends with Kale, the other guy over there."

I look back at Alex and his friend, Kale I presume, and he smiles at me. Or at least I think he does. I raise my hand, and then let it drop. Overly friendly people in small towns is another thing about my new life I'll have to get used to.

"Well, I should get to class. See you later."

"Bye!" Christina calls after me, since I'm already a quarter of the way to my locker.

When lunchtime rolls around, I explore outside the back of the school, past the woodshop classroom and near a tool shed, about as far as I can get without going off campus. I don't have an off-campus pass. My new foster mother wouldn't sign for it. There's too much trouble I could get into, Connie said, listing a bunch of crimes former foster girls of hers committed when given just an inch of freedom. Shoplifting. Doing and selling drugs. Prostitution, even.

I kick the dirt in front of me. That's pretty much all there is out here other than a few cottonwood trees. Dirt, mounds of it, a few tumbleweeds—of course, there would be—and a lone wooden bench. No Christina asking me why I won't eat lunch with her. No new friends trying to get to know me.

I sit on the bench and unwrap my tuna sandwich. I lift it to my lips, and then set it back in my lap. Minutes pass. I wait for the bell to ring, alone.

CHAPTER
TWO

I consider knocking as I step over the Welcome Home mat outside the front door after I walk home from school.

I bet Connie would like that. Instead, I turn the knob and walk right in, heading straight for the foster kids' room. She calls it the girls' dormitory, weird as that is.

"Hold it!" Connie calls from her favorite spot, sunken into the large couch in the living room. She pulls her bare feet off the coffee table and stands, smoothing her gray sweatpants as she does.

"Where do you think you're going?"

"My—uh, the bedroom," I answer.

But then, down the hall, the bathroom door opens and out steps my social worker, Mindy. I gasp, a thousand questions flooding my mind. I haven't seen her in two weeks, not since I woke up on the tattered, urine-smelling couch in Fran's office with Mindy standing over me, introducing herself as my social worker.

"I thought Fran was my social worker." I sat up, rubbing my sore back. Blinking my blood-shot eyes, dry from all the crying.

"She's the emergency response worker. Whole different job. I'm your case worker, and I'll be your point of contact with CPS from now on."

My eyes rolled at the word *job*. This, Mindy just reminded me, is her job. Fran's job. A bunch of people's job. Their work is how they see this, I thought, not my life that they're messing with.

I stood and followed her out of the office. Fran was nowhere to be found, gone to take some other kid away from their family or something. Mindy drove me out of Reno to this joke of a town I'd never heard of.

"Hello, Victoria." Mindy smooths a piece of her dirty-blonde hair away from her face. "Just who I'm here to see."

I step forward. "Have you talked to my dad? Am I going ho—"

Connie waves a thick hand in front of her. "Have a seat."

I rush by Connie, take my backpack off and sit on the loveseat. Mindy walks around me, glances at the small love seat and then the space next to Connie on the other couch.

She sits with Connie, setting her large purse full of paperwork and binders at her feet. Connie drags her legs out of the way to make more room.

Behind me, giggling noises come from Annie's bedroom, loud enough for me to hear over whatever cartoons she's watching in there. Since she's Connie's real kid, the one she actually gives a damn about, she gets her own room while all three foster kids share one. Sometimes Connie keeps four foster kids all in the same room.

I lean forward and open my mouth to ask Mindy again when I'm going home.

Connie clears her throat and my words evaporate. She looks at Mindy. "Would you like something to drink?"

Mindy adjusts herself in her seat. "Water would be lovely, thank you."

Connie hauls herself up and makes her way through the living room to the kitchen. Standing at the fridge, she doesn't offer me anything. She returns with two bottles of water and hands one to Mindy. My leg bounces and I look back and forth between the two of them as they take their sweet time. Mindy opens her water and takes a sip. She sets the bottle on the ratty wooden end table and turns to face me, folding her hands neatly in her lap.

"So, how was your first day of school?"

I blink quickly. "Fine. So, what's going on with my family? Have you talked to my dad? Does he want me to come home?"

Mindy leans back into the couch and shoots Connie a side-glance. Connie's face falls, but she quickly readjusts when she sees me looking at her. Mindy exhales. "Well, no, Victoria, he doesn't."

I hold my breath and wait for her to say something else, but Mindy just sighs quietly and watches me. Heat rises in my body.

Mindy clears her throat. "Do you want to tell me about what happened with your dad? Why you're here?"

I dig my fingertips into the armrest and squeeze the

fabric. "Nothing happened," I push out from my gritted teeth. "Nothing. It was just a misunderstanding."

From the other side of Mindy, Connie sighs, folding her thin lips into each other.

Mindy leans closer to me. "Look, if you just tell me, maybe I can help you. You just have to be honest with me, tell me about your dad, what's been going on at home."

Connie, too, leans closer so she can hear my response. I close my eyes. My father's face flashes in my memory. Him crying about missing my mom, about her dying. The depression. The drinking. He was confused. He was sad. Drunk. He didn't know what he was doing.

Maybe I imagined everything.

Maybe it *was* my fault.

I shudder and open my eyes. Mindy and Connie are still staring at me. Waiting.

I swallow. "And tell you what? There's nothing to tell."

"He said that you made sexual advances on him, that you . . ."

My stomach turns, my throat goes dry as Mindy looks at me expectantly. I shake my head. *No.*

Outside, through the open window, I see an elderly couple stroll by the house, hand in hand. They pause by the bushes to look in—they probably hear us in here. They can watch my life unravel from the outside looking in, like it's a reality show. Entertainment. Then they can walk by, as they're doing now, and go back to their regular lives. Just like Mindy will when she leaves today, and Connie will as soon as I move out of here.

Mindy takes another drink of water. Her long dress swishes as she crosses her ankles in front of her. "Okay," she says. "Has he hit you? When the emergency response worker picked you up a few weeks ago, you didn't have any bruises. So, there's no physical evidence of abuse."

"Let me get this straight," I scoff. "You won't believe that I didn't do anything wrong unless I tell you my dad beat me?"

Neither of them answers me. But they share a glance. Sympathy maybe? It makes my fists curl. The kids' song playing from Annie's room grows louder. She must have turned the volume on the TV up, so as not to be inconvenienced by the noise out here. I run my right hand over my other arm and up toward my shoulder.

Bruises. That's what Mindy wants.

Months ago, I caught Tiffany putting makeup on her arms. I went to the bathroom she and my dad shared because I had a headache. I wanted some Tylenol. But she was there, covering a bruise on her upper arm and shoulder with concealer.

Tiffany snapped her long face in my direction. "Don't you have your own bathroom? Don't you knock?"

I took a step back and started to stutter an apology. But Tiffany wasn't hearing it. "Why would you?" She shook her head. "You never do a damn thing I say, anyway."

Tiffany slammed the door. I can almost feel the air hit me in the face, like I'm there with her rather than in this living room with Connie and Mindy.

Mindy's voice is calm, her words slower, after my

outburst. "No, Victoria. I'm not saying that we won't believe you. I'm just trying to get the facts."

Connie coughs into her hand, loudly. We meet each other's eyes, and rather than her usual scowl, Connie's brows are pushed together.

"You can trust us, Victoria," Connie says.

My eyes widen. *Trust them?* Mindy, the woman who stuck me in this dump? Connie, the woman who takes government money to house me here only to treat me like a servant? *Please.*

Dad's face close to mine intrudes, breaking into my thoughts.

I trusted *him.*

I still want to.

Mindy looks at Connie again, then around the house. A few of Annie's toys are scattered around the faded carpet. The toys four-year-old Annie is allowed to play with but won't share with Lizzie, our foster sister who is a couple years older than her. A small wooden table and TV are at the edge of the room just before the door, next to Annie's toy chest. What does Mindy think of this place?

I steady my voice, breathe slowly. "What about my stepsister and her mom?" I ask Mindy. "What have they said?"

Buzz. Buzzzzzzz. Mindy closes her eyes for a second. She pulls her cell out of her bag, looks at the name of whoever is calling and sets the phone on the couch next to her.

"I'm sorry about that," she says, before blinking several times. It takes her a moment to seemingly get back into our conversation.

Mindy shakes her head. "Look, Victoria, Tiffany and Sarah aren't exactly forthcoming." She clears her throat. "I've interviewed them, together and separately, and they say they haven't seen anything to verify your father's story, but they believe him."

My mouth falls open. I put my hands on either side of me on the couch, fighting the pain in my chest.

"Wait." Mindy puts a hand out. "What I mean is, Tiffany says she believes your dad, and your stepsister says she doesn't know what to believe. That you and she weren't exactly close, but she didn't think you'd ever do anything like that. But she doesn't believe your dad would lie, either."

Connie scowls, rolls her eyes.

Tears begin to well up. I look up at the ceiling, try to stop them from falling.

"I'm starting regular home visits with your family, once every two weeks," Mindy adds. "But yes, at the moment it's just his word against yours"—her phone starts buzzing again and frustration cracks through her sympathetic demeanor—"not that you've given us a lot to go on."

Connie's water bottle crunches in her hands. Mindy turns to look at her, and Connie sets the bottle on the coffee table in front of them. Her face is flushed red, but she nods at Mindy to keep on talking.

"In any case," Mindy says, staring her phone, "I will keep an eye on the situation and make weekly phone calls to Sarah and Tiffany in addition to the home visits. I admit we try not to remove one child from the home and leave the other, but this situation is complicated." Mindy finally meets my eye.

"Your stepsister doesn't seem to be in any danger, none that we can prove, at least. I'll make sure your stepsister is safe, that's my job, and you make sure you do well in school and follow the rules here. That's your job. That's all we can do."

"I want to go home." The words pour out of my mouth. "This is a big misunderstanding."

Connie opens her mouth to say something, but Mindy beats her to it. "Victoria," she pauses, as though searching for the words. "It's not that easy. Your father threatened . . ." she stops again, as though she's thinking. "Not only did he kick you out of the house in the middle of the night, but he also told the police officer if you stayed he'd lock you in the closet. He said that in front of a police officer, and I am assuming he knows better than that—he's a lawyer after all. That kind of punishment is unacceptable, regardless of what happened with your father and you that night, and we can't ignore that comment." She tilts her head at me, as though she feels sorry for me.

It makes me want to scream. Instead, I clench my jaw. Hold my breath. Until Mindy's phone buzzes, again, and I have to use every ounce of self-control I have not to lose it on her.

"Should you get that?" I ask between clenched teeth.

Mindy and I lock eyes. I don't blink. She finally sighs, grabs the phone and reads a text message.

"I'm sorry, I have a lot of kids on my caseload." She swallows as her eyes meet mine again. "But they'll just have to wait. I'll turn this on silent for the rest of our visit."

Connie blows a raspberry, seemingly as annoyed as I am.

But for different reasons, I bet. She would probably rather be watching TV than dealing with this right now. Seems I'm an inconvenience to them both.

Mindy continues, "During the time you've been here at Connie's, I've done a follow-up investigation. I haven't come up with enough to take your stepsister away from her mother. While Tiffany says she and her daughter are safe in that house, I can't do anything because I have no proof that that isn't the case. But you and your father clearly have something going on that isn't healthy, one way or another, and when I told him what he has to do to get you back, he made it clear to me that he's unwilling to go through that process."

I shake my head quickly. "I don't understand . . . why can't I just go home?"

Connie sits up in her seat. "Victoria, if you're not safe there, you shouldn't want to—"

"Your dad won't go to counseling," Mindy interrupts, ignoring Connie and staring straight at me. "He won't take parenting classes. He won't submit to home visits and school visits by social services to you if you were to return. Tiffany, on the other hand, to keep from losing her daughter, has agreed to cooperate with us and allow me to visit her and her daughter to check in. But we can't force your father to cooperate, so you won't be going home."

I start to feel dizzy, as though the room is spinning around me. Dad, he shouldn't have done . . . I'm sure he didn't mean . . .

But he's my *dad.* That's my home.

I force my eyes back to Mindy. "So forget about parenting classes and counseling then. I don't care, just let me go home. My dad didn't do anything, okay? What if I say that, tell the police officer that? Can I go home then?"

Mindy reaches out and pats my knee. "If you want to talk about it, we can. You have the right to say what happened. And if you tell the authorities—"

"No." I jerk my knee out from under her hand.

Mindy sighs softly. "Would you like to take individual counseling, then?"

I look at my lap, deflated all of a sudden, and whisper. "Can I go home if I do?"

"No, you can't," she says. "But it might help you . . ." Mindy hesitates, then goes on, ". . . adjust to your new life here."

I shake my head. "No counseling."

Connie sits quietly on the other side of Mindy, staring out the window. Mindy's light-brown eyes look straight into mine.

I blink a few times, quickly. Grasping. "You said when you brought me here that it was possible I wouldn't stay long. If I'm not going home, where else can I go? A foster home closer to my school?"

Mindy shakes her head. "Like I said when I called Connie last week, unfortunately it's been more challenging than I thought it would be to find somewhere for you in Reno. There aren't any homes with availability that will accept a teenager with the behavioral problems your dad said you have."

I glare at Connie. She hasn't told me about a phone call.

She only said we had to wait until Mindy visits to get more information. Connie clears her throat, looking at Mindy, not at me.

"I think you'll do just fine here with Connie." Mindy glances at her wristwatch. "It's getting late. I've got a two-hour drive back to Reno. I'm supposed to see you once a month, so I'll be back here to check up on you sometime in February. Do me a favor and behave yourself here, okay? Try to make the most of this situation."

Mindy grabs her phone, quickly becoming engrossed by the many messages she probably missed while talking to me.

That's it. All of my hopes for seeing Mindy, for getting out of this godforsaken house, were obliterated in just a few minutes. Gone.

Mindy uses her hands to push herself out of the couch—she'd sunken in with Connie on the other end. She picks up her bag, adjusts her dress and grabs the half-empty water bottle, putting it in her purse. Connie stands, and they shake hands, before Mindy turns back to me.

"See you soon, Victoria."

Connie sees Mindy out the door, and then returns to stand in front of me. Outside, I hear Mindy's car engine start. She drives away.

"Look," Connie says, twisting her hands awkwardly, "I know you must be angry. I understand—"

"How could you possibly understand?" I snap.

Connie's face flashes mad, but then she takes a deep breath.

"Your father"—she pauses for a moment—"doesn't want

you there. He'd give up his parental rights but with you being so close to eighteen . . . when's your birthday, in a few months? With you turning eighteen in April, there's hardly a point in all that."

Great. I'm too old for it to be worth Dad's while to *officially* give me up, so he can just let me rot here until I'm legally no longer anyone's problem, that's what Connie is trying to tell me. I cross my arms and glare past Connie, at the round wooden table where we have our "family" meals.

Connie stares at me for several seconds. "That's what I know, so now we're on the same page." She puts her hands on her hips. "Let me see what you've got in your bag."

I hand my backpack over, looking away. *Rule number four: All foster children and property subject to search, at any time, especially before and after entering or exiting the residence.* Connie begins sifting through my bag, pawing at my textbooks, notebooks, and pencils. Not once, but twice. She shakes my backpack for a few seconds and then tosses it to the ground.

"No drugs today," she rasps.

I roll my eyes at her. "No drugs any day."

Connie leans down to meet my eyes.

"I'm just trying to help you," she says. "And I could do without all the backtalk." She plops on the couch and looks at me.

I grit my teeth and force out the words I have to say to be able to move in this home. "Can I go to the dormitory now?"

Connie waits a beat, tilting her head forward.

I bite the inside of my cheek. "Please?"

Satisfied, Connie nods. I yank my backpack off the

ground and head for the "girls' dormitory," passing stupid photos of Connie and her ex-husband Bill and Annie. In their family photos, Annie is a pudgy baby rather than the toddler she is now. Connie and Bill smile big, toothy grins for the camera.

My stomach twists.

The knob to the door squeaks as I open it. I walk to the bottom bunk of the bed closest to the barred window. A baby monitor perched on the windowsill reminds me that Connie's listening, even though she's in the living room watching her soap operas. Connie can always hear us in here—which, of course, is the whole point—although I'm alone this afternoon. Jamie's pink-and-purple covered bed is made, but she's not here. Just her boy band posters taped on the upper half of the wall with the band members smiling at me.

Jamie must be at Child Protective Services visiting her grandma, who's too frail and old to take care of her twelve-year-old granddaughter, but who still makes the drive to come see her every now and then. At least Jamie has a grandma. Dad's parents died in a car crash before I was born, and Mom never knew her father. She was raised by a single mom who had her late in life, so she, too, died when I was too young to really know her. Both my parents were the only child in their families, just like me. Until Sarah came along.

It had always been just Sarah and her mom, since her dad was a deadbeat who took off the second he found out Tiffany was pregnant. Maybe that's why Tiffany hovered over Sarah like a helicopter. They were all each other had. Like Dad and I once were.

I picture Sarah. Fourteen and a freshman in high school, the apple of her mom's eye, without a care in the world. Sarah, who didn't tell Mindy that I must be telling the truth. Sarah, who is going on with her life, with my dad and her mom, without me. Like I never existed.

I grab my pillow off the bed and squeeze it. Take a few deep breaths. I could scream into it. No one else is in the room with me. I squeeze harder and harder, until I can't anymore, swallow the urge and put the pillow back in its place. I slip under the covers of my previously perfectly made bed, and pull the bedspread up to my chin.

I turn five words over in my head, the ones my mom told me again and again before she died. *Everything in life is temporary,* my mom told me. *Everything in life is temporary, honey, the good and the bad.*

I pull my backpack off the ground. Take out my personal statement for my scholarship application for Truckee Meadows Community College in Reno. I've already been accepted to the school, but now that I don't have Dad to foot the bill for college I need to get serious about applying for financial aid. I wrote a draft of an essay by hand my first week here, after Connie finished searching my things for drugs and money before finally leaving me alone. I need to make some edits before I type it up at school and finish the rest of the application.

Why do I want to go to college? That prompt is easy to answer since I already wrote something about that for my

UNR application. I sigh bitterly. I was supposed to go to the University of Nevada in Reno. I applied and was accepted early. But without Dad's help, TMCC is the only school I'll be able to afford while working whatever job I can get to pay for some tiny apartment in Reno. Thanks to my dad, of course, for kicking me out and leaving me with absolutely nothing to pay for the education he always stressed was so important for me to get.

My best friend Jess and I won't share a dorm, like we planned. We won't take classes together. We won't do anything, because I won't be there. She's in Reno and I'm stuck here in the middle of nowhere and I will be until I graduate.

I start working on my breathing again. Focus.

TMCC is my future now. It's what I have to do to get my life back on track.

The real point of the scholarship essay is to explain how financial aid will help me go to school when I otherwise might not be able to. I look down at the paper, scan until the part about why I need the money.

I always thought my family would pay for my school, as that is what my father has promised me. But now that I am in foster care, I don't have that assurance anymore.

I fight the urge to crumple the piece of paper up and toss it in the trash. Instead, I drag an eraser over the line, scrubbing it out.

I inhale deeply and start rewriting. *Due to my recent change of circumstance, I have to pay for college by myself if I want to go. Now it's more important than ever that I go, so that I can take my life back.*

I close the notebook and hold it up to my chest. At least with my acceptance to TMCC in hand, I'm not completely screwed. But as I sit in a room with barred windows and a baby monitor with Connie listening to my every move, college seems too far away.

I put the notebook in my backpack.

Just finish the semester. That's all I have to get through. After I graduate, I can move back to Reno, get a job, and go to college. It will be like I was never in foster care. Like this was all a bad dream.

CHAPTER
THREE

*J*jolt awake to the alarm blaring at me from the windowsill. "It wasn't real," I tell myself. I stab a finger at the alarm until it quiets.

Sinking back into bed, I can still feel Dad's warm breath on my face as he whispered to me. And then he moved closer. Too close.

I couldn't move, I couldn't think.

Dad's eyes were glossy, his voice husky and words slurred. "All I want to do is love you."

My stomach sinks, twists. I pull my legs closer to my chest and roll over. Let the nausea wave over me.

Maybe I'm sick. Maybe I did this. Maybe there's something wrong with me.

I look up at the ceiling, try to focus on the air bubbles rather than the memory. I force out the breath I've been holding. Then suck air back in, feeding my lungs, faster and faster. I wipe sweat off my forehead but pull the covers closer to my body anyway.

I'm here, now. Focus on now. It's Tuesday, so I'm last in the shower line-up. My foster sisters are already in the living room with Connie. I grab my toiletry bag, full of the Dollar Store shampoo and soap that Connie says is all she can afford based on the *measly stipend* she gets.

I swing the door open and call out. "Connie, may I go to the bathroom, please?"

Connie doesn't seem to hear me over the show she's watching on TV. Some ridiculous melodrama that no one else wants to watch. I lean against the wall and listen to tension-building music and reunions of long-lost lovers.

"Connie," I try again.

The TV goes silent. "Come in here, girl," she calls as she stomps to the dining room.

I walk down the hall, rage bubbling beneath the surface just like every time I have to ask to go to the freaking bathroom. It's inhumane.

Connie looks at me, noticing my scowl, I'm sure, because she returns it in kind.

"This isn't fair," I blurt. "I shouldn't have to—"

Connie interrupts. "If I didn't have foster girls before you who snuck around this house, hiding their drugs, climbing out the window to meet their boyfriends, and getting knocked up, maybe you wouldn't have to ask before entering or leaving a room in my house."

My toiletry bag dangles at my side as I twist my fingers around the top of it, tamping down my anger. Or trying to. Connie plops in her wooden chair, leaning forward to reach the cup of coffee in front of her. "When, or *if,* I should say, you leave this placement and haven't landed yourself in jail or pregnant, you'll thank me. Mark my words."

In the living room, Lizzie's on the floor using crayons

to draw in a coloring book the teacher at daycare gave her. Her long, black hair falls in front of her face as she scribbles away. Annie's in her bedroom, watching TV. Jamie sits on the couch doing homework. She turns her head to look at me, with her brown eyes that almost seem too big for her smallish face, and shakes her head to remind me—like she first told me when I moved in—that every interaction with Connie is easier if I keep my mouth shut.

Connie clicks her tongue, looking at me. "You've got something to say? Spit it out."

I ignore Jamie's warning and look straight at Connie. "You get paid to have me here. Don't act like you're Mother Teresa."

Connie sets her mug back on the table. "Not nearly enough. Barely enough to feed you, and definitely not enough to deal with your sass."

I cross my arms. "Can I take a shower now?"

Connie growls what I take to be a yes, and I head to the bathroom.

After my five minutes of hot water run out, I throw on the same jeans I wore yesterday and a T-shirt. The tag sticks out. I tuck it back in, praying that no one at school will see my name written on it. My jeans, shirts, even my underwear now say "Victoria Parker" or "VP" in big, black letters. Connie made me take a sharpie to all my belongings for inventory when I first moved in—her house protocol. Apparently, kids she had in the past stole from each other.

My new foster sister, Jamie, sat on the ground with me in the living room that first day, handing me each piece of clothing out of my garbage bag for me to letter. Once she reached the first pair of my underwear, my face flamed. Jamie grinned. She peered over my head to make sure Connie wasn't watching and then leaned in to whisper. "She's worried we might steal *her* underwear, not each other's."

I sputtered, and Jamie's grin widened. She lifted my underwear overhead, her eyes popping. "She's worried we might steal her granny panties and *use them as a tent!*"

I smile at Jamie in the living room now and, as if she knows what I'm remembering, she wiggles her eyebrows at me.

In the kitchen, I set several rows of bacon on a baking sheet and put it in the oven, and then grab bowls for Lizzie, Jamie, and me. I take the box of Cheerios out of the cupboard and put that out, too. I scramble eggs, and then set the milk and drinking glasses out. The sound of cartoons fills the living room. Annie has graced the rest of us with her presence.

"You better get a move on. It's nearly 7:00." Connie shouts to me from the couch. "Come on, baby," she calls softly to Annie. She bounces over as Lizzie and Jamie take their seats at the table.

Once the bacon's ready, I bring it with the bowl of eggs to the table. Connie takes it from me and begins serving it to Annie and then herself. "Well, don't just stand there. Eat your breakfast," she says.

Jamie, sitting in between me and Lizzie, catches my eye and smiles, revealing the small gap between her two front teeth. Connie looks away and Jamie whispers, "Eat it, before Connie does."

I choke on a laugh so Connie won't notice, but then Jamie's answering smirk plunges me into a memory. My throat tightens as my thoughts flash to Sarah. It wasn't even two months ago, not long after I saw Tiffany in the bathroom, when Sarah wanted to talk. I had been lying in bed, with my bedside lamp on, reading after I thought everyone had gone to sleep.

Tap, tap, tap. Someone was outside my door. I froze. Dad hadn't been drinking that night, I thought. I pulled my blankets close, until I heard the soft voice of Sarah on the other side of the door.

"It's me," she said. "Can I come in?"

Lizzie eats her breakfast, unaware of the loud crunch she makes with every bite. She catches me staring at her and grins, the freckles on her nose bunching up. Like Sarah's freckles.

I went to the door and opened it a crack. Sarah stood barefoot, her thin frame nearly lost in her too-big pajama set. "I could see the light through the door." She smiled at me, sheepishly. "Can I come in?"

I opened the door wide for her. She walked inside and sat on the edge of my bed. Once back against my pillows, I watched Sarah. She held one of her feet in her hands, staring at it. "Are you mad at me?"

I stuttered. "I, um. No. Why?"

Sarah let go of a long breath. It was a moment before she spoke again.

"I don't know, things just feel different." Her blonde bangs fell into her eyes, and she blew them out of her face, looking at me.

I held her gaze. She was right, of course. Dad and Tiffany had been fighting more and more and somehow that had translated into Sarah and me being weird with each other. Me, especially, since Dad had been wanting to spend more time with me, and not Sarah. I wouldn't admit it, but I liked the attention.

I look back at Jamie, her chin-length, wavy blonde hair falling into her face as she settles into her bowl of cereal quietly. Jamie and Lizzie are too good to be here, to be treated like this. We all are.

"I don't know what you're talking about," I said to Sarah that night. "I mean, yeah, we haven't hung out as much lately, but we're busy. You've got less time now that you're in dance, and I'm planning my life after high school, getting ready for college." I shrugged. "It's normal."

Sarah nodded, her freckled face turned down. I forced a laugh and playfully shoved her shoulder. "I miss you, too. I guess I kind of like you, now that I think about it."

At the table, I shake my head, quickly, involuntarily, as if a bug flew near my face. I didn't know that would be the last time we were in my room alone together. Sarah must have forgotten the late nights we stayed up talking about school and her many friends. Forgotten how I promised I would drive her around if she helped talk Tiffany and Dad into letting me get my license. Forgotten how I'd sit with her while she binged her stupid reality shows, just because she wanted someone to squeal with.

I choke on my eggs and push them away, filling my bowl with cereal. I've been here for more than two weeks, and Sarah hasn't done anything to get in touch. I'm not allowed to call her, and Connie would kill me if I tried using a school phone. But Sarah has a cell phone now that she's a freshman. She could call me here, I bet. If she wanted to. But maybe she wants nothing to do with me, after whatever my dad must have told her about that night. Why he would do that, how he could even *think* that I wanted—

I can't think about it. I won't.

The discussion around the table flits in and out of my ears. Lizzie tells Connie about what she's learning in pre-school, and Connie seems mildly interested until Annie declares she is the smartest one in her whole class.

I stab my spoon into my cereal, imagining Dad and Tiffany picking Sarah up from school—my school—and helping her with her homework. Him and Tiffany beaming at her with pride as she performs with all her friends on the dance team at basketball games. Being a family now that the one thing keeping them miserable, apparently, is gone.

"Careful, girl, or you'll owe me a new bowl." Connie scowls in my direction.

Jamie nudges my glass of milk toward me, but I don't reach for it. I close my eyes. Breathe.

Before Dad . . . did what he did, he seemed unwilling to be around his wife for long periods of time, so Tiffany spent more time with Sarah. I was a spare—except when it was just me and Dad, alone. He acted so different then. But otherwise, I was invisible. Tiffany only had time for Sarah.

Sarah, let me do your hair for the game. You look so cute when I do it.

Sarah, baby, are you eating enough? You need more calories now that you're in dance.

Sarah, you shouldn't be staying up so late with Victoria. You need to get more rest.

Sarah. Sarah. Sarah.

I stare at the milk carton in front of me, but I'm not here, at the table.

In my head, I'm back in my room with Dad. With his probing hands, with him pushing up against me. I shudder. *No.*

My mouth starts to water, as though I'm going to be sick. I take a drink, let the milk slowly slip down my throat.

What if Dad's right? I could be imagining it. He acted wrong, he was being so strange, but he's my *father.* He loves me. He didn't mean to . . .

No.

I can't tell Mindy what happened, not only because she doesn't really care about sending me home, not only because I don't understand any of it.

I blink a few tears back.

I can't say it out loud. I can't tell anyone what happened that night.

I squeeze my eyes shut and open them. No. I'm not telling Mindy or Connie or anyone.

Connie sips her coffee, before scanning the table looking at each of us. "Well aren't you all a bunch of talkers."

No one responds.

⬤

Jamie and I walk to school together through our boring residential neighborhood: one-story houses sitting next to each other in small lots, the sidewalks cracked but clean. The farther we get into town, away from Connie's, the greener the grass gets. Jamie hands me one of the earbuds for her iPod—*her* caseworker let her take it from home—but I shake my head. "No, thanks."

"What's wrong? You were so quiet at breakfast."

I shrug. "I was just thinking about home."

Jamie's silent for a moment. She twists the cord to her headphones around her fingers. "You know what I like about Connie?"

I stop, stunned. *What in the world could she find to like in that woman?*

Jamie grins. "Not a damn thing."

I laugh so hard I snort. Jamie chuckles. "My grandma taught me that joke."

We walk in silence, until the last couple of blocks when Jamie and I split up so she can head up the hill to Silver Valley Middle School. We say our goodbyes, and I watch her walk away, her green backpack bouncing behind her as she goes.

At school, I follow a horde of students coming from the parking lot onto the lawn and walk through the double doors. I catch Christina's olive skin and long black hair out of the corner of my eye. She walks by with a couple of girls wearing letterman's jackets, including the one with perfect hair who whispered about me my first day—Taylor, I think her name is. Christina turns back to wave at me. I keep walking to my locker, unload my backpack and grab what I need for first period before hurrying toward class. The bell should ring any second.

"Hey, we haven't met yet, but I'm Kale."

I whip around to see who's talking to me. It's the guy with the light-brown hair who was with Alex in the hallway—Christina's friend. A couple of kids try to walk by him, and he moves closer to me to get out of their way. I clutch my book to my chest. "Um. Nice to meet you."

Kale opens his mouth to say something, but I notice Christina several paces behind him. She hung back near the door to English class. I step around Kale and walk into the classroom without waiting for him to respond.

Christina follows me in, grinning. She takes the seat next to me. "It's only your second day, and you're already making friends. I approve, obviously. Kale's like one of the only cool guys in this school. I've known him since we were practically babies."

I nod. Making friends. Not at all what I'm going for—what would be the point when I'm counting the days until I can get the hell out of here and put this part of my life behind me? But there's no way to say that without sounding like a jerk. Or getting asked *why*.

From the front of the class, our teacher Mrs. Langley

catches my eye. "Victoria," she says. "Can you please see me up here in the front?"

I steel myself and head over.

"Victoria, I just got a call that you're wanted in the principal's office. You're not in trouble. He just needs to speak with you."

My chest tightens.

"You'll want to bring your belongings with you," she says.

Several students give me curious looks as I walk back to my desk. "What'd you do?" Christina asks.

"I don't know." I put my book in my bag before heading out of the classroom. Maybe Mindy found a foster home for me in Reno, after all. Or maybe the principal knows I'm a foster kid and wants to give me a talking to about how I better not do drugs or prostitute myself at his school, like Connie seems to think we all do. I head down the hallway, past the stupid plaques and trophies, and round the corner to where the guidance counselor's office is. The principal's office is the first one after the school's entrance.

The young woman at the front desk smiles to greet me. "Victoria, thanks for coming so quickly," she says. "I'm Becca Branson, but you can just call me Becca. No Mrs. Branson or any of that."

Her smile widens, revealing just about every tooth in her mouth.

"Okay."

She looks at me expectantly.

"Okay . . . Becca."

She beams at me. "Just wait here a moment. I'll go get

Principal Nelson." Becca turns and disappears into the office behind her.

A moment later, Principal Nelson opens the office door behind Becca's desk. He takes two large strides and he's standing in front of us, towering over me. He smiles.

"Nice to meet you, Victoria." He reaches out his large hand. I shake it. "Please follow me."

I follow Principal Nelson around a copy machine and filing cabinet into his office. He reaches behind me and shuts the door. "Please have a seat," he says, and I do.

Principal Nelson sits in his black leather chair, behind his ancient-looking wooden desk. He folds his hands together on the only open space on his desk, the rest of the surface covered with paper and clutter.

"You're probably wondering why I called you in here, but you're not in any trouble," he says with a smile. "How are you liking SVHS so far?"

"It's okay."

Mr. Nelson scratches his head full of curly salt-and-pepper hair, which matches his thick mustache. "All right, down to business, then." He sighs. "I'm sorry to have to tell you this, but one of your old classes doesn't meet the requirements here."

I close my eyes and pinch the bridge of my nose. What did I expect? When your life falls apart, apparently, it's just one thing after another. My eyes sting with tears, and I look at my hands.

Mr. Nelson tilts his head to the side and frowns. He grabs

a paper cup off the top of the water cooler next to his desk and fills it. I take it from him and gulp it down.

"Which class?" I stammer.

"Pre-calculus."

"But I'm in calculus—I need it to graduate!"

He nods. "Yes, you do, but you need pre-calculus as well. And you can't take calculus without pre-calculus."

I shake my head, crunching the paper cup in my hand. "Why doesn't the class I took from my school in Reno count? I passed, it should count!"

"I know, it should," Mr. Nelson says. He leans forward. "I'm sorry, Victoria. My hands are tied. The regulations for coursework come from the superintendent and the school board, not me."

"So, I'm not going to be able to graduate on time?" My voice breaks.

"If I can help it, you will," he says. "Let's get you enrolled in pre-calculus and calculus at the same time. Get you re-enrolled in the extra class, in sixth period, which would have been your free period. You'll be with the juniors, and you'll also need to stay in calculus. But at least this way, I think I can make the case that you should still graduate on time."

I shake my head. "And what if you don't? What's it to you if I don't graduate? What do you care, except that you have to deal with me for another year?" Tears start to fall, and I hate myself for it.

Mr. Nelson fiddles with his mug. "I know you live with Connie."

My jaw clenches.

His voice softens. "Most of the time she takes younger kids who end up at the elementary school or the middle school. I haven't been able to help any of them; they usually end up moving after a few months. But my wife's a fifth-grade teacher and from what she says I know living in that home is no piece of cake."

Mr. Nelson stops and looks out the window to his left. On either side of it are plaques naming him Principal of the Year or coach of a championship-winning basketball team. His eyes trail over them before he looks back at me.

"I was adopted when I was a toddler," he says. "My mom and dad adopted me, and if they hadn't, I don't know what would have happened. Something bad, probably. I know it's not the same thing as what you're going through, but I want to help you. Trust me."

I flinch at the word *trust*. Mr. Nelson frowns as he waits for me to respond.

I tear at a piece of skin near my right fingernail. "Thank you," I force out. "Can I go back to class now?"

Mr. Nelson's eyebrows furrow. "Yes, Victoria. Just remember, I'm here if you ever need anything. And I'll keep working on your math requirement."

I nod. Chest tight. Another problem, another weight crushing down on me. As I walk out of the principal's office, I rearrange my features. Blank face. Because I'm just another student out here in the hall, that's what I want people to think. Everything's fine.

Everything's fine.

CHAPTER
FOUR

I sit on my bed, cross legged. It's morning, but I can't find the motivation to move. I feel stuck, like my body is heavy, my legs weighted down on the bed. My mind is a million miles away.

Thinking about Mom.

Sometimes it seems she's been gone forever, like the years I had with her and Dad, *before,* were just a dream.

She and I had been so close at one point, but that seems even further away. Before I started pulling back, little by little. I was scared it made Dad unhappy. Even though I couldn't figure out why.

I close my eyes, remembering.

Mom loved old romantic movies. Like *Groundhog Day* and *The Princess Bride.* And even *Pretty Woman.* (Mom always covered my eyes during the steamy scenes.) When we weren't cleaning up around the house or I wasn't doing school work, we'd watch them together, curled up on the couch, eating popcorn. Happy.

It was Valentine's Day, years ago, and Dad was still at the office working late. Mom was a little sad. Though she didn't say anything, my ten-year-old self could see it by the way she sighed when she sat the phone down after Dad called.

"Another late night," Mom said. She looked down at her slinky black dress and heels. She'd dressed up for a date that now wasn't going to happen, her curly hair tied into a tight knot and lips painted red. She was beautiful. But then again, she always was.

"You're my Valentine, Mom!" I exclaimed, my voice high and excited. Mom staying home meant I had her all to myself. No babysitter.

Mom grinned that movie star smile of hers as she stepped into the other room to change and call the babysitter. All the while I came up with a plan to make her feel better.

Tears trickle down my cheeks as I remember. I so badly wanted to make her happy.

Mom came back to the living room with pajamas on, her hair now falling down her back in soft waves, and still looking down. I had two wine glasses out, filled with apple juice, on the coffee table. I put a candle, unlit—I wasn't allowed to use matches—in between the glasses. Mom's mouth fell open.

"What's this, sweetheart?"

"You're my date, Mom! We can have a movie marathon! All the best romantic movies until Dad gets home!"

Mom beamed. She walked toward me, swept me in her arms, and kissed my cheeks.

"You are the sweetest. This is the best Valentine anyone

could ask for, Victoria," she breathed in my hair. "Thank you."

That night with Mom was perfect. Until Dad got home. Late, as we started the third movie of the night, Mom and I turned as we heard Dad's key click the lock.

He opened the door, briefcase in one hand and a single red rose in the other.

"Daddy!" I called. "Happy Valentine's Day! Mommy's my Valentine!"

Mom and I were cuddled on the couch together. Dad dropped the rose to his side, looking a little confused as he saw the empty wine glasses.

Mom chuckled. "It's just juice, Jeff."

"What are you doing up, Victoria? It's almost midnight."

Dad's eyebrows bunched up. He was grumpy from work again, I could tell. He always seemed grumpy lately.

Mom stood and walked toward Dad, taking his briefcase out of his hands and his jacket off.

"Looks like you two were having a great time, Leah. Don't let me keep you."

Mom hung Dad's jacket in the coat closet. "Victoria wanted to cheer me up, since you had to work late, Jeffrey."

Dad harrumphed a little, and I sat up on the couch. "We could finish the movie together, Daddy." I pointed to the TV. *Say Anything* was on, and it was almost to my favorite part when John Cusack held the boom box up on his shoulders so he could show his love.

"I'm beat," Dad said, heading to their bedroom. "Going to bed."

Mom tilted her head slightly. "Okay, we'll be quiet out here so we don't keep you up."

Dad turned toward her slightly.

Mom and he looked at each other without saying anything. It's like they were having a conversation without words. "Fine," Dad finally muttered. "Finish the movie. Goodnight."

The door slammed behind him, and I flinch now. Like I'm there.

And though Mom and I cuddled back together on the couch, we were quiet. Daddy was mad at us, I could tell. I just didn't know why. But I didn't ask. And Mom didn't say.

That night when I went to bed, I heard Mom and Dad arguing, even though he said he was going to sleep when he went to their room.

I couldn't hear them from my bedroom, not really. I just heard bits and pieces.

From Dad: . . . *my daughter, too!*

From Mom: *Don't be ridiculous.*

And something from my Dad about *ungrateful.*

I let out a loud, angry sigh. Dad and Mom fighting. Dad and Tiffany fighting. Dad always getting his way, the common denominator.

I had planned to ask Mom about their argument the next day. It was before Mom told me it was better to just ride out Dad's anger, better not to say anything when he was mad, and let him cool off. It was before I watched him yell at her more and more as I got older, less and less behind their closed bedroom door and more in the living room and the kitchen.

Before I saw her shoulders slump and her mouth push into a thin line. Before she told me that's just how men were, they could be sensitive even though they acted so tough. It's just easier to obey your father than to fight, she instructed me.

But that morning after Valentine's Day was before all that.

During breakfast Mom didn't seem to be in the mood to talk. She ate her eggs quietly, and she didn't ask me about what I had going on in school that day like she usually did.

Dad stood up from the table, and Mom flinched. Dad didn't seem to notice; he was smiling at me. "I'm taking you to school today, Victoria, on my way to work. Isn't that great?"

I looked at Mom. "I've got a lot of work to do around the house anyway." She patted my hand, cleared our plates and disappeared into the bathroom.

I shiver, although it's warm in the dormitory.

Dad was chatty on our ride to school, asking me questions he normally didn't ask about my friends and what classes I liked. I was sorry he and Mom weren't getting along and scared it was my fault.

"Daddy, did I do something wrong?"

His eyebrows furrowed from the driver's side. "No, Victoria. Why would you say that?"

He laughed like it was silly, like I was imagining something, as he turned back to the road. So I dropped the subject. Enjoyed my time with Dad.

But that was the first and last time Mom and I ever had a movie marathon together.

At lunch I head for the library. It's not much, just a half-dozen tall bookshelves, a few long tables, a small computer nook, and the librarian's station.

It's empty, no one is in here but the librarian. Good.

I walk to the first computer desk and clear my throat. "Excuse me," I say to the woman, her head bent over a book at her desk. "Can I use a computer?"

She smiles. "Of course. We have a content block, so only age-appropriate web searches are allowed."

I slip the straps of my backpack off my shoulders. "I just want to fill out some scholarship application stuff. That's all."

The librarian nods and gestures in front of me. "Then go right ahead." She returns to her book.

I set my backpack on the floor and pull my handwritten financial aid essay out of a binder. Typing it doesn't take long. It's easy enough finding the financial aid portal on TMCC's website and submitting the essay, but it's still a relief to get it done. When I'm in college, it'll be like none of this ever happened, I tell myself for probably the millionth time. I can move on.

I glance up at the wall clock. Still ten minutes until lunch is up. But then I feel someone behind me. I turn to see Christina's friend, Kale.

"All alone in here?" At his side, Kale holds a few books. Topping the stack is a pink children's book with what looks like a unicorn on it.

I keep my eyes on the unicorn. "Good story?"

Kale holds the books out in front of him, as if inspecting the picture book. "You know, I didn't think unicorn and fairy princess books would be my thing, but don't knock something until you try it." Kale's long eyelashes flutter as he looks up, still smiling. Not just with his mouth, but his whole face. The florescent light seems to dance off his pale-blue eyes as he continues to stare at me.

I look at my shoes suddenly, drag them back and forth on the carpet.

He laughs and brings the books back to his side. "It was for my sister, although I'd be lying if I told you I haven't read it. Many times. That girl can get anyone to do anything for her." He steps closer to me, and I look back at him, unsure of what to say.

Kale nods. "It's pretty good, actually. The book." He lifts it again, slightly, and he's still looking at me. "I checked it out for her. In case you didn't know, this place doubles as the public library."

"That's handy." I smirk. "Is there a horse and buggy service I can take in lieu of a school bus?"

Kale raises an eyebrow at me. "No, but my favorite neighbor is a goat by the name of Charlie. Would you like me to introduce you two?"

My face goes hot. I should say something else. *Something less aggressive.*

"Your name's Kale, right? Is that like the vegetable?"

Kale's face lights up. "Exactly." He grins. "Which means I'm good for you . . . and trendy."

He winks.

I laugh, despite myself. I feel that I'm blushing, so I look down to clear my throat. "And the rest?" I nod to the other books he has curled up his left arm.

Kale grins. "Sherlock Holmes, of course! Have you read any of them?"

As if just deciding now is a good time to look up from her book, the librarian calls out to Kale. "Good to see you back in here so soon, Kale. You have something for me?"

He turns toward her. "Yeah, I'll be there in a second, Ms. K. I'm just getting to know Silver Valley's new student here." He tilts his head toward me.

She nods, shaking her head at Kale with a smile. Maybe he's in here bugging other girls all the time. "When you're ready, though," the librarian, Ms. K, continues, "I'll be happy to discuss my thoughts on the book *you* recommended I read."

Kale grins. "Oh, don't worry. I haven't forgotten, Ms. K. You aren't getting off that easy." He looks at me conspiratorially. "I have excellent taste."

I stare at him mutely.

"In books," he finishes.

My face flames again, but I don't know why. I shake my head to clear it. "No, I haven't read any Sherlock Holmes."

His face animates. "I highly recommend them, any of them. All of them. I've read so many of the stories, a bunch of times. It never gets old, the mystery. The intrigue." He raises his eyebrows at me. I force a laugh. And then a smile.

"What about you?" Kale asks. "You're in the library. What do you like to read?"

I look around the empty room. "Oh, um. I'm not here

for books. I mean, I like to read. Nonfiction mostly. But I'm just using the computer here."

"Nonfiction, like biographies?" Kale points behind me. "There's a whole section on those just behind you, aisle four, I think. I could ask Ms. K if she knows of any new ones—"

"No, no." I interrupt. "Just here for the computer, like I said." I realize he's about to ask what for, so I offer, "college prep stuff."

"Got it." Kale swings the books at his side a few times, and then glances at the computer station behind me. I quickly log out of the computer, stash my notebook in my backpack and stand. "See you later."

Kale's face falls slightly. "Nice talking to you," I add. He nods, smiling again, and waves his library books in the direction of Ms. K. "I better return these. See you around."

I walk around him and out of the library. Quickly. My hand slides to my back pocket, where I used to keep my cell phone. If I had it, I'd text Jess. Tell her about Kale. Maybe I'd even turn around and sneak a picture of him to Snapchat to her.

Hey, look at this cute guy I met! He talked to me today, and I didn't even embarrass myself as much as I could have!

But I don't have a phone, and I'm not Snapchatting anyone. Thank you, Mindy, for closing all my social media accounts for me. At least she did that. It hurt at first, but the last thing I need is anyone here seeing photos of my old life on Facebook or Instagram and asking questions.

So I can't talk to Jess. There's nothing to say anyway. Nothing that I want to.

There would be too many questions about Dad.

There would be too many questions. Period.

My shoulders sag as I walk. Four years ago, I let it slip that my dad sometimes cried about my mom, before Tiffany came along. Jess told her parents and they invited Dad and me over for dinner. It was crystal clear they were worried about him. They tried to set him up on a blind date. They invited him to church. They meant well, I know that, but Dad didn't care.

Afterward, Dad wouldn't let me go to their house again for two whole months.

No. No reaching out to Jess to tell her about Kale, or about anything else. No new friends, or old ones. They're a luxury I can't afford until I get out of Connie's, out of Silver Valley, and start my life in college.

After stopping at my locker, I walk into the math classroom. Every seat is taken except one in the first row, right next to Kale, and one in the back row. I hesitate.

He must feel me staring, because he stops doodling in his notebook and looks up. "Hey. I didn't expect to see you in here."

I shake my head—*figures*—and set my backpack on the ground between us, before pulling my book out.

"Aren't seniors supposed to be in calculus?"

I zip my bag forcefully. "So you know I'm a senior? What else do you know about me?"

Kale watches me silently for a moment. I can feel my face turning red again.

He chuckles. "You're new here, so I guess you haven't noticed"—he pauses to look around the small classroom as if this helps him illustrate the point—"but there are only a couple different classes each grade level can take per period. So, with a little deductive reasoning . . ."

"I *am* a senior," I say, in a much softer tone. "It's just my old school's pre-calculus class didn't transfer, apparently." I wave my hand, resigned, as his face creases with concern. "Whatever, it's fine."

Kale stretches his feet out on the floor in front of him. Other students chatter around us, even as the second bell rings. Kale starts tapping his pencil on his notebook, absent-mindedly, before his eyes land back on mine. "So, what brings you to Silver Valley? It's not every day we get new people."

I open my mouth but nothing comes out. Thankfully, the teacher greets the class and begins the lesson for the day.

When the bell rings, I say goodbye to Kale and head out fast so that there's not enough time for much else. Christina's standing at the door as I walk through it. I don't even know her, yet she's already everywhere I go.

"What happened? They flunk you already?"

I walk around Christina. She seems to like me for some reason, but she's the opposite of any friend I've ever had. Christina is outgoing and chatty. Persistent. Jess and I bonded over being quiet and shy in middle school.

Christina catches up with me, so I have to answer her. "The pre-calculus class from my last school didn't transfer."

She sighs sympathetically. "No wonder you're so grumpy. I'd be pissed, too."

We both head in the direction of my locker, which is just a few lockers away from hers. "I can't help but notice Kale's also in pre-calculus." Christina's brown eyes flash at me.

"And?"

"Have you asked anyone to the dance?" she answers. "I think you should ask Kale. We're going together as friends, but I'm sure he'd love having an official date. And it would be nice to hang outside of school so you and I could get to know each other, right?"

I choke, but quickly start to clear my throat.

"No." I sputter. I step around a couple kids standing in the middle of the hallway, who apparently can't be bothered to not block the way for everyone else. "I mean, no I don't want to ask Kale out. I'm not going to the dance."

Christina walks by them, too, and is back at my side. "Why not?" she says. "What's wrong with him? He's cute, not my type because ew gross, but objectively I still think he's one of the better-looking guys at this school."

I tighten my grip on my books as we walk. "I just got here. The last thing I want to think about is a school dance. And anyway, I don't know him."

"Still, you should come with us," she says, her voice matter-of-fact, as if it's clearly the only acceptable thing to do. "He's really awesome, and I think he thinks you're cute."

I stop at my locker and start fiddling with the digits to my combination. "I thought you didn't want to go to the dance? What about all that stuff you said before, about that comic strip the school is theming it after being archaic? And, more importantly, why do you care?"

Christina watches me unload my stuff. "That was mostly to piss Alex off." She flips her hair out of her face. "And, to answer your other, slightly rude question," she looks at me sideways, a smile playing on her full, glossy lips, "you're different. I can tell, and I like that. If you haven't noticed, there aren't a lot of people like me in this school."

I pause for a beat. Not sure what she's getting at. "You mean, because you're Mexican?"

Someone bumps into my back as their group passes me in the hall. "Sorry," the girl says, sounding anything but apologetic when I turn to glare at her. I turn back to Christina.

"I prefer Latina, seeing as I'm American. And, yes, that does make me different." She raises one of her perfectly shaped eyebrows as if she's explaining something obvious. "But being Latina is not what I was talking about, at least not exactly. My grandparents on both sides came to the US for a better life, and my parents have given me everything they could, but they haven't left this one-horse town. So yeah, I want to do better. My family worked hard so that I could."

I abandon the pretense of searching for a book in my locker and turn to Christina.

"And I don't think people here get that." She grins at me, seemingly pleased that she finally caught my attention. "I need to get out of here, not just Silver Valley but out of Nevada entirely. I need to shoot higher, go bigger."

The bell rings, and Christina and I drift toward class with the last stragglers. "Obviously I'm not like other people here because I'm fabulous, forward thinking, and ready to get the hell out of here as fast as I can," she continues. "Like I said, you seem different. And either way, you're not from here, and I could use less Silver Valley in my life."

"I didn't mean to offend—"

"You didn't," she cuts me off. "So, anyway, I've been meaning to ask you. What's your story? Why did you move to this joke of a town?"

"Oh, you know, the school dances."

Christina laughs and waits for a more suitable answer. I stare at her, my lips sealed.

"Got it, none of my business. Good luck keeping a secret, though. Nobody around here has anything better to do than pry and gossip."

My stomach sinks. Perfect.

Jamie walks home with a couple friends in the afternoons. Their houses are all on the way to Connie's, so they never actually see where Jamie lives. And I walk alone through quiet neighborhoods of older, small houses until I reach Connie's front lawn, complete with yellowing grass and a sinister-looking garden gnome. Charming.

I've slowly gotten used to the routine. I get home, let Connie check my bag for drugs and other contraband, do homework and wait for dinner, since it's Jamie's turn to cook tonight. I can't help her. Connie says the two of us would be loud, and noise in the kitchen interrupts her show. That ridiculous, over-the-top soap opera she's obsessed with.

Only a month before I got thrown out, Netflix had a new documentary on hunger in developed countries versus underdeveloped ones. Dad saw it saved in my queue. He'd been out in the living room, checking his email from the couch.

"Why do you watch this crap?" he asked, his green eyes not leaving the TV. "What do you care about all these problems other people have? You have food, you want to go around moping about something you'll never have to deal with?"

"You're a divorce lawyer," I replied from the other end of the couch. "You deal with other peoples' problems every day. Isn't that what you're doing now?" I nodded at his laptop.

Dad grimaced, the bags under his eyes making them look droopy. He set the remote on the end table and adjusted the computer. "And look how happy it makes me."

When Connie calls us to the table, I sit and quietly eat the chicken casserole Jamie baked for dinner. Connie shoots contemptuous questions at us in between mouthfuls. "How was school? You learn anything?"

"We're dissecting a frog in science class. It's gross," Jamie says, watching Connie with a grimace that I'm not sure is related to her or the frog. "Why is that something we need to know how to do? I don't think I'll ever need to pull apart a frog's guts."

Connie snorts but nods, seemingly in approval of Jamie's assessment. I don't want to picture dead frogs or dead anything, so I stare at the red Kool-Aid in front of me. We never drank sugary drinks at home. "And what else have they been teaching you kids?" Connie asks.

Jamie elbows me in the side. She's already answered a few questions, so it's time to share the love.

"Sorry. I'm just tired," I finally mutter, pulling my gaze from the Kool-Aid to Connie. Annie giggles at the glare her mother gives me. Her big eyes and pudgy cheeks almost make the little girl cute. Almost.

Connie snorts. "No doubt from horseplaying late into the night." She glares at me. "I heard you girls. You know nothing gets by me and those monitors. You'd think you'd be a better example."

Lizzie watches Connie glare at me, her eyes wide. Most of the time, she doesn't say much. Her social worker brought her in after her mother was arrested for drug dealing, and her mom apparently never got her act together afterward. This should be a safe place for Lizzie, but she's scared of Connie. Seeing Lizzie cower when Connie talks to her, this little girl who should be showered with attention by any parent and yet is afraid of Connie, makes me want to throw things.

I unclench my jaw. "We weren't," I say. "We were studying. You know, so we can get good grades and one day get out of this hellhole."

Connie chokes on her food and her thin eyebrows shoot high up on her forehead.

"This hellhole? I'm guessing you think you're too good for this town, huh? You're from the city, so you're too good for Silver Valley?"

Under the table, Jamie's hand grabs for mine. She tries to squeeze it, to signal for me to stop. I yank it away.

"I didn't say anything about being too good for the town." I stare straight at Connie. She clutches her fork. "Just here."

"Here?" Connie speaks so quietly I can barely hear her. "You couldn't possibly . . ." she stutters, her voice cool, yet fierce. "My home?"

Jamie tries to grab for me again, but both of my hands are balled in fists.

"I'll let you figure it out. You're a smart woman. You did make it all the way up to the sixth grade, right?"

Connie slams both of her hands down and the whole table shakes. A piece of chicken falls from the pan and smears cheese on the table. Lizzie begins to whimper.

"To the dormitory," Connie hisses. "Stay there until you're ready to apologize and change your attitude. Come back in when you see that you're lucky I let you live here. Aren't many foster homes that want a stuck-up, ungrateful brat like you!"

I avoid Jamie's stare and walk away.

On my bed, I wrap my arms around my knees and rock back and forth. This is real. This is my life now. But just over two weeks ago, I was at home. I went to the same school I'd gone to for all of high school, I did my homework, I came home, and I ate dinner with my family. It was boring, but it was my life. I had a home. A father. A drunk, depressed father, but still, he's my dad.

Or was. Now I'm alone.

Connie's rough drawl travels from the kitchen. Complaining

about something, though I can't hear what. *Nope, not alone.* Being alone would be better than this.

That's all I wanted, before—to be on my own. Away from Dad and Tiffany's fighting. Away from Dad when he was drunk. Not having to ask Jess to let me stay the night at her house when I knew he was in one of his weird moods.

I put my hands over my eyes. Maybe I should have told her. I should have told her how he was acting.

I exhale, holding onto the blackness. I know I'd never do that. It would be too humiliating. Jess and her perfect family with her perfect still-together parents wouldn't know what to do with any of that information. Or worse, they'd try to help.

I open my eyes and look out the barred window to the backyard, where discarded broken toys decorate the yellowing and patchy grass. Still, my mind drifts back to my old life. I wish I could tell Jess about Christina, about Kale. I laugh softly to myself, thinking about the way Jess and I used to talk about boys. Jess was a virgin, too, but unlike me she held out for religious reasons.

I was just too scared of what would happen if my dad found out about it. When I started high school, he told me if he ever caught me messing around with any boys I wouldn't have to worry about him keeping us apart because after what he'd do to him—my dad never elaborated on this part—the kid would never want to see me again. I barely talked to any guys at school except our friend Bryan, who Jess knew from church. Jess and I both talked to him on the phone sometimes, and then immediately called each other to share the play-by-play. It was all harmless, though. We talked about stuff at school, bands we liked. Jess and I both were ecstatic just to have a cute guy who was our friend and were happy enough with that. Dad really had nothing to worry about in that department.

But he thought he did.

I clench my jaw. Not going to think about that.

Jess and I had a plan. Once we got away from our parents, we would be free to figure out who we wanted to be. We'd live in the dorms at UNR, wear whatever clothes we wanted—Jess couldn't because her parents were strict about that kind of thing—and study whatever we wanted, away from Dad and his jabs about history. Because what job worth having could I get with that, he'd say.

Even if I wanted to tell Jess what happened—which I don't—I can't. I can't even make up some story of where I went and why, because I don't have my phone. And like I'd ever ask someone at school to borrow theirs. That would be a stupid way to blow my cover. That's the last thing I need: everyone at school knowing I'm in foster care, feeling bad for me, or knowing the messed-up stuff Dad's been saying.

I need to get out of here, out of this room, this house, this town. This life. Once I do, I won't have to lie about where I live, or worry about anything or anyone else but me.

I close my eyes again. In my mind, I hear Dad's voice, soft and calm. Not angry. *Victoria,* he says. *I'm so sorry. I didn't mean any of it. I want you to come home. We all do.*

I hear Connie stomping through the hallway, and I wipe

the wetness off my eyes with the blanket before she opens the door.

"Now that you've had time to calm down, we need to have a little talk." She huffs. "My house, my rules. You don't follow them and I'll have you thrown out. And if there aren't any other foster homes that will take you, you'll have nowhere else to go but juvie."

I stare at Connie silently. Then I hang my head. She wouldn't be the first person to throw me out when I became inconvenient.

Maybe my dad and I won't work things out. Maybe he's forgotten all about me and moved on with his life. With Tiffany. With Sarah, who can take my place of being his daughter now that I'm gone.

Connie clicks her tongue, waiting for a response.

I could tell her I hate her. I could tell her she's the most horrible person I've ever met. That no one likes her. It would be so preferable to curling into a ball and sobbing.

Instead, I nod.

She eyes me and for a moment it's like I see sadness or sympathy in her eyes. The way they turn down, along with her mouth. But in a flash, she's back to normal. "I'm a stubborn and righteous woman," Connie says. "I may make a respectful child out of you yet."

"I'm sorry." That's it. I don't elaborate. Connie waits another beat, and then sighs before leaving.

About twenty minutes later, after she's finished doing the dishes, Jamie comes into the room.

"You okay?"

"I'm fine," I lie. "I just hate it here."

Jamie sits on the bottom bunk. She's watching me with her big brown eyes. "I know," she says. We sit in silence for a moment. "Me too," she finally adds. "But you're almost done. When you turn eighteen, then no one can make you stay here anymore. Then you can go home."

I pull my legs close to me, into my chest. "Home? I'm about as wanted there as I am here."

"Your dad doesn't want you back?" Jamie asks. I've avoided this conversation with her until now. She twists a piece of her short, strawberry-blonde hair as she watches me from the foot of my bed.

I shake my head.

"And neither does your stepmom?"

I speak slowly, controlled, without looking at Jamie. "Tiffany, my stepmom, probably wanted me gone from the beginning. She was jealous—at least that's what my dad said."

Jamie nods, but doesn't reply.

Suddenly, I'm back in my old house—or at least it feels like it—as I imagine what it would be like to be sitting in my bed there, instead of this bottom bunk in Connie's prison. Sarah's bed flashes in my mind, with her sitting on it. My dad walks into her room. He leans in close to her, his lips brushing her earlobe as he whispers something.

The hairs on the back of my neck stand up, and I shake my head quickly. *No, he wouldn't.* Nothing like that would happen with Sarah. Dad said I was special. And even if Dad wanted to—I shudder at the thought—nothing would ever happen with Tiffany always so close by.

Jamie clears her throat, staring at me.

I lower my eyes, blinking rapidly to regain focus. Tiffany's always around. She wouldn't leave Sarah alone long enough for my dad to bother her. Sarah could barely sneeze without her mom knowing about it.

"My dad blames me, I think, for his problems with his wife," I finally say.

Jamie pulls lightly at the sides of my comforter, dangling her legs over the side of the bed. "Why?"

I shake my head, not able to form the words. Maybe I liked the attention, but I didn't want him to—*No*. I shake my head. Nothing happened. It was a mistake, a misunderstanding.

"I'm tired," I say to Jamie. "Don't worry. I'm fine."

I stiffen as Jamie hugs me, wrapping her arms around my legs still pulled against my chest. She climbs up to her bunk and grabs her iPod, then lowers herself down, into bed with me. I scoot over to make room. She hands me one of her earbuds and puts the other in her ear.

I smile. She's trying to cheer me up. "I'm really not in the mood for one of your boy bands," I say.

Jamie scoffs, pretending to be offended. "Okay, fine. You choose."

I take the iPod and scroll down her now-familiar playlists until I find a bluegrass band and hit play.

Jamie takes the iPod back from me and leans her head back into my pillow. "You're so predictable."

"Quiet, child." I put the earbud in my ear. "You know nothing about music."

We settle in and listen for about a half hour before Connie hollers for us to turn the lights off and go to sleep.

CHAPTER
FIVE

*S*aturdays, as Connie told me my first wretched day here when she handed me that stupid binder full of rules, are room inspection days. I woke up at six this morning to get started on washing my clothes, before I took a break to study. And then when the clothes were washed and dried, I folded them and put them away. But I still need to dust.

Most of the cleaning supplies are in the laundry room. I find a dust rag and some cleaning spray next to a big white bottle of bleach. Back in the bedroom, I slide the rag over the windowsills and countertops, then put freshly washed sheets on my bed and Lizzie's, too.

Lizzie is coloring a piece of paper torn from one of Annie's coloring books. Must be, because she finished all the pages in the one she got from preschool days ago.

I kneel beside her to whisper. "How'd you manage to get that without Annie seeing?" Lizzie whips her head in my direction, her black hair falling in her face, her eyes wide.

"Don't worry, I won't tell." I add quickly.

Lizzie smiles, relieved. "Annie was in her room watching cartoons when I tore it out," she whispers back.

I look at the Disney princess wearing a big ball gown. Lizzie colored it bright pink. "It's beautiful," I say, and Lizzie beams. Jamie sits cross-legged on her bunk, watching me. I pat Lizzie on the head, and she goes back to coloring.

Grabbing the baby monitor off the windowsill and putting it in between my two pillows, I walk it over to the other side of the room. I slide my pillows in between Lizzie's pillows. *Try to listen in on us now, you cow.*

Jamie doesn't acknowledge what I'm doing, but continues watching me.

"You should really make your bed. Connie will flip if you don't."

"Have you ever had a boyfriend?"

"No. Why?"

"Oh, I don't know." Jamie sighs. "There's this guy at school. I really like him."

I laugh and shake my head. "I don't have much experience in the guys department, sorry."

Jamie shrugs, and stares out the barred window wistfully.

I set the dust rag down and climb the wooden ladder to sit with her. "What's he like?"

Jamie lights up, apparently eager to share this information. "He's really cute and nice and funny. And everyone likes him. He talks to me, like a lot, even in front of his friends."

Jamie's face can barely contain her smile. "He held my hand today."

I grab her pillow and hit her with it. "You really buried the most important information there!"

Jamie ducks out from under the pillow, breathless. "Yeah," she says. "He asked me to be his girlfriend, and I said yes." Her face is practically glowing.

She laughs, her voice happy and carefree. "I don't know, maybe living here isn't that bad. Wait—" She stops after catching the look on my face. "What I mean is," she says, "I've made some friends, and I like going to the school here. Middle school isn't like the best thing in the world wherever you go, but here the kids are really nice, and they pay so much more attention to me than kids at my old school did."

I fiddle with the edge of her bedspread. "Have you told anyone you live here?"

Jamie shakes her head quickly. "Nope. No way. Have you?"

I shake my head, too, but try to pull the smile back on my face. "I'm happy for you." I look down at the dust rag I left below. "I better keep cleaning. I don't want to provoke the wrath of Connie."

Jamie fixes her bed and cleans up her area. She settles on top of her covers and takes a nap, and I use the rest of the afternoon to study, study, study.

Connie bangs on the door with the restraint of a bulldozer a couple hours later, and Jamie climbs down from her bed. Connie opens the door as I put my schoolbooks in my backpack.

Connie walks into the room, clipboard in hand. Lizzie moves to stand in front of her bottom bunk bed and Jamie and I do the same in front of ours, just as instructed for weekly room inspection. With white gloves on her hands, Connie traces her fingers over the windowsill next to Lizzie's bed.

She pulls her hand up and inspects her fingertips, still white. Connie makes a few fast, dramatic marks on the sheet of paper.

"Corners of the sheets tucked just like I taught ya, Lizzie." Lizzie smiles at me in gratitude. Connie moves up to the shelf behind Jamie's bed, feeling the wood as she looks behind Jamie's few belongings. She does the same thing to the shelf near my bed, and our shared dresser, before stopping to look at me.

Connie waves her white, dustless glove at us. "Good job, girls. I'm happy to see you took my instructions cleaning this room seriously. This place looks great and, as your reward, free time for the rest of the day!"

I force a smile. Like this is a treat, not having Connie bark at us to cook or clean for half a day. Connie looks at us, to see if we have anything to say.

"Thanks," I mutter. Connie's face falls slightly, but then she flashes me her trademark scowl as she leaves the room.

Now that we're free of the witch, Lizzie pulls her coloring page out and settles onto her bed, and Jamie puts her headphones in and starts writing in a notebook. I should study. What an exciting Saturday I have planned. Not that

I used to have the most epic Saturdays at home, but they were definitely better than this.

My mind drifts to my stepsister. The last time I spent a Saturday just hanging out with Sarah, watching our shows and stuffing our faces with junk food, she fell asleep on the couch. If I had known it was the last time we'd *really* spend together, just her and me with no fighting or parent drama looming over us, would I have paid more attention? Would I have told Sarah what she means to me?

My mom knew about lasts. Our last conversations were all about me not giving up, me remembering to keep on going no matter what, taking care of myself and Dad. Mostly taking care of Dad. And how much she loved me.

Those last hugs where she held me tight and wouldn't let go.

Mom's last words to me are written in a letter she had Dad give to me after she died from breast cancer, four years ago. I've read it over and over again to remember Mom. To feel her with me, even when I can't feel her arms wrapped around me, even when I can't hear the sound of her sweet laugh.

Everything's different now. Everything. Mom is gone, I'm completely out of Sarah's life, and my dad's, too. Sarah and Tiffany believe lies about me, and who knows what Jess thinks. Did she ask my dad? Does she even care I'm gone?

Maybe no one misses me.

I grab my backpack out from under the bed, sifting through until I find the letter. At least I had the good sense to bring it with me when Fran took me away. I lay back down to read it for probably the millionth time.

Dear Victoria,

If you're reading this letter, it means I'm no longer with you. I'm so sorry, sweetheart. I wanted more than anything to watch you grow up into the lovely young lady I'm sure you'll become. I'm sorry to miss your high school graduation, your wedding day, meeting your children. But I'll be watching you, baby. I'll never truly leave you if you keep me in your heart.

I know this won't be easy on your father. Please take care of him. It'll be just you two now, and your father isn't as strong as he'd like everyone to think. I know sometimes he loses his temper, but he loves you. Please remember that. He loves you so much, just like I do. You're so pretty and smart and kind. I know you're going to do great things, sweetheart, and I'm so proud of you.

Please don't let my dying hold you back. It's normal to grieve, but I want you to move on, Victoria. That's normal and healthy and I want your father to move on, too. He'll need someone to take care of him, so please don't give him a hard time if he finds someone new to love. And I hope you'll take care of him, too. You're so good at that. I love you for that sweet heart of yours, baby. I love you both so much. I just want you both to be happy.

If you can promise me one thing, please lead a happy life. Choose to be happy. It's a choice. Don't let this or any other hardship define you. Like I told you, everything in life is temporary, the good and the bad. Be strong like I know you are.

I love you. You're my biggest achievement and my greatest love. Thank you for that.

Love,

Mom

A single tear falls from my face and hits the letter. Quickly, I wipe it off. Softly blow it dry. Gingerly folding the paper, I put it back in its envelope and stash it back in my bag.

I know this won't be easy on your father. Please take care of him, she wrote.

I did take care of him, Mom, or at least I tried to. But it wasn't enough. I wasn't enough.

Everything in life is temporary.

Even this. Missing home. Foster care.

I remember Mom telling me over and over again *everything in life is temporary* as she was dying. Those few months went by in a blur, mostly spent by myself as Dad took Mom to doctor's appointments and chemotherapy. At home, Mom put on a brave face and Dad cried alone in his room. He thought we couldn't hear, I think. But it was temporary. She died, and then Tiffany and Sarah came along.

Happiness. Suffering. Even life itself. All temporary. Everything, good and bad, ends, so I'd have to pick up the pieces after she died and move on—that's what Mom told me. *Okay, Mom. I won't let tragedy define me. I'll be strong. Like you.*

I grab my stupid pre-calculus book. Getting good grades and going to college is the only way I can make a new life for myself.

But the words in the textbook blur out of focus. I read and reread them, still remembering. For my mom, I wanted to go to college and get good grades and become the person she was certain I would. I wanted to make her proud of me. Even if I wasn't sure that she was out there somewhere, in Heaven or whatever, I didn't want to let her loss define me. That, like she said, would be the best way to honor her memory.

It was after she died when I decided I wanted to major in history, even though Dad thought it was a stupid major. One that wouldn't *align with real world success.* It makes me think of a book I read about a year ago that was all about becoming an expert at something. It said you had to jump on the right opportunities and practice whatever it is you're passionate about for ten-thousand hours. I thought about that book for weeks. I couldn't imagine loving anything except history enough to focus on it for that many hours, to be that committed.

I read the introduction to the math lesson again.

Jess and I did a campus tour with her parents last year. We were going to read books on the quad together when the weather was nice, just like the girls we saw when we visited. We were going to get jobs on campus and save money for spring break, to go somewhere with a beach.

I shake my head and hold onto the textbook tighter.

I can't think like this. I'm still going to go to college. It might not be UNR. It might not be what I hoped for or dreamed of. But that dream is dead, just like Mom. It's gone and it's not coming back.

I pull out some financial aid forms I got from the school's guidance counselor, Ms. Claire. She told me about a grant that offers money to help foster kids pay for school and living expenses if they make good enough grades and turn in a budget and financial plan. I'm pretty sure I can live in a studio or one-bedroom apartment near the community college for about one thousand dollars per month, including utilities. Now I take out my college preparedness notebook and add up the price of rent, add what I think I'll spend in groceries and other incidentals per month. Plus the cost of tuition and fees and textbooks.

I stare at the number for a long time. That's a lot of money.

I never had a job. Dad wouldn't let me work. He said school was my job. At the time, I thought that was nice of him. He did give me an allowance and I had a savings account, which of course I no longer have access to. I've never had to worry about money, I mean not really. I saved for an iPad, which I had to leave at home—of freaking course—but that's about it. Dad covered clothes, gave me lunch money. He was going to pay for college, rent, and books. Now I have nothing.

I put my head in my hands. *Temporary. Everything in life is temporary.* Then I get back to number crunching.

On Sunday morning, Connie takes us to church. To the outside world, Connie seems to be a good, Christian woman. At least, that's how she thinks people see her. She holds her head high as we walk into the one-story building with a sign that says "All are Welcome" in the foyer. Ahead, there's a big wooden cross behind the podium, and stained-glass windows behind that.

Maybe right this minute, Jess is in a church like this

back in Reno. Maybe she and her parents are praying for me. She always asked me to come with her Sunday mornings, but I never did. I didn't see the point in it. Mom believed in God—though she didn't go to church—and look where that got her, dead from cancer.

Connie shakes the pastor's hand heartily before marching us to our seats. The pew in front of us is full of little old ladies, widows and divorced women, wearing hats and bonnets and long, pastel dresses. And they seem to *love* Connie.

The frailest looking of them turns and leans over the back of her pew to talk to Connie. "I've said this before and I'll say it again," she says. "It's so good of you, Connie, to take these poor kids in." The woman scans each of our faces briefly before looking back at Connie. "They're all so lucky the Lord gave them a second chance and blessed them with a mother like you!"

I snort, but that turns into coughing when Connie shoots a glare my way. Jamie sits quietly next to me, not wanting to provoke the beast. I contain myself and put my hands in my lap on the tattered, two sizes too big, mess-of-a-skirt Connie bought me when I told her I couldn't go to church with her because I didn't have anything formal enough. I cross my ankles as I sit up in the church pew and smile innocently at Connie until she returns to her conversation. Jamie stifles a laugh.

Yeah, this church is fun all right. If there is a God, he certainly isn't here.

And he wasn't back home in Reno that night with my dad, either.

The sudden lump in my throat tells me I need to get out of here. "May I be excused, Connie? I need to use the bathroom," I whisper so I don't disturb the pastor as he readies to give his sermon.

"Of course, dear," Connie answers loud enough for everyone within a two-pew radius to hear her.

The lump turns to bile and I swallow it down. I head to the bathroom and almost walk into the door as it opens from the other side, revealing one of the last people I want to see here: Shampoo Commercial Girl from school. My mind grasps for her name.

"Taylor," I mumble. "Sorry, sorry about that." I try to walk past her into the bathroom. I can feel my face turning bright red.

"Victoria," she says coolly, looking perfect in a pretty, pink dress with her glossy hair straightened expertly. "I didn't know you go here."

My chest tightens. If she sees me with Connie, she'll know.

"No, no," I stammer. "I'm actually just helping out—volunteering, you could say." Taylor eyes my second-hand outfit. *Really?* her face says.

I clear my throat. "Yeah, volunteering for a friend of my mom's. Connie, she takes in foster kids, bless her, but it's hard to get them all ready for church and to get them to sit still, behave themselves, so I volunteered to help her. I thought it would look good on my resume, when I try to get a job next year."

Taylor smooths a piece of hair away from her face.

"Who's your mom? What does she do? I mean, your family moved here for a reason, right? It's such a small town, maybe I know them."

"Nope, not them," I say quickly. "Just me and my mom, and it's a long story. We'll have to sit together at lunch sometime, if you aren't too busy. I mean, you have so many friends."

Taylor continues looking at me, waiting for me to elaborate. Because she probably knows I don't eat lunch with anyone. I've continued dodging Christina and Kale's attempts to get me to sit with them all week. That bench outside practically has my name on it.

I step around her. "Sorry, not trying to rush, but I want to hurry up in here and get back to the sermon. You know, since I'm supposed to be helping with the kids and all."

I walk by her and into a stall. Why did I do that? Lies are harder to keep up with than avoidance. I rest my head against the wall, doing everything I can to not run. Not just out of the church, where old ladies look at me with pity and mild interest, but no actual compassion. Out of this town, where I'm a stranger, only exciting because I'm new.

When I return to the pew and sit, Connie reaches to put her arm around me. I flinch and scoot away from her. I look back to see Taylor sitting a few pews behind us, smirking in our direction.

Connie turns to see who I'm looking at and seems to register that I don't want to be seen with her. Her face falls. I grab a Bible from the seat in front of me, pretending not to notice.

Connie pulls her skirt down and looks at me again, but not like before. Her lips a thin line, her eyebrows furrowed, she stares at me with her beady eyes, using them to shoot daggers at me.

I can't help it. I look back at Taylor, who is now whispering into the ear of a pretty woman who is also perfectly coiffed. Glossy hair, flawless makeup. Probably her mother. The woman nods. They're both looking at Connie.

And just when I thought my life couldn't get worse.

CHAPTER
SIX

hird period P.E. I stare at my gray T-shirt that says Silver Valley High School on it and the accompanying blue shorts in my locker. I hold on to the door, even after the locker room clears out after the first bell rings.

"What are you waiting for, an invitation?" Christina claps her hand on my back and I flinch. "Whoa, sorry about that," she says quickly. "I didn't mean to scare you."

I force a laugh. "I'm fine."

Christina fiddles with her phone. It feels like it's been forever since I had my own phone. I stare at it, remembering, for a moment too long, because Christina notices.

"So, hey. I was looking for you on Instagram last night and couldn't find you. What's your handle?"

I stare into my locker, like I'm looking for something, even though I'm not. "I don't have an Instagram."

Christina chuckles. "Well look who's a small-town girl now. So what, then? You're only on Facebook?"

I hold my P.E. clothes in one hand and shut

the locker with the other. "No, I actually don't do anything. I, uh, I used to, but I had a bad experience."

Christina raises her eyebrows at me. "I'm waiting."

I sigh and scan the room. Nothing but lockers, no people around. "It's a long story." I face Christina again, racking my brain for a believable excuse. "It involved some pictures. And a party. Yeah, a party, and my mom was pissed. And she closed down all of my social media accounts and won't let me reactivate any of them until I turn eighteen."

"Brutal! What a hard ass."

I bite back a laugh. As if not having a phone was my biggest problem in life. "You're telling me."

Christina looks at the door to the gym. "Well, hurry up and get dressed! You really don't want to piss off Ms. Oak, speaking of hard asses."

She puts her phone in her locker, next to mine, and locks it. I change quickly and trail behind Christina.

As soon as I reach the edge of the court, Ms. Oak calls to me in her raspy, deep voice. "Hustle up!" She's standing in the middle of the gym, to the right of a volleyball net, with about twenty students around her. Blue, silver and white banners saying Silver Valley Wolves and Wolf Pride line the wall behind us, along with several rows of blue bleachers.

A flash of Tiffany, Sarah, Dad and me playing beach volleyball at Lake Tahoe every summer crashes into me. Me and Dad versus Tiffany and Sarah, or sometimes Sarah and me versus Tiffany and Dad. My team always won. Mom played in high school and taught me how to play, after all.

"You know Lauren, right?" Christina whispers quickly.

I nod at the freckled-faced brunette next to her. She has so many freckles that she almost looks tan. I recognize her from some of my classes and because she usually hangs out with Alex, Kale, Christina, and Taylor—who I'm still successfully avoiding, not that she's tried to talk to me since church.

My jaw tenses. Most of the time Lauren is attached at the hip to Taylor. I try not to stare, afraid to see if she's looking at me funny, or is showing the interest—or even distaste—Taylor seems to have for me. Do they suspect I live with Connie? Have they told Christina about it?

Ms. Oak bounces the volleyball. She's saying something, but her words are drowned out by the *thud* the ball makes each time it hits the ground. Thump. Thump. Thump. It doesn't matter what I was focusing on before, because being near something that's *so Mom* means she's all I can think about now.

I'm back in my bedroom with her, a couple weeks before she died. No volleyball net. No kids standing around waiting to play.

"Baby girl, my strong, sweet, beautiful girl," Mom said. She ran her fingers through my hair as I watched a tear cling to her long eyelashes.

"I need you to promise me something," she began.

I scooted closer to her on my bed. "Anything," I whispered.

"Promise me you'll be strong when I'm gone."

I shook my head. "You're not going to die, Mom. You can't give up. The chemo—"

Mom bit her lip as the tear rolled slowly down her cheek.

"It's not working, honey. I've stopped taking treatment. I want to be myself for the last bit of time I have."

I shook my head again, holding tears back.

"No."

"Please, Victoria. Please, just listen to me. I need your help, baby."

"I'd do anything for you, Mom. You have to know that."

My voice was shaking now. Mom reached for my hand.

Christina and Lauren are whispering to each other, but I'm not listening.

"Take care of your dad. It's going to be really hard on him when," she hesitated and looked down at her lap, "when I'm gone."

It would be hard for me, too, I thought. Unbearable.

Which is exactly why she couldn't die.

Christina elbows me in the side. Ms. Oak calls my name again. I hadn't realized she was taking roll.

"Here," I mutter.

"Where are you today?" Christina whispers.

I shake my head quickly. "Didn't sleep well last night. I'm just tired."

Ms. Oak goes back to roll call.

I stare at the volleyball net. Mom was outgoing when she was my age. She loved to play volleyball, and high school was actually fun for her. She had so many friends. But she had her pain, too. She used to tell me how much she wished she had a dad growing up. How independent her mom was, how she never listened to anything any of her boyfriends said, and that's why they always left. Mom told me she and her mom were always moving around when she was young, from boyfriend's house to new boyfriend's house. And how much it hurt whenever her mom made her say goodbye.

Mom told me if her own mother had been less willful, she could have had a dad. And that men needed to be respected and uplifted by their wives and children. That they had to see that they were needed to feel loved.

"Just don't let him lose hope, honey," Mom told me. "Show him life will go on. Don't let him lose himself. Don't let him stay sad forever. I want him to marry again. Maybe he'll give you that brother or sister you used to want so badly."

I close my eyes as I remember Mom's sad smile. Me pushing my lips into a thin line, nodding. Watching my mom watch me. Needing me.

"I promise, Mom," I told her. "I'll take care of Dad."

Christina is saying something, and I blink several times to focus. I don't want my face to betray me. I force a smile. This is just a normal day in P.E. playing volleyball, no big deal.

"Okay, volleyball today," says Ms. Oak. "Team captains are Christina and Lauren, so you girls come to the front and pick your teams."

Christina flips her perfectly curled black ponytail behind her shoulder and walks over to the left side of Ms. Oak. Lauren heads to the right side and flips her ponytail just like Christina did. She smiles at me, revealing flawless, extra-white teeth.

Ms. Oak nods at Christina. "Christina, you first," she says.

Christina perks up. "Oh, well that's easy. I'll take the new girl, whose name is actually Victoria, who knew?" She grins at me and I walk to her side.

I'm here, right now. Not all in my head, not with Mom.

"How do you know if I'm any good?" I whisper to Christina as Lauren chooses Alex for her first pick.

Alex grins at Christina. "You don't stand a chance." He blows a kiss at her.

She rolls her eyes and turns back to whisper to me. "I don't, but there's only one way to find out. And I'm not letting my friend get chosen last in P.E.; you'll never live that down in this crowd. Just try not to suck, okay?"

At that I laugh, letting go of the tension in my chest. "I'll see what I can do."

"Great," she says, and then loud enough so everyone else can hear, "Next up I choose Zach."

The burly guy who sits with Alex in history heads in our direction. He attempts to high-five Christina, but she just looks at him awkwardly until he lowers his hand. Alex guffaws, Christina shakes her head at him, and she and Lauren continue picking people until the teams are full.

Christina and Lauren flip a coin. Our team wins, so Christina leads us to the right side of the volleyball net. "Zach, you take left front," she says as she points to the far-left side of the net. "Victoria, let's see how you do as a middle back. Stand in the middle, in the back," she explains. "That'll be Cassie in the back with you, and Jack to serve.

That leaves Kevin up front and I'm the setter." She walks over to me and extends her forearms facing out with her hands held together and thumbs out.

"That's how you hold your arms if the ball comes to you, and then you hit it like this," Christina says as she extends her arms up.

"Got it," I say, trying to suppress a smirk. There's no reason to tell her I'm good at volleyball, when I can show her. "No problem."

"Bump, set, spike, hit, that's the way we like it." Lauren chants in a singsong voice as she shimmies her hips back and forth on the other side of the court.

I hold back the kind of laugh that Lauren probably wouldn't like and turn to look behind me.

Jack stands with his left foot extended slightly in front of his body and both feet behind the line, bouncing the volleyball up and down. Ms. Oak blows the whistle. Once Christina's in place, with her knees bent, her hands reaching up in a setter's position and ready for the ball across from the net, Jack tosses the ball up and serves it. His force makes the ball soar to the middle of the other side of the court. Lauren scoops it up with her forearms just before it can touch the ground. One of her teammates gets under the ball and sets it, and Alex spikes the ball right down at us. Zach and Kevin are too far up in the court to stop it. That just leaves me.

I scramble to get in position, but won't make it quick enough so I dive, extending my arms just in time to bump it to Christina before I hit the floor.

Christina steps forward and sets it gracefully to Zach,

who slams it down just over the net. Too fast for Alex or Lauren to stop it.

The balls slams into the floor. "Nice!" Christina hoots. She raises her hand up in a high-five, and I oblige. "I didn't know you could play!"

I shrug. Christina smirks at me. I grin and, for once, it's not forced.

"Well, that's decided," Christina says to me after we win the game and are heading back to the locker room. "You're trying out for the club volleyball team. Regular season for school is already over—we lost in regionals—but there's a club team that meets after school."

"Um, no."

"What do you mean, 'no'? It would be such a waste if you didn't!"

I shrug. I didn't want to play on any sports teams back home, and that definitely hasn't changed. Plus, Silver Valley is more likely to become a booming metropolis overnight than Connie is to let me join any teams. "Sorry, Christina. It's just not for me."

She sighs. "Season's over anyway, so I guess it doesn't matter." After we reach and open our lockers, Christina starts undressing in front of me, taking off her uniform and putting her regular clothes back on.

Lauren calls "See you in class" as she walks toward the gym, pulling her letterman's jacket on as she does. I wave to her.

"And anyway," I say to Christina, "it's not like you don't have any friends on the team." I nod at the doorway Lauren just walked through.

"Lauren? She's too busy hanging out with Taylor." Christina shrugs, like it's no big deal, but her frown says otherwise.

I hesitate at my locker until the rest of the stragglers leave the locker room, and Christina nods toward the bathroom stall. "Go ahead."

I give her a small smile—I guess she noticed me changing in here before class rather than actually using the bathroom—and take my clothes with me. Christina follows and waits on the other side.

"What's wrong with that?" I finally say. "I mean, aren't all of you friends?" *Even with Taylor.* I slide my jeans on, scowling at the tag that shows my initials on it.

From the other side of the door, Christina sighs. "We're friends." But her annoyed tone makes me think there's something she's not telling me.

My throat tightens. I don't know why, but her silence makes me uneasy.

Christina waits a beat before talking again. "So, speaking of which, Taylor's been asking about you. She says she thinks you're *mysterious.*"

My stomach drops as I yank my shirt over it. "Oh?" Now my tone of voice—shrill—gives me away.

I hear her laugh from outside the stall. "Don't worry about her. She's just nosy. We used to be closer, but we hardly talk anymore—except I guess now that she sees we're hanging out. New people excite us in this one-horse town, as I've told you."

I inhale deeply before opening the bathroom stall. The class bell rings, but Christina doesn't seem to mind that we're going to be late.

"So what's the deal with you and Taylor, then?" I try to sound like I don't care much, casual. "You said you hardly talk anymore, but you're friends?"

"We are, I guess." Christina twists the ends of her hair, as if this conversation is boring her. "But she's a gossip, can't be trusted as far as you could throw her—you wouldn't believe the secrets of mine she's told practically the whole school about—and overall she's kind of annoying." Christina lets go of her hair and looks at me. "To be honest I'm just pretty much over most of the people in Silver Valley. Good thing you showed up, for my sake anyway."

I nod. Although I would hardly count my moving to Silver Valley a good thing.

Two weeks later, Santa smiles at Christina and me as we walk into his classroom. "So, do you ladies have a date to the dance this Friday, or are you keeping the entire male student body on pins and needles waiting for them to ask you?"

I smirk as we take our seats. "Pins and needles."

Christina shifts around in her chair. "Um, I sort of asked Alex to the dance this morning." She scrunches her nose and looks my way.

I whip my head to face her. "I thought he was a Neanderthal?"

"Yeah, well, he grows on you. Plus, the dating pool isn't exactly wide so it's either that or no one, probably."

A crumpled-up ball of paper sails in between our desks, narrowly missing Christina's head.

"Hey!" She turns around. Alex laughs and Christina flushes. Perfect. Now that I'm officially the only girl in this freaking school who hasn't asked a guy out, it's going to be a lot harder keeping people from bugging me about this stupid dance.

"I couldn't help it," Christina says. "He grows on you. And he's charming, kind of like your boyfriend Kale. Plus, I had a secret crush on him freshman year," Christina takes in my expression. "Alex. Not Kale! He's like my brother!"

I lower my voice so only Christina can hear. "Kale is not my boyfriend. I mean, yeah, we get along in pre-calculus, we joke around a little—well, mostly he does and I'm just there," I ramble. "But that doesn't mean anything." I add.

Christina's eyes dance with laughter. I glance at the seats behind me to make sure Taylor and Lauren didn't hear that. Taylor and I still haven't gotten together to talk about my "volunteer work" over lunch, like I promised her at church, weeks ago. Since then, neither Jamie or I have gone back. Connie doesn't like it—I bet she'd love to parade us around for those old church ladies to see—but technically, legally, she can't make us go, she told us after I complained.

So, for once, Mindy—or the threat of telling Mindy something—was actually helpful. Not that *I* talk to her. She supposedly calls and speaks to Connie occasionally, to check on how I'm doing.

Christina laughs. "It's not that hard to ask a guy to a dance, Victoria."

I shake my head and open my textbook, pretending to be suddenly very interested in today's reading assignment.

After the bell rings, Christina gathers her stuff, and we walk out together.

She's quiet for a moment. Then she stops walking. "Is something bothering you, other than the dance? You can tell me, you know."

I stop to look at her.

If only my biggest problem were this stupid dance.

I'm in foster care. A ward of the state of Nevada is the actual term, according to Mindy. I have no freedom. I have no family. All I have is a dream to go to college, to get out and start over when I graduate. It's the only thing that keeps me sane, keeps me from tearing my hair out and crying myself to sleep every night.

Christina lowers her voice. "We are friends now, right? Even though you never sit with me at lunch." She looks away.

Apparently, Christina takes it personally that I eat outside by myself all the time or spend lunch breaks in the library working on stuff for college. I usually tell her I need alone time at school for inner peace in order to rebuff her attempts to join me.

A few freshmen walk around us. I guide Christina to the right, a habit from my old school, where you'd get shoved if you stood in the middle of foot traffic blocking the way.

I force my face to match the lightness of what I'm about to say. "Need I remind you that you sit with practically the entire senior class at lunch? I'm an introvert. I think that's reason enough for me to prefer the solitude of the great outdoors, don't you?"

Christina leans her shoulder against the locker to her right and laughs. She stands straighter. "Okay, yeah. I guess I see your point, but we could always sit at a smaller table. And don't change the subject."

"I'm fine," I say as we start walking to our lockers. "Nothing's bothering me, but I am sorry for being a jerk. I'm glad you and Alex are going to the dance together."

Christina sighs and then looks at my jeans, the same pair I wear almost every day. "If you need something to wear, you can borrow something of mine."

My face tenses. "Thanks, I'll think about it."

Kale appears to the side of her. "Hey, since I ran into you, Victoria, I just thought I'd give you one last chance to ask me to the dance this Friday. It's Monday. Time's a runnin' out."

Christina beams. "I'll leave you two alone." She heads in the other direction before I can respond.

Kale grins. "Christina said you were working up the nerve to ask me."

My mouth falls open. "I never— "

"Hold on, hold on." Kale's hands shoot up quickly, as if fending off an attack. "I'm kidding. But she has mentioned a few times she thinks we should go together."

A moment passes and he drops his hands and puts them

in his pockets, his bravado fading. "But don't worry. You don't seem into it, so I'll just . . ." he trails off.

I swallow, my mouth suddenly dry. "Wouldn't you rather go with someone who asks you without you having to ask them to ask you?"

We stop at my locker, and I start shoving my stuff in there, not looking at him.

"I like you," Kale says. "I just think you're cute, you're funny—in a sarcastic way. I just thought we could have fun together if we went to the dance." He shuffles his feet and looks around the hallway as people walk by us. "But look, you don't want to go with me, that's okay. I'll stop bugging you about it." Kale takes a step backward. "See you later, then."

The back of his arm brushes against my shoulder as he turns around. It reminds me of something, but I don't know what. I hold tight to my locker door.

My father's back flashes into my mind. My skin crawled at the smell of whiskey on his breath, still lingering in the air after he pushed me onto my bed.

And I'm not staring at Kale's back anymore, at Kale walking away after I told him no. I'm back in my room. Watching my dad walk away. I said no, I said no, I said no.

And he left me.

My dad's back, his legs, turning around and stomping out of my room, I'm there again. The crash of the door as he slammed it shut, before he stormed back in moments later to physically throw me out of the house. He left me. In an instant, it all slams into me.

I whip around to face Kale. "Wait!" *Don't leave.* Kale turns to me, looking unsure.

"Go to the dance with me?" I blurt.

Kale's eyebrows furrow in confusion. I stare at him, breathless, waiting.

"Why the sudden change of heart?"

I tighten my grip on the locker. "I want to go with you, okay? You talked me into it."

His eyes search mine. "You're sure?" He tilts his head and lowers his voice. "Like I said, I think it could be great to go together. But I don't want you to feel like you have to . . ." he puts his hands back in his pockets. "Really, I'm sorry I bugged you so much. Date or no date, I'll be happy if we can be friends. If you want. I'd like that. Friends."

He chuckles, and I can tell he's embarrassed.

I look down at my feet, my face turning red. "It'll be fun. If you still want to, that is."

I look back up. Kale grins at me, his eyes animated, back to normal. I swallow.

"Yeah, I do." That smile's still lighting up his face. "See you later?"

I shake my head vigorously. "Yeah. See you."

He turns and walks away.

I breathe a few short and fast breaths. I can't help but smile, surprising myself, when I think about what I just did.

Is this a date? My first date?

And then it hits me like a punch in the gut.

Dad's words, *If I ever catching you messing around with any boys I'll make sure they never, ever make the mistake of chasing after my daughter again.*

I close my eyes.

No.

Dad's not here. He's not here, but I am, because he doesn't want me. So I can go to a dance, I can go on a date.

He can't stop me.

CHAPTER
SEVEN

*T*he next day at school, the high of asking Kale out has faded. Not that I'm not excited, but just getting through a day at school, pretending everything's fine, that I live in a normal house with a normal family, hiding my past, hiding my secrets . . . it's all so exhausting.

In between classes, I head for the bathroom to collect myself. I need to be alone, but don't have enough time to go outside to my bench.

Alone.

I've been *alone*, it seems, for years. Since I was eleven, since Mom got sick.

Inside the bathroom, I sling the door to a stall shut behind me. My backpack on the ground, I sit on the toilet with my head in my hands. I'm not here, at school. I'm there, in the past.

Dad had been worried, lately. I figured it was just work stuff getting to him, like usual, but Mom was acting off, too.

I thought maybe they were fighting. They'd been having so many hushed conversations behind their bedroom door that I couldn't hear. Dad had been moping around more than usual, talking to me less and less, seemingly everywhere Mom was when he was at home.

Mom picked me up from school, like any other day, but we drove home in silence. She held my hand, and I was grateful for her touch. Sometimes it felt like she was my best friend in the whole world. We talked about school and volleyball—though I loved playing with her at the YMCA when she sometimes took me, I'd never sign up to play a sport at school. Unlike Mom, who could make friends with anyone, I'd always been shy.

But even though we had all those things to do together, sometimes she seemed far away. Like when Dad was around, sometimes it was like I wasn't even there. She catered to his every need: took his shoes and jacket off for him when he got home, gave him massages, cooked all of his favorite foods. But when she didn't pay attention to him, if she and I were talking or playing a game, he got cranky, and she stopped.

Dad just felt left out, I guess. I wanted us all to have fun together, but it never really seemed to work out that way. It was either him and Mom—or Mom and me. Or sometimes Dad and me, if I caught him on a good day when he wanted to play Frisbee or watch TV with me.

But there Mom and I were in the car together that day, holding hands without talking. And I felt like everything was fine the way it was, even if our family was a little odd.

When we walked in the door, Dad was sitting at our round kitchen table, his head in his hands.

"Dad," I said, startled. "What are you doing home from work early?"

Dad raised his eyes to look at me. They were the most vibrant green, yet puffy and bloodshot. He'd been crying.

"Daddy." I moved toward him and he hugged me, wetting my shoulder with his tears. I froze.

Mom came up behind me, put her hands on my shoulders and sat me down. She sat next to me and grabbed my hand again. I felt hers shaking in mine.

"Baby, I'm sick," she said, her voice cracking.

"Do you need some medicine, like Dayquil or something?"

I knew it was more serious than that by the way they were acting, but my chest was tight and my head was spinning and I needed this not to be real.

Mom explained to me that though many people survive breast cancer, her cancer was advanced. It had spread to other organs.

I shook my head *no*. But Dad was crying, and Mom's face was pinched and her eyebrows were furrowed and I'd never seen her look so sad. I crumpled, shaking my head, saying no no no over and over again. It was as though if I said it enough this wouldn't be real.

But it was. Mom started going to more and more doctor's appointments and Dad holed up in his room, depressed. He wouldn't talk to me, I couldn't understand it. He crawled into himself, it seemed, and left me alone to watch Mom die. I watched her lose her hair. I combed her wig for her and told her she was still the most beautiful woman I'd ever seen. I saw her crying in the bathroom. I held her in my arms and told her she was the best mom in the whole world. That she could get through this.

It was like Dad couldn't take seeing Mom get so thin and frail or her skin turning yellow. She was so tired after he'd drive her home from chemo and then go back to work.

I cooked for her then, I took care of her then. And Dad either hovered over Mom, always there but not really helping, or hid in his room.

Until one day, when I came home from school and Mom wasn't home. When neither she nor Dad answered their phone for hours, I knew something was wrong. Dad came home in the middle of the night, his skin pale, his eyes red and puffy, wearing the saddest look I've ever seen on anyone in my entire life.

"She's gone," he said.

I was only twelve, too young to lose my mom. Blackness crashed down on me. Air couldn't make it into my lungs. Whatever words Dad was saying didn't reach my ears. I rocked back and forth, back and forth, for hours, even after Dad left my room. I'd never felt so alone.

The toilet in the next stall over flushes. I hadn't realized anyone had come in. I blink back a few tears. The bell rings. I'm going to be late to class if I don't start moving before the second bell. But I'm shaking, and I can't pull myself out of the hole I've fallen down. The place I try so desperately not to go—remembering for too long—it's dangerous. But now that I've started, I can't stop.

I hold my breath until I hear the water run, the girl in here with me washing her hands, and then the door close behind her as she leaves.

I walk out of the stall, stare at myself in the mirror.

Mom's gone. She's been gone for years. And now, Dad is, too.

He hasn't called. He doesn't miss me. He doesn't want me back.

I haven't been able to shake this feeling that I've been trying to ignore so hard that it hurts. I'm looking in the mirror and I can't lie to myself anymore.

Thinking back, remembering. Dad's been sad for so long, but what happened with him wasn't a misunderstanding. I know that now. What he did was wrong.

So at lunch, I go to the library and sit at one of the computer stations.

I type *What happens to fathers who touch children inappropriately?*

My heart beats fast as the content blocker pops up.

I sigh. Try again.

Reporting abuse, I type, *parent child*. I scroll through the list that the search engine brings up. A bunch of domestic abuse stuff, but toward the bottom, I see a link that makes my breath catch.

Signs of Sexual Abuse, Molestation and Wrongful Touch of Children

I shake my head, *no*, keep looking. Type more search words in.

Is the Child Victim Of Sexual Abuse Telling The Truth?

I feel my heart in my throat.

I tilt my head back, look up at the ceiling. Decide to try again, adding one more word to my search: *jail.*

My jaw clenches. More questions about if the child is

telling the truth. Another item is about what to do if you are accused of *molestation*. A few links down is one about sentencing and punishment. I click on it.

I stop breathing. Years in prison. *Years.* Up to a lifetime, depending on the circumstances, this website says.

Oh my God.

Dad's face flashes before my eyes, where the computer screen should be. Tears make his green eyes look bright, and his mouth quivers underneath his mustache. He told me he didn't know how he could live without Mom. I told him it would be all right. *It had to be.*

The librarian coughs and it's like a defibrillator just smacked me in the chest. I look around, no one else is here. No one can see what I'm looking at.

I remember promising Mom I would take care of Dad when she was dying. Even when her hair had fallen out from chemo, when her skin and eyeballs had turned yellow, when she was so weak she could barely sit up in bed, she reached her shaking hand for mine and made me promise one last time.

I close my eyes for a second, controlling my breath, controlling myself.

I can't do this to Dad. I have to take care of him, like I promised.

"Mom! One of the foster kids took my toy!" Annie shrieks later that afternoon. She's sitting on the living room floor among heaps of dolls, stuffed animals, and other toys. Lizzie, sitting cross-legged a few feet away from her, freezes, her hand clutching a doll. Wide-eyed, with fear practically permanently stuck on her face, she looks at Connie.

"No manners, hand it over!" Connie shouts. From the kitchen sink where I'm washing dishes, I watch Connie heave herself up from the couch and stomp to the corner of the living room.

Lizzie's bottom lip quivers as she gives Connie the doll. Connie hands it back to a pig-tailed Annie, who smiles deviously at Lizzie before tossing the doll behind her, missing her chest full of toys that she could not care less about as long as Lizzie isn't playing with them. Lizzie's shoulders begin to shake, her eyes welling up with tears.

Connie leans down to whisper something to Annie. Annie scowls and gets the toy, before handing it back to Lizzie, but she's still crying.

I want to go to her, hold her, tell her everything will be okay, tell her that she's more than just a government check.

But I don't. I hate myself for it, but I have to stay on Connie's good side for the possibility of her letting me work at the library on a group project with Christina this Friday night. Which is a lie, of course, but I can't tell Connie that. She'd never let me go to the dance. And I can't spend the night at a friend's house without CPS doing a full background check on her parents.

Kale's grin, his blue eyes lighting up as I tell him I want to go to the dance, flash in my mind. It might not have been my idea at first, but asking Kale out was worth it, just to see that smile. I don't want to keep pushing him away.

I don't want him to stop coming around. I don't want him to leave me.

Lizzie's wide eyes shift to me for a moment. She covers her face with her long, black hair when Connie turns back to her. "Go on, now! Don't be such a crybaby. Next time ask first to play with a toy. Learn some manners. And stop crying already. She gave you back the doll, didn't she?"

Lizzie sobs and runs to the dormitory. She didn't ask Connie permission to leave the room first, like usual.

I stare at the discarded doll on the floor. Annie doesn't pick it up, just goes back to playing with her other toys. Connie, already situating herself back on her couch throne, snaps at me. "What, you gonna cry, too?"

I take a deep breath, set the last of the dishes down to dry. But I say nothing.

Annie brings a handful of toys over to where Connie sits and flops down on the floor next to her. Connie kicks her feet out in front of the couch. "All of ya, a bunch of criers! Toughen up if you want to do any better than your parents. You'll all turn out just like them, those people who aren't smart enough to avoid getting their kids taken away and thrown in here."

I want to snap back. Smart enough, I'm not sure, but my parents were educated. My dad's a lawyer—but Connie doesn't want to hear that, or that my mom graduated from college but chose to be a stay-at-home mom and take care of me.

I look down at my hands resting on the tile countertop. Stare at my fingers, prune-like from washing so many dishes.

Here I am, leaning over an empty sink, just like my mom spent so much time doing. Is that what she imagined her life would lead up to, a marriage and a kid and a mountain of dishes? Until she died early, and all of her time to live was gone.

I walk over to the edge of the kitchen. "Can I sit down?"

Connie nods, surprised. I hardly ever sit in the living room with her, mostly because I can't stomach having to ask to do so. And because I don't have the desire to watch her crap TV shows. I move to the loveseat opposite Connie and look up at the screen. A voluptuous woman slaps a tall, dark and handsome man for cheating on her. Riveting.

I sit up straighter on the loveseat. "You're right, Connie, about our parents," I say. "Most of them weren't smart or tough enough to make the right decisions for their kids, but I don't want to be like them."

Connie looks back at the TV. I clear my throat. "I just want to do what you say, become smarter so I can live a better life. One where I can have a nice family and a nice house, like you do. So, I've been trying really hard at school."

Connie gives me the side-eye. "You trying to mock me? Because I won't stand another minute of your sass." Annie stops brushing her princess pony's mane to look up at us.

"No, no! Not at all," I answer quickly, my voice shrill. "I'm just saying being in this home has been a good influence on me, that's all. Just like my social worker said it would."

Connie tilts her head and smiles slightly. She pats Annie on the shoulder and twirls one of Annie's pigtails through her fingertips.

I stand. "I'm just going to go study in the dormitory now," I say. "My friend Christina and I are partners for a project. I'm compiling research—"

"Go on and get then, if you have so much work to do!" Connie waves an arm at me as she turns up the volume with the remote control. The woman who just slapped the man is now kissing him passionately.

Satisfied that I've laid some groundwork, I head to the room and open the dormitory door—to find Jamie crying in her bed. I quickly move closer.

"What's wrong?"

Jamie wipes at her face. "Nothing."

I climb up the ladder, pausing on the top step. "Did something happen?"

Jamie sits up. "I'm just homesick. I miss my parents."

I hesitate. Other than a few conversations that didn't delve too deep, our parents are mostly unchartered territory as far as the two of us go.

"Do you want to talk about it?"

She shakes her head. "No. No, I don't."

I sit at her feet and stare at my hands.

Jamie sniffles. "I'm glad you're here," she says. "I don't think I'd be able to do this alone."

I swallow the lump in my throat. "Me, too, Jamie. Me, too."

"Even though I haven't found Kale crushworthy since

we kissed," Christina says to me, "I can totally see why you like him."

I don't respond to the bomb Christina just dropped. *She and Kale kissed? When? And I'm just hearing about this now?*

I stare ahead rather than look at Christina. We're sitting on the bleachers watching Kale run laps around the track with the rest of the cross-country team below us. I'm supposed to be walking home from school now, but I told Connie this morning I wanted to stay late to ask a teacher for help on an assignment.

I just wanted to feel normal, for one hour, and hang out with a friend after school.

Christina tilts her head, glances from Kale to me, before readjusting her back on the bleachers. I'm biting my lip. Waiting.

Christina has chosen now of all times to be quiet. Although we're a few rows up on the bleachers and Kale—who breathes steadily as he jogs who-knows-how-many-laps—is unlikely to hear me, I'm careful to keep my voice low and unaffected. "Oh, you guys kissed?" I clear my throat. "I thought you said he was like a brother to you?"

Christina laughs and playfully shoves my shoulder. "You're too easy! Yeah, in eighth grade, spin the bottle. About as many sparks as kissing my grandma."

I grin and watch as little beads of sweat trickle down Kale's brown hair and onto his flushed, though still pale, face.

I look up at the clear blue sky and listen to the sounds of the runners' feet hitting the pavement as they go. There's not much else to listen to out here, other than a few birds chirping in some trees to the right of the field. At my old school in Reno, there'd always be the cacophony of cars driving through the intersection just outside of campus. But not here. In Silver Valley, the noises come from trucks, tractors, or animals. I've seen a coyote lurking at the edge of the bushes just outside of the school, and supposedly there are wild horses all around here, I just haven't seen any yet.

"Although I was surprised that he used a little tongue," Christina muses. "Apparently Alex dared him to, and trust me, Kale and I both regretted it." She wiggles, as if the thought alone is gross. "You know, if he was that much of a daredevil then, I'm sure he'll be quite a handful now." She looks at me with exaggerated wide eyes. "Tell me this, what are your thoughts on handcuffs?"

I start coughing. Like, a lot.

She smiles and flips her hair like she always does, with that self-certainty I admire. I guess having a friend in Silver Valley isn't the worst thing that could happen.

But then Jess, her round face and blue eyes, flash in my mind, and I suck in a breath. I haven't thought of her for days.

"Whoa, I was only kidding!" Christina raises her thick, black eyebrows at me.

I shake my head, try to conjure up a smile to match our easy conversation. "If he thinks he can try any of that with me at the dance, he's got another thing coming. I demand at least three dates before any talk of handcuffs, as a general rule."

Christina's eyes widen, and she laughs so hard, I can't help but laugh, too.

"And I never said I *like* him." My eyes land back on Kale

as he makes his way around our side of the track. He catches my eye and grins. I hope Christina doesn't notice me blush.

But her huge smile tells me she does. "You didn't have to say it." She laughs. "He's the best—I've probably never met a nicer guy. I always wanted a brother, and for me he's like the closest thing. You should see him with his sisters, how he plays with them and takes care of them."

I turn to her, remembering the picture book. "Takes care of them. What do you mean?"

Christina eyes the runners for a second, lowers her voice. "His dad isn't around much," she says. "He works a lot, as a truck driver. And you know, four kids are a lot for Kale's mom to handle at once—three, if you don't count Kale. He just kind of fell into that role, I think, taking care of everyone."

Christina shrugs, like that's the end of it. But my stomach tightens. "I feel like there's something you aren't telling me."

She sighs. "Look, I shouldn't have even brought it up. It's really not my business to tell, but his dad drinks, like too much. When he's around, that is. And he fights with Kale's mom. Not like physical or anything, but it gets ugly. So as much as he can, Kale makes sure his sisters don't see it. He takes them to the park or to his aunt's. I've even picked the girls up a few times, while Kale stayed home and tried to get his dad to calm down. I'd call the cops, I really would, if I thought he'd ever lay a hand on his wife, but Kale swears his dad never has."

I sit up, moving my feet off the bleachers in front of me, and clutch my knees to my chest.

"I had no idea," I whisper. "That sounds awful."

Christina inhales deeply and then lets out a long breath. "Yeah, I know. But look how Kale is despite it all. It's pretty impressive, you know?" She laughs softly. "If I had half his chill about much smaller stuff, stuff that doesn't even matter in the grand scheme, I would be better for it."

The coach yells at the players to speed it up, improve their time. In the front of the pack, Kale pushes to go faster. I watch him, the way his limbs flow as he runs. How his chest rises as he breathes almost rhythmically. I guess I don't know that much about him. We all have our secrets.

I clear my throat. "Christina, I have a problem."

Christina's dark eyes narrow. "Is everything okay?"

"Everything's fine. It's just my, uh, my mom, like I said before, she's really strict. There's no way she'll agree to me going to the dance."

She scoffs. "Why not? Are you Amish or something?"

I swallow a laugh. "No, it's just I'm grounded. I guess I've been slacking off on doing my chores, or so she says. But I was thinking if I told my mom we're working on a class project at the library, that could work."

Christina eyes me quietly for a moment. "Lying to your mom—I didn't think you had it in you, Vickster."

"Vickster?"

"You know, rhymes with trickster. Eh? Eh?"

I release my legs to a regular sitting position. "So, you'll do it, then?"

Christina looks at the track just as Kale laps one of the other guys, smacking his backside and laughing as he goes.

"Do what?" Christina asks, looking back at me. "You're the one lying, not me."

I shake my head. "I just wanted to make sure you knew that I'll be stretching the truth a little and that you're okay with it."

We both look back at the track just as the cross-country coach blows the whistle and the team huddles around him. Christina chuckles. "Anything for young love, and to keep me from having to spend too much time alone with Alex. Wouldn't want him to get any ideas."

"Thanks," I breathe. "And what do you mean, ideas?"

Christina shrugs. "Oh, you know, the usual. Handcuffs."

I laugh at that as the team starts to disperse.

I scoot forward. "I should go home now."

Christina's arm shoots out in front of me. I follow her eyes and see Kale's on his way over.

"And to what do I owe this pleasure, Victoria?" Kale smiles at me as he wipes the sweat off his forehead with his forearm, climbing the bleachers. "Staying after school to watch me practice?" Kale wiggles his eyebrows dramatically at me.

My first instinct is to usually laugh at Kale's silliness but I'm not sure what to do or say after all I just learned about him. "I, uh, it wasn't my idea. It was Christina's."

As Kale jumps over the last bleacher between us, Christina gives me a knowing look, then turns back to Kale. "It's a nice day, and I thought Victoria could use some sun. Her skin was starting to blind me."

After winking at me, Christina unzips her bag, pulls out

the hand towel she uses for volleyball and tosses it at Kale's face. He snatches it out of the air before it hits him.

"Thanks." He uses it to wipe the back of his sweaty neck. His fair skin glistens in the sunlight, and I know I should find him totally gross right now.

But I don't.

Christina puckers her lips at me. Thankfully the towel is covering Kale's face, so he doesn't see.

I clear my throat. "I hope you don't sweat this much at the dance."

He finishes up with the towel. "I will if it means you'll be checking me out as much as you were this past hour." He grins.

I choke, but try to cover it up with coughing.

He slides onto the seat next to me.

"I know, I know. I'm much better looking than any guy you've ever seen. Where was your old school again? Reno, right?

I slide my backpack on. "Yep," I say. "Good old Reno."

"Do you miss it there? Do you go back and visit your friends much?" he asks.

Christina perks up a little, watching me. I don't talk about Reno or my past if I can help it. It's too risky. And, if I'm being honest, it reminds me of everything I left behind. Everything that I can't go back to or change. Everything I have absolutely no control of.

I pinch my forefinger and thumb together. "Not really. I mean, we talk on the phone, but I've been pretty busy with homework and stuff."

"We should go!" Christina says. "My parents let me go shopping there sometimes, you know, because there aren't a ton of stores in Carson City. We could all go some weekend soon, after the dance. Catch a movie or go bowling. And you can invite people. We could meet your friends!"

I hold the straps of my backpack closer to my shoulders, tightening my grip. "Yeah, we should," I say slowly. "I mean, I'll ask my mom. She's strict, like I said, but I'll ask." I stand. "I better go."

"Want a ride?" Christina asks.

"No, I like to walk." Another lie.

Kale stands up beside me. "I'll walk with you."

"No, really, I'm fine."

He faces me. "Well, can I at least get your number? I'll text you, coordinate for the dance."

"Nope," I call over my shoulder, already bolting down the bleachers. "No phone. Long story, Christina can tell you."

I don't hear them say anything else, because I'm already too far away for their words to reach me.

After dinner that night I stare at Connie's plate, which is littered with crumbs from the Hamburger Helper I made for us. "Here, let me get that." I take Connie and Annie's dishes to the sink, before making round two for everyone else's.

"What do you play me for, girl, a fool? I know you want something," Connie calls to me. I turn around.

"What do you mean?" I ask in a high-pitched voice. I clear my throat and force my voice to return to normal. "I just thought I'd get the dishes done early so I can work on that project I told you about."

Jamie stands. "Can I be excused?"

That's probably the first thing I've heard her say all night, I realize. She's been quiet all day. I try to catch Jamie's eye, but she won't look at me. She fiddles with the end of one of her long sleeves and tucks her arms into each armpit under my stare.

Connie watches Jamie for a moment. "Go ahead," she says.

Jamie rushes to our room. In her back pocket, I see something shimmer. Something shiny. Connie sighs heavily, seemingly not noticing. Lizzie looks down at the table, saying nothing, per usual.

Connie turns her attention back to me. "What's this project you've been talking about?"

My breath catches. I hadn't thought of that part yet. I look at Lizzie. She's only six—she should be in kindergarten already, but no one taught her any of the stuff she needs to know, like colors or whatever kids her age are supposed to have learned, so she's in day care with Annie. Scared, timid, not old enough to know how truly messed up all of what happens in this house is. She just knows it hurts. And that she misses her family.

I turn toward Connie, thinking quickly. "It's for health class." Never mind that I'm not even in health. "We're supposed to write a research paper and give a presentation. I chose to focus on the importance of brain development for young children, like toddlers." I take a breath and force a smile. "It's supposed to be really important they are nurtured and cared for at that age to make sure they turn into healthy, good people."

Lizzie watches Annie leave the table, without permission, and go to the living room to play with her toys.

"I was inspired by you, actually." I look back at Connie. "That's why I picked the topic. If some of the babies and little ones you take in didn't live here, who knows what would have happened to them, right? You aren't just keeping them from being homeless. You could be *saving* them."

Connie stares at me. No expression. Lizzie, on the other hand, looks at me like I've grown a third eye.

Suddenly, Connie stands and walks over to me. She raises her arm—I flinch slightly, but that doesn't stop her from patting me on the back.

"That's a good project." Connie nods vigorously. "I trust you'll let your classmates know where your research is coming from? There's a lot you could learn in this house, like I always say." She grins and practically bounces to her spot on the couch. Lizzie and I watch her from the table, motionless.

"If there's anything I can do to help, you just let me know," Connie says as she sits. "I'm happy to help teach those classmates of yours a thing or two. This town could use more people like me. That's what those nice ladies at church say."

"Well, actually, there is something," I call after her. "Would it be okay if I work with Christina on our project after school Friday? The library stays open until nine-thirty at night for tutoring, so maybe I could stay until nine or so?"

Connie looks back at me. I hold my breath.

She remains still for a moment. Finally, she nods. "All right. You'll have teacher supervision, so yeah, I suppose. But only because it's just the kind of project I approve of, not any of the crap they usually teach in health class."

"Thank you!" I rush back to the sink to continue cleaning before Connie changes her mind. When I'm finished, I practically skip into the dormitory.

Jamie's sitting on her bed, and she quickly pulls her blanket over her lap as though she's hiding something. I pause, give her a questioning look as I walk in. She scowls at me.

I stop short. "What's gotten into you?"

"Oh, nothing," Jamie scoffs. "Just the usual. My life is a living hell, I have no family, and I'm practically a slave in this home. No biggie."

I walk over to the little wooden ladder that leads up to her bed but hesitate at the bottom of the steps. "Can I come up?"

Jamie shrugs and turns away, so I make my way up and sit at the foot of the bed. She pulls the blanket closer to her lap, as though she's protecting herself.

I reach my hand out and let it hover near Jamie's legs. She moves her watery, angry eyes toward me, and I snatch it back before she can see.

"I've lived here for months," she says. "This wasn't supposed to be my permanent home. My caseworker said I'd only be here for a little while, but nobody wants to adopt me. I'm too old."

I rest my hand on the edge of the bunk. "I thought you

liked living in Silver Valley, or at least your school. What about that boy, your boyfriend? How are things going with him?"

Jamie glares in the other direction. "Who cares about him? He's just a guy. He doesn't even know me, and we broke up anyway."

"What happened?"

Jamie's face reddens. "What does it matter? I don't care about him or anyone at my stupid school! I just want to get out of here. I just don't want to feel like I'm in jail. I want to live in a different foster home, anywhere else but here."

I lean closer to her. "You'll get another placement." *It's more of an emergency home than a long-term placement,* Mindy told me. I don't know much about other foster homes, but they can't all be this bad. "You have to be patient. There are so many good things about you. Someone will want you, I promise."

"I'm not a puppy!" Jamie shouts, and I flinch. I look to the door, but if Connie's heard us, she still doesn't come in.

I turn back to Jamie and tell her what I've been saying to myself every time I almost fall apart. "Everything is going to be fine," I whisper. "Trust me, you'll get out of here. We all will."

Jamie wipes a tear as it slides down her cheek. Her anger seems to fade. Like she believes me, even if I'm not sure that I do. "Do you want to get adopted?" she asks.

"I don't even know that I could be. I think Connie says my dad still has parental rights or whatever. Plus, I feel like I'm too old. I'll graduate high school and be on my own soon."

At the word *graduate*, Jamie bristles. I could lean forward and hug her. But instead I step down the ladder.

This is only temporary, I think. Everything in life is temporary.

CHAPTER
EIGHT

*F*riday, early in the morning, I wake in a cold sweat. It's pitch black in our room, and Jamie's soft snores tell me I didn't make any noise during my nightmare. I'd been dreaming that I was hiking the Pacific Crest Trail, like Cheryl Strayed did in *Wild*. I hiked and made friends for the first part of the dream until suddenly I realized I had no boots. Unlike Cheryl, I didn't have boots that were the wrong fit. I didn't have shoes at all.

Rather than wondering why the hell I was hiking barefoot, I called my dad and asked him to send me some.

"You're reading that feminist crap again," he spat in the dream. That's what Dad called the book when he found me reading it in my room. He took it from me and threw it in the trash. I fished it out later—since he was drunk, he didn't notice—and finished reading it. It made me want to escape to college and figure out who I was on my own, without Dad judging me, more than ever before.

This memory didn't sit well with me in the dream. I started to panic, breathing quickly and looking for a way out. I needed to run. Suddenly, the trail turned into a dark nightclub, flashing blue and purple lights, with pulsing techno music and college students grinding up against each other, laughing and having fun.

I felt someone breathing behind me and whipped around to see my dad, scowling.

"So, this is why you want to go to college, Victoria? To become a little slut?"

I turned to run, until the floor fell out from under me. I dropped farther and farther into a black pit of nothing.

And then I woke up.

Now I'm sweating, my heart thumping madly in my chest. In my head, I keep seeing an image of Dad in handcuffs, in a prison jumpsuit, because of what happened. Because I told.

But I haven't told anyone, and I won't.

It feels like it takes hours, but I finally doze off.

In the living room the next day, my backpack is full of schoolbooks ready for Connie to check before I go. Today's the day of the dance. My stomach knots, but I force a big smile as I reach Connie.

Connie's sunk into her indent on the couch. She looks up at me. "Well, you seem excited for this project."

I drop my backpack at her feet. "I like studying; it makes me feel like I'm actually in control of something for once." The irony is that it's true, even though I have no plans to study tonight.

Connie says nothing as she unzips my bag and starts to inspect the contents, moving my books around and shaking it.

Apparently satisfied, she zips it back up. "Have fun tonight."

I nod and head for the door.

"Hey, wait up!" Jamie calls to me as I round the street corner.

I turn, flushed from hurrying out of the house. "Sorry, I didn't mean to leave you, I was just—"

Jamie takes one big step, closing the distance between us on the sidewalk, and interrupts me. "My social worker called this morning when you were in the shower, and it looks like there's a couple that wants to adopt me." A smile slowly spreads across Jamie's face.

I stop walking and allow myself to smile, too. "That's great—I knew it would happen! I told you so!"

Jamie laughs as she scratches at her arm. "Hey, wait. I didn't even say anything about them. They could be psychos for all you know!"

I catch a glimpse of a scab on Jamie's inner forearm. "What happened? Did you fall or something?"

Jamie shakes her head. "Nope. Caught my shirt on a nail in the hallway at school. That place is literally trying to kill me!" Jamie laughs, but the smile doesn't reach her eyes. "Anyway, back to me moving in with potential psychos, and you don't even care?"

I keep my eyes on her. "You look, I don't know, happy or relieved or something, but whatever it is, it's definitely good."

Jamie nods, and her eyes begin to water. Actual happy

tears. "They're an older couple, both in their late forties, and it's their second marriage. She didn't have kids before, and the husband's kids are grown up already. They just moved to Reno from Carson. They seem really nice. I met them when I visited my grandma at CPS last month. And Grandma's happy because they said they'd drive me to see her more often, since she's so old and it's getting harder for her to drive." Jamie exhales. "I'm sorry I didn't tell you. I was scared I'd jinx it."

I look down at my feet. "Don't apologize. I'm just happy for you." I make myself look at her. "When do you leave?"

"Eight days. But who's counting?" She laughs softly. "I'm going to miss you."

"I'll miss you, too." Connie's home will be unbearable without her. I chew on my bottom lip for a beat. Don't be selfish, I tell myself. This is the best thing for Jamie. "But it's not like you're moving to another country. Maybe after I graduate they'll let me come visit?"

"I hope so."

We're both quiet for a moment, until we start walking again, past the last few houses that line the street. I hug Jamie as I say goodbye. She takes her usual turn to walk up the hill toward the middle school.

Inside SVHS, the whole place screams Valentine's Day. What with the red paper hearts plastered on several lockers and teddy bears and flowers a few girls are holding, how could I miss it? Up ahead, Kale walks toward me. When we reach my locker, he pulls a single red rose from behind his back.

"Thank you," I say quickly, "but you didn't have to."

Kale leans against my locker. "I know I didn't have to. I wanted to."

I tuck a piece of my hair behind my ear and blush, despite myself. "You really are a gentleman, aren't you?"

"Yes!" Kale exclaims, his eyes popping. He laughs when he sees the look on my face and feigns indignation. "I'm so glad you're finally seeing me for the charming man I really am."

I shut my locker, with a big, fat, stupid grin on my face. "Yeah, yeah. Don't make me regret it."

Kale laughs and hands me the rose. He takes my books and walks me to class.

After lunch—during which I sit with Kale, Christina, and Alex at a small table—I head to Ms. Claire's office. She's been great since my first week of school, giving me paperwork to fill out for scholarships and whatever else she thinks might be helpful. The guidance counselor at my old school never paid students this much attention, or at least, she didn't for me. Outside Ms. Claire's open door, there's a big sign that says, "Your future awaits."

I knock twice and then open the door a few inches. "Do you have a few minutes?" I ask.

"Of course, have a seat." Ms. Claire points to the loveseat across from her desk. She shuts the door behind me and tucks a stray red hair away from her freckled face. "What can I help you with, Victoria?"

Tuition and fees, books, rent, food, transportation costs. A minimum of nine thousand dollars for my first semester alone, by my calculations. I adjust in my seat. "I applied for the FAFSA to get grants for college. And I'm working on the education training voucher thing we talked about, but I don't know if I'll get that much or not. I don't know if I should take out a loan."

Ms. Claire scoots forward and leans over her desk. "You can take out a loan, if you need to, but have you heard how much grant money you're getting? I've known a few other kids in foster care who applied for aid and got quite a bit. You might not need any loans."

"I haven't heard back yet. Is that normal?"

"When did you say you sent in the financial aid application?"

"Just a few weeks ago." I lean forward. "I would have turned it in sooner, when I got in after I applied, but I thought I was going to UNR."

"I know," she says softly. "You should hear back soon, and if not, you definitely will before you graduate. Sometimes paperwork takes a while to process. TMCC will send you an award letter. Did you let the school know about your change of address so they'll send the letter to Connie's rather than your father's house?"

"Yeah." I squirm in my seat, the thought of my dad receiving my mail and reading it flashing through my mind.

"Good." Ms. Claire rolls her chair to the side of her desk and opens her filing cabinet. She thumbs through several folders in the P section until she finds *Parker*.

Ms. Claire rolls back to the front of her desk, opens my file and writes something quickly on a piece of paper, before looking back at me. "Sit tight for a few more weeks, see if you hear anything, and try not to worry about loans until after you know how much you'll be getting in grants. You'll have time."

Don't worry. Easy for her to say. I get up to leave. "Okay. Thank you."

"Wait." Ms. Claire stands. "I think it's great you're preparing, that you're so determined to go to college as planned." She stops after she sees my mouth fall open and corrects herself. "Well, almost as planned, in spite of all you've been through this year."

I press my lips together as Ms. Claire clears her throat.

"Really, all you've done over the last month and a half, since you started school here," she goes on, "all this work you've done to get scholarships and go to community college, and getting excellent grades, it's remarkable. Your teachers, and I, well, we're all very impressed by you."

I look at my feet. "Thank you."

Ms. Claire smiles when I bring my gaze back to hers. "I think it's all going to work out."

I force a smile. You'd think my cheeks would hurt with all of this forced smiling, but it's become second nature to me. "Thanks."

I walk back outside, past the "Your future awaits" sign and through the hall. Loan or not, I'm getting out of here. A few weeks ago, Connie mentioned extended foster care—which basically means I sign a document giving the state permission to keep taking care of me by allowing me to stay with Connie after I turn eighteen in April, until I graduate. But I don't know if she and I can stand each other for that long.

If not, maybe I can get a job. Maybe there are some cheap apartments I can look into. How much could it cost to live in Silver Valley? I can work in town at one of the tourist gift stores or restaurants until I graduate . . . if I graduate on time. Another *if*. Mr. Nelson said not to worry about fulfilling my math requirement, that he'd try to convince the powers-that-be to let me take two math classes and graduate. I just have to hope he's doing everything he can to convince the school board.

There's so much I can't control.

Graduating on time.

Where I live.

Not being allowed to talk to Sarah.

My head starts to feel foggy, dizzy. Voices start to blend together, the words and sounds around me losing meaning.

I dig my fingernails into the palms of my hand, dragging my feet as I walk.

I can't do this here. I can't worry about things I have no control over when there are so many of them. I steady my breathing. Release my balled fists. And the noises of the hallway, the conversations and laughing, the Valentine's Day paper hearts come back into focus.

Christina sees me from across the hall, and weaves through the kids walking between us. "So, everything good?" she says. "Your mom still buys your story?"

"What?" I blink a few times, focus on Christina. "I mean, yeah, she did." I take a deep breath. "So, I'll hang out around school for a while until the dance starts and I'll see you when you get here?"

Christina gasps. "You kidding me? No offense, but I'm not letting you go to the dance like that!"

Heat rushes into my cheeks.

"You'll come to my house after school," Christina continues. "I'll make you look presentable for a date."

I cross my arms. I'm wearing the ratty old skirt Connie gave me for church that one time, rather than the same pair of jeans I wear basically daily. Christina's wearing leather boots, dark jeans, and probably a designer top.

Christina throws her hands up in the air. "Oh my gosh, don't be like that. It's fun to go glam, get dressed up and everything. We can do something with this." Christina takes a piece of my unruly hair into her hands. "I mean, we can curl this—"

"It's already curly, wavy . . . well curly-ish, but—"

"Obviously it's curly enough; I mean curl it with *intention*."

My arms drop to my side, but I'm smiling. Christina's determination is impossible to stifle for anything she sets her mind to, so there's no point in trying. "Okay, I get it. But won't your parents mind, me showing up unannounced?"

Christina chuckles. "Not at all. They're totally chill, and my mom's been dying to meet you anyway. So meet me in the gym after your last class. I'm going to practice with the other seniors on the club volleyball team, so we should finish up at around the same time."

"Okay, um, sure. And Christina," I say, as she's about to walk away. "Thanks."

"Don't mention it," she says with a smile. "And I'm the one who should be thanking you. This dance will be so much better now that you're coming!"

CHAPTER
NINE

I meet Christina in the gym as planned. We walk outside toward the parking lot and her family's pickup.

Taylor walks by, heading toward her shiny red Mini Cooper—one of the only non-trucks in the parking lot. Alex and Kale are close behind her, getting into Alex's massive black truck and waving at us. "See you later, ladies!" Alex calls.

We wave goodbye to the guys. Kale keeps his eyes on me until he closes the truck door behind him. My stomach flutters as we climb into the pickup.

To keep Christina from making mock googly eyes and talking about me and Kale, one of her favorite pastimes, I begin, "So, where are you going to go to college? I know we've talked about the places you're applying, but have you decided which one is your number one?"

Christina smiles like she knows what I'm up to. "I'm applying to UNR," she says, "but you know I'd rather go to George Washington or Georgetown in D.C. Georgetown would be my number one, though."

Christina starts the engine before sweeping

a piece of her long, black hair out of her face to look at me. "It takes longer to hear back from their admissions departments. I shouldn't know until sometime in March." She watches Alex's truck as he turns outside the parking lot and disappears from view. "What about you, are you planning on transferring to UNR after a couple years at TMCC?"

I shrug. "I'll have to see how things go." If I can afford to stay in school.

We drive out of the lot and head in the opposite direction from the way I usually take. Christina pulls onto the highway and we drive by farmhouses, barns, and sweeping pastures with spotted cattle eating grass and horses galloping in their pens.

Sarah loves horses. She begged our parents to sign her up for riding lessons. Tiffany wouldn't have it, though, not until Sarah is older, at least. She said horseback riding was too dangerous.

My hair whips in my face, and I roll the window up and turn to Christina.

"You said you always wanted a brother. Does that mean you're an only child? I never thought to ask."

Christina sees I rolled my window up and rolls hers up, too.

"Yep. My parents say I was a handful enough as it was." She smiles, like this is a compliment. "What about you? Do you have any brothers or sisters?"

I'm not telling her about Sarah, since she's in Reno and not here. "I'm an only child, too."

We pass more horses, and I imagine Sarah here with

me. She would ask to stop the car, so she could get a better look. She would love it out here, probably, even though Silver Valley is so small. She would like the outdoors and the animals. The people who are friendly and all know each other so well.

My throat tightens.

"I'm sure you'll get into Georgetown. You have practically perfect grades."

Christina exhales. "I hope so. It just really sucks not knowing. Even if I do get in . . ." She pauses, smirking. "*When* I get in, that's just the beginning. The classes are going to be really hard, and going there is going to be super expensive. At least you won't be buried in loans like I'll be." She shrugs and then smiles. "I'm going to live in the dorms, but you should totally get an apartment near TMCC. I'm sure they have something similar to student housing, even as a community college. I can come visit you. And you should come see me, too!" She pulls off the highway onto a winding road.

I nod, but don't even want to think about how expensive a plane ticket to visit Christina would be. "So, where's Alex going to go? UNR?"

Christina bites her lip and shakes her head, staring at the road. We pass Victorian-style houses as we make our way near the foothills. "He's not exactly the college type. He'll probably stay here and take over his dad's car-parts store someday. He'll get married, have a few kids, save for retirement." She laughs before making a turn. "Not that there's anything wrong with that, *per se*. It's just not the life I want."

"So, what's next, after college then? Do you know?"

Christina chuckles. "You ask a lot of questions, Vickster! But that's okay," she adds without skipping a beat. "I'll answer. Like I said, I want to move to D.C. and go to school there to study political science and women's studies, get elected into student government, after which I'll intern for a senator on the Hill and continue my rise to power. And then, of course, I'll become the first Latina president." She elbows me like she's kidding. I don't think she is.

"What about you?" she asks.

"Oh, pretty much the same thing. Except a few minor details."

Christina turns her face from the road slightly to raise an eyebrow at me. "Like what? The Latina president part?"

"No," I quip. "The women's studies part."

We both laugh, and she turns again. "Okay, here we go."

Ahead there's a dirt path, leading up a hill the height of a double-story building.

"Wait, where's your house?"

"Almost there."

The truck chugs along as we slowly climb the hill.

Once we reach the top, my breath catches. About a dozen cattle graze in a pen, blocked in with metal rods that keep them in the green valley beneath us. "Wow," I breathe.

The road starts to descend and we drive to the bottom. We pull up in front of two small, wooden houses and a barn to the right of the cattle pen.

"Are you guys ranchers or something?"

Christina parks near the pen and kills the engine.

"Sort of." Christina hops out of the truck. "We don't

kill these bad boys, if that's what you mean." I follow her to the pen as she steps close to pat the backside of a cow. "Go ahead. You can touch her."

I set my hand on the cow, next to Christina's hand, and feel its coarse, white-and-brown spotted hide.

"So, what do you do with them, then? Sell the milk?"

Christina nods. "My dad mostly does the milking with a suction cup machine, but he makes me help him every now and then. They're mostly for show. For tourists. The owners of the ranch are super rich, they live in Tahoe, and they let us live here for a discount if we manage the property. We keep the cattle healthy, water the plants, basically do all the stuff they don't want to."

She waves an arm in front of her. "And as you can see, this place is huge. The upkeep is a ton of work. My mom rents out the guesthouse for extra money. She does it as a bed and breakfast, so she's always busy cooking for the guests and cleaning up after everybody. I help her sometimes, but she doesn't let me do it often because she says it's her job and my job is to go to school."

My eyes turn down. My dad used to say my job was going to school. "Nice mom." I take my hand off the cow.

"The best," Christina says. She pats the cow and starts walking again. I follow her. "Speaking of which," she says over her shoulder, "she's very eager to meet you. She's met everyone in this town already, so you're exciting."

Perfect. I'm sure *everyone* includes Connie, then. I'll have to be careful what I say in front of her.

"Exciting, that's my middle name," I grumble as we step

over the welcome mat and walk into a small sitting area on our right. Christina hollers, "Ma! We're home!"

"Coming, *mija*," a soft voice calls from the kitchen on our other side. A petite woman with a head full of black waves and a big smile emerges from the other side of the kitchen island. She runs her hand over the granite countertop as she approaches us.

"Mucho gusto; you must be Victoria. Pretty name for a pretty girl. My name is Maria, and I'm so glad to finally meet you."

I stiffen as she wraps me in her arms. I feel her soft hair toss over my shoulder and get a whiff of lavender and sunshine. "Nice to meet you, too."

Christina swats at her mom's back. "All right, that's enough. We have to go downstairs and get ready."

Christina's mom lets me go. "What, no time to chat?" She grins at me.

Christina glares at Maria, a look she normally saves for Alex when he teases her.

"Oh, okay. Don't mind me, then," Maria says with a giggle. "Let me know if you need anything. Advice on hair and makeup, what to wear, booooooys."

Christina grabs me by the arm, leading me through the sitting area and down three wooden steps that turn into another longer flight of stairs.

"I live in the basement. It's the only way to have some space in this place," Christina says loudly, exaggerated so Maria can hear.

Maria laughs and starts making noise in the kitchen,

unloading the dishwasher by the sound of it. Appeased, Christina smiles and leads me down the second flight of wooden stairs.

Christina and her mom have everything, and she doesn't even know it.

"I thought you said you live in the basement?" I say, to change the subject in my mind more than anything else. "This is more like its own apartment."

Christina walks over to the first section, separated from another room.

"I'll give you the tour in a sec. I have to run to the bathroom real quick. Make yourself comfortable."

She waves her arm in front of the couch. It's covered in purple throw pillows.

I sit as Christina disappears around the corner.

I can hear her mom upstairs, singing a song in Spanish. Her voice is beautiful, though I don't understand the words. Christina thinks I'm lying to my mom about where I am tonight, but even that's just another lie. They are starting to stack like Jenga pieces, piling on and on, tipping, but not yet toppling over. Christina's life seems worlds away from mine. I'm not like her, I don't have a room of my own. I don't have a mom.

The days and weeks after Mom died blur together in my memory, as though I'm watching them on a slideshow.

Cue the first slide, Dad telling me she's gone, holding me as I cried. But he was crying, too. His sobs shook his body. "What am I going to do?" he wailed. "I can't do this. I can't do this without her."

I wanted him to tell me everything would be okay, that Mom was in a better place, that I'd see her again someday. That we'd be okay.

But he didn't.

"I don't know how to live without her," he finally said. And I couldn't explain why, but suddenly I felt sheer panic. I'd already lost Mom. I couldn't lose Dad, too.

Fear plummeted down, landing hard like a rock in my gut.

And in this moment, looking at the walls in Christina's room, with posters of Hillary Clinton and a couple other women I don't recognize, my chest tightens and I feel that fear now, like it's happening, even though it was years ago. The harder Dad cried, the harder I cried.

I blink quickly. No tears, not in Christina's room. Not here.

"She was everything," Dad said back then, in between gasps. My shirt was soaked from his tears and mine. "What am I going to do?"

My tears dried up almost instantly. I had a sense that I needed to do something, to take control. I wiped the tears away from his eyes, like Mom used to for me.

"It's going to be okay, Dad." My voice was strong, like it belonged to someone else. "We're going to be okay."

The toilet flushes in the bathroom. My thoughts speed together, frantic, almost out of control.

Second slide, Dad and I spending more time together. Him crying about Mom, me listening. I learned not to break down about her in front of him, it only made him worse. He couldn't handle it, I could see that.

My heart races, and I grab the edge of the couch, digging my fingernails tight. Christina will be back any second, but I can't pull myself out, I can't stop thinking about the past, what I don't have, even as I hear the faucet running.

Dad didn't cry at the funeral, and I thought we were going to be okay. But after the service, after we ate the casseroles Jess's mom and her church friends brought, we slowly ran out of food. And Dad didn't go shopping. He didn't go to work.

When my stomach wouldn't stop growling, I took money out of Dad's wallet and walked to the grocery store after school—I started going back to class a couple days after Mom died because I couldn't bear to be around Dad crying all the time. I bought us food, cooked Dad spaghetti and meatballs, just like Mom used to.

I stand and start walking around, as though I'm looking at the posters on the wall. I'm not.

Dad went to work the next day. And I kept cooking.

Maria must have left the kitchen. I don't hear her singing anymore. She seems like a good parent, not the kind who would ever make Christina fend for herself or take care of her.

Cue the third slide, it's been a few months since Mom died and Dad and I were watching romantic movies together like Mom and I used to. We're talking about everything— school, his work. We're best friends, just like Mom and I used to be, *before*. Before it hurt Dad's feelings so much.

And Dad didn't cry so much anymore.

The door to the bathroom opens. I inhale deeply as Christina approaches. I've become an expert at pretending everything's okay. That I am.

Christina waves for me to follow her, and I do. "And here's the closet, every girl could use a walk-in closet."

I blink rapidly. Nod my head, like Christina asked a question, before I realize she didn't.

We stop in front of a full-size mirror and enter a closet big enough for a twin bed to fit in. "This is huge."

"I'm pretty lucky my dad knows how to do this kind of thing," Christina says. "He built this closet for me—the owners let him—and those wooden shoe racks, too. He didn't build the bathroom, though. That was already there."

Christina pauses for a second, then looks at me and my clothes.

"Actually, now that I think of it, I have a few pairs of pants I can't fit into anymore, since I gained weight recently. I bet they're your size. Wanna try them on? If you want them, they're yours!"

My stomach sinks. She feels bad for me, but I can't let her see how much that hurts.

"Can we do it later? I want to get ready for the dance."

"Sure, I'll bring you some to school and if they don't fit you can just give them back, and I'll donate them to the Salvation Army."

I extend my arm toward the bathroom. "Okay, so on with your tour. The bathroom?"

"Right over here." Christina grins and leads me to the

opening between rooms. "So, here's the room, but the bathroom's over here on the right."

Large purple pillows and a white comforter cover Christina's queen-size bed. A patterned rug decorates the floor, and she's even got an old, black reclining chair in the corner.

I share a bedroom with two other girls and a baby monitor where Connie is always listening. Waiting for me to do something worth punishing me for.

I squeeze my lips shut.

Christina pauses a beat, but then lets it go. "This-a-way. Here's where we will get you ready for tonight!"

I let out a long exhale and look around. Christina's bathroom shares the purple theme she's got going on in the other rooms. Purple shower curtain. Purple rug. Purple towels. Makeup brushes and assorted lip glosses cover the bathroom sink. Christina hands me a flat iron.

"This, my friend, is a straightening iron. Use it."

I shake my head and hand the straightener back to her. "It won't work. Trust me, I've tried. You can't tame the beast." I grab a chunk of my hair and scrunch it in front of her face, for good measure. "And I thought you said we were curling it, anyway."

Christina grabs a piece of my hair with her free hand and inspects it. "You *can* tame this beast. By curling it."

"I think that would be counterproductive."

Christina waves the iron at me. "Haven't you ever curled it into smoother curls? That's how my mom does hers. Your mom must have straight hair, otherwise she probably would have told you."

I purse my lips. "Yep, my mom does. Have straight hair, that is."

My mom's hair was just like mine. Curly. Wavy. A little bit of both. She just died before I hit that age where you teach your daughter about hair, clothes, and makeup. And boys.

A couple of years ago, Tiffany helped me with my hair. I was getting ready for a school dance, actually. "Can I come in?" she asked, pausing outside the bathroom door. She must have seen me from the hallway, battling, trying to get it to not look so frizzy. "Maybe I can help," she said, with less bite in her voice than usual.

I agreed, begrudgingly, and Tiffany pinned my hair into a half-up style that looked pretty good. She told me my auburn hair was pretty; she liked that it was unique and contrasted with my fair complexion. With a soft laugh, Tiffany said she'd always thought that but didn't know why she hadn't told me. I wasn't surprised. It wasn't like the two of us ever spent time together, without Sarah or Dad.

Dad always said Tiffany didn't know how to relate to me because I was my mom's daughter. He always said I shouldn't take it personally, that I reminded Tiffany that my father was in love with my mother before her and that she was insecure.

Christina clears her throat, subtly reminding me I'm getting weird again.

"And she's not really girly anyway, my mom, so I don't know how to do any of this stuff," I finish.

Christina's eyes narrow at me for a moment. But she doesn't say anything. She leans back onto the bathroom counter, the mirror behind her reflecting my reddening face. I look away.

"Okay, well it's lucky you have me tonight," Christina says. "And trust me, Kale is going to *die* when he sees you. You'll look even hotter than usual!"

My stomach sinks. Hot? I look in the mirror at my messy hair, unremarkable face, and second-hand clothes. I would have loved to have been called hot before what happened with Dad. I was a late bloomer and excited when I started to fill out. But then Bryan, the cute guy who went to church with Jess, started noticing me, and Dad started freaking out. Paying even more attention to me, and less to Tiffany. Becoming the most controlling he'd ever been.

Christina reaches under bathroom cabinet and pulls out a medium-sized curling iron for herself and plugs it in. She squeezes my shoulder.

"I'm glad you're here," she says.

I nod. "Me too."

"Lip gloss: Berry Splash, check." Christina holds her hand out for the lip gloss, after we finish eating the sandwiches her mom brought downstairs for us. I hand her the Berry Splash, and she stashes it in her purse. "For later," she says, "in case it gets all rubbed off from kissing Kale!"

I whip my head around to face her. "What? Nobody said anything about kissing," I say quickly. We're going to be at a chaperoned event, so jokes about handcuffs aside, I hadn't really considered the possibility.

Christina puts her hands on my shoulders and turns me to face the mirror. My cheeks warm, but I can't help but smile at myself. I look good. I'm wearing a black, strappy dress Christina lent me, with a glittering, silver scarf wrapped around my shoulders, and a pair of her black, high-heeled boots. The clothes I wore to school are stashed in my backpack. I'll leave it in Christina's car and change back after the dance before she takes me home, or a couple of blocks away. As far as she knows, I told my mom I'm walking home from school after studying with her for our big project.

I pull the dress down, eyes still locked on my reflection, almost in disbelief. I didn't want a dress so revealing at first. Christina talked me into it. Plus, no one will be thinking about how much skin I'm showing when they see Christina in that red mini-dress.

Christina slides a hand through my hair, curled into shiny waves and softened from styling product and whatever other magic she did to make it look good for once. My eyes look bigger from the soft highlighting she did with different tones of brown and gold eye shadow, and from the mascara she put on me that makes my lashes look long and thick.

I smooth the lip gloss by rubbing my lips together.

Christina wiggles her eyebrows at me. "You look hot, I'll say it again." She laughs at my expression. "And trust me, when Kale sees you, he will have kissing on his mind, nice guy or not. He's not dead!"

My stomach goes from being warm and tingly to

cramping and downright painful. My mind flashes to my father again.

"I don't know if I can do this."

"Woman up!" Christina shakes my shoulders softly, a smile still playing on her lips. "I'm going out with Alex tonight, too, and you don't see me falling apart."

"Girls," Christina's mom calls from upstairs. "You about ready? The dance starts soon."

"Yeah, Ma! Just give us a sec!"

Christina grabs the mascara and quickly puts it on her own eyelashes. A quick dash of gloss to her lips and she calls, "Ready!"

"Come on," she says, grabbing my arm. "Tonight is going to be awesome!"

CHAPTER
TEN

*W*hen Christina and I get to school, the parking lot is already halfway full of cars and people, some leaning up against their trucks with the music on, just hanging out.

I pull my dress as I carefully step down from my seat in the pickup. It's freezing out; snow covers the mountaintops but doesn't reach us down in the valley. I can't believe Maria let us out of the house like this. Christina's dad was still at work by the time we left, which might have something to do with it. At least we brought jackets.

Lauren hops out of a black SUV. She says goodnight to her mom and saunters over to us.

"Hey, you clean up nice!" Lauren says with a smile. She, too, has a full face of makeup on, masking the freckles that I like so much.

I wave my hand at her floral dress and black booties. "You, too."

"Dances are a big deal in this town." Lauren laughs. "We have to entertain ourselves however we can." She smiles at me. "You guys ready to head in?"

Christina follows Lauren, walking in her

heels gracefully, and I fumble along trying not to fall. Blue-and-white balloons hang from the twenty-foot-tall, gray archway in front of the school that we walk through toward Mr. Nelson. He's behind a wooden table set in front of the school entrance. Even though he's sitting, he's still almost as tall as us.

"Five dollars each," he says. "The school needs to make money somehow. And don't you ladies look lovely tonight." An open cash box is on the table, along with a stamp-maker.

Oh, no.

How could I forget about this? School dances cost money, and I don't have any.

A group of sophomore boys start to form the line behind us. Lauren takes cash out of her purse and pays Mr. Nelson.

Christina hands Mr. Nelson a ten, and he gives her back a five. I'm not asking her for money. I'll just have to go—

Mr. Nelson nods at me. "And you're good to go in, Victoria, since you paid me ahead of time this morning."

I swallow, nod quickly and try to thank him with my eyes.

After Christina and Lauren go in, Mr. Nelson reaches a hand out to stop me. "Everything's settled with the school board and your math requirement," he says. "I just got the final word today. You're set to graduate with everyone else, provided you pass your classes. Shouldn't be a problem for a good student like you, though." He winks.

I stare at him, unable to find words.

"Victoria," Christina calls from up ahead.

"Thank you, thank you." I whisper.

"Go on." Mr. Nelson nods in the direction of the dance.

"There you are," Christina says as I catch up. "Paying early was a good idea. I'll probably ditch this bag in my locker by the end of the night." She grabs my arm and leads me farther into the hallway with Lauren.

Red-and-white balloons tied in clusters and tacked to the wall lead us to the front of the gym entrance. Other than the balloons, visually you wouldn't know there was a dance tonight, since the fluorescent lights are still on in the main hallway. The hall's empty, save a couple of freshmen making out next to one of the blue lockers near the math classroom. But the music—now that's different. Some remixed techno song blares through the doors.

"Let's go!" Christina shouts over the music. She grabs my hand and rushes forward to the double-doors, taking us through them.

My eyes adjust to the dim lighting. On either side of the gym, kids and a few teacher-chaperones stand against walls or sit in groups on the blue bleachers. A cluster of freshmen girls dance together in the middle of the basketball court.

"Where do you think the guys are?" I shout into Christina's ear.

"Who cares?" she yells back. "They'll find us. Let's dance!"

Lauren, already positioned with her back against the wall and a glass of punch in her hand, laughs at my bewilderment. Zach walks over to her and starts a conversation. Even he dressed up for the dance. He's wearing a button-up shirt that makes his neck look thicker than usual.

"You coming?" Christina calls over. Lauren hands Zach her punch and joins us as we head for the dance floor.

Christina starts moving with the music. Watching her and feeling the beat, I bob my head slightly. My stomach flutters as my thoughts turn to Kale, and I scan the gym looking for him. But, just as soon as the warm feelings come, they morph. My palms start to sweat. I don't have the best record at school dances.

The last school dance I went to, when I was a junior, was nothing like this. My high school sprung for the community center, not our gym, and actually paid a DJ, rather than letting some teacher or kid plug their iPhone into the speakers.

Jess and I hung out with Bryan that night. We both obviously had a crush on him, but it wasn't competitive. It was more like a game. Who did Bryan talk to in class more often that week? Who did he look at more? Was he flirting with one of us or both of us? It was hard to tell.

Bryan was cute. He almost looked like Jess, except for being a guy. They both have blue eyes and light-blonde hair. He was so nice and smart, and I thought he probably didn't like either of us that way. At least, not until that dance. He followed me outside when I left to get some air, standing closer to me than usual.

"Maybe we should go back in, check on Jess," I said. He stepped closer to me and said there was just one thing he wanted to do first.

And he kissed me, softly. My first kiss. I expected to like it more than I did. I didn't tell Jess, even though I knew she wouldn't be mad. She'd be happy for me, even if I wasn't sure I was happy for me. That's the kind of friend she was.

Bryan called me the next day. We talked on the phone for an hour. Even though I wasn't ready for more kissing, I liked feeling like he was interested in me. It felt new and exciting. Like I was special. I don't even remember what we said to each other, other than the usual stuff I talked to Jess about: moving to the dorms and what I hoped college would be like. He wanted to go to UC Davis, but we agreed to stay in touch.

Bryan called again the day after that. We talked for another hour.

And the next day we talked for two whole hours. Tiffany and Sarah were out grocery shopping, and they had decided to get dinner out, just the two of them. So I was supposed to cook dinner for Dad and me, but I lost track of time. Dad opened my door, he didn't even bother knocking.

"What are you doing in here?" he barked, looking around the room, like I was hiding something.

I covered my phone with my hand. "I'm on the phone, Dad."

He was quiet for a second, staring at me, like he was trying to read my mind or something. It was weird. "It's dinner time." Dad slammed the door behind him.

After I made chicken and rice and we sat down to eat, Dad asked me who I was talking to all the time. I didn't think to lie. I told him my friend, Bryan.

"So what, you have a boyfriend and now you don't have time for your father?" Dad said, his words low and cold.

"He's not my boyfriend, he's my frien—"

"Yeah," Dad snapped. "Your mom had a lot of *friends* when she was your age, too. And in college. Is that why you don't want to live at home? So you can sleep around with any guy in the dorms who pays you attention?"

I choked on my chicken. "Dad!" I swallowed, my face burning. "No, that's not even—"

Dad slammed his fork on the table and walked away. Just like that. I sat there in shock, watching his closed door. I felt ashamed, even though I didn't know why. I hadn't done anything wrong, had I?

The next day, I kept an eye on the time to make sure I would get off the phone with Bryan before it was dinner time. Tiffany was home to cook and Dad wasn't back from work yet anyway, so it didn't matter. Or so I thought. Because only a few minutes into our phone call, I heard Dad's car pull up into the driveway. I started to tell Bryan I had to go, that I'd see him in school tomorrow, when I heard Dad's fist banging on my door. I'd locked it.

I hung up, cutting Bryan off. Answered the door. Dad yanked my phone out of my hand. "You're not responsible enough to have your own phone," he said, "seeing as how you didn't listen to a word I said yesterday. You're too young," he sputtered, "and what have you done to that boy to make him call so much?"

I opened my mouth to speak but Dad cut me off.

"No daughter of mine is going to be easy. You want me to pay for college, pay for you to live in those dorms? To trust you to live on your own?" Dad's face was red, and a vein was sticking out of his neck. "Then you better follow my rules. No more boys in high school. You're done with Bryan. Do you understand me? Done."

I tried as hard as I could to hold back tears. If I cried, it would only make Dad angrier. I nodded. And Dad stomped away.

All the goodwill between Tiffany and me earlier vanished as soon as it came. She was on Dad's side. *I had to set a good example for Sarah,* she said. They were a team, not Dad and me. Not her and me.

Back at school, I apologized to Bryan, but didn't explain. I only said I didn't want to talk to him anymore. It was easier for me to just ignore him, pretend like nothing happened. After a few weeks, Dad finally gave me my phone back. I never called Bryan again.

And it was all thanks to that school dance.

Someone grabs my elbow and I whip around. I gasp, scared, until I see who it is.

Kale.

His light-brown hair looks a bit darker with gel in it. His blue collared shirt brings out the color of his eyes.

My stomach warms.

"Hey." He smiles at me.

Christina bumps into me, on purpose maybe. I turn to look back at her and she bumps me again. Right into Kale's arms.

"Dance!" she commands.

At that, the tune fades away, replaced by a slow song. Perfect timing, I guess, but still awkward.

Kale grabs my clammy hand. His hands are soft, not like my dad's. My stomach clenches.

From the wall, Lauren waves off Christina's calls to join the rest of us. Zach and Taylor appear across the gym, dancing. All the freshmen who were moving to the music before clear out, and a couple of sophomores embrace. Locked together tightly, they quickly start making out.

Great.

I clear my throat and smile up at Kale.

"Dance with me?"

I nod, and he puts his hand, the one that isn't already holding mine, on the small of my back. His feet move slowly to the right, and I follow him, looking at his chest.

Alex appears at our side with Christina, dancing. And pretty much glowing. She plays it cool with him, but here she is, clearly having a great time. She grins at me as Alex spins her away in another direction.

Kale moves us slowly in the shape of a square, nothing fancy or creative, thankfully. His hand is warm. I take my hand and quickly wipe it off on my dress and glance at him sheepishly, before putting it back in his.

"You look great," he says. "You always do, but now, you know." He breathes out, laughing at himself. "You look very nice tonight."

I giggle at him fumbling his words. Kale clears his throat.

"I don't think you're supposed to look at my chest when you dance," he says. "I mean, why would you when you've got this great view up here? Although I've got some pretty amazing abs, too."

I cough out a laugh and Kale smiles, leaning just a little closer to me.

My dad's face flashes where Kale's should be, and I stop breathing for an instant. I inhale quickly, shake it off, and force a smile.

Kale tilts his head, and questions me with his eyes. I look away but come back. His light eyes and long eyelashes hold my gaze.

"So, uh, Christina tells me you guys kissed a few years ago." I raise an eyebrow at him.

Kale exhales a little laugh. "Ha. Yeah, a long time ago. Don't tell me you're jealous?"

He adjusts his hand on my back and turns me just slightly away from Christina and Alex.

I look back up at him. "No, she said it was gross."

He pretends to be affronted. "The nerve." He nods in agreement, though.

"We've all known each other since preschool," he says. "After a while, it can start to feel incestuous."

Incestuous.

Dad's dark hair and green eyes come back to me by force. His smile. The smell of alcohol on his breath. But this time, instead of stomping out of my room, he's hovering over me as I lie in my bed.

"I need you, Victoria," he said, as I kept my eyes closed, pretending to be asleep. "We both need each other. You're my favorite girl."

I remember that moment when he snuck into my room late at night months ago. I wanted to be my father's favorite.

But it felt wrong when he did stuff like that, everything was *wrong wrong wrong*.

I blink several times. *No, not here.* Swallow. Stare at the freckles on Kale's nose. Kale's eyes narrow at me in confusion. I quickly look away.

I steal a glance at Christina. Alex's talking to her, and she's laughing. I focus back on the conversation. "You guys seem to be really close. I mean, best friends, even."

He smiles at me. "We don't have friendship bracelets." He waits a beat. "Yet."

I accidentally step on the edge of his shoe. "Oops, sorry." I blurt. "Maybe your sister, or one of your sisters, can make them for you. How many do you have? Sisters that is?"

Kale lifts his eyebrows. "So, Christina's been giving you intel, huh? You can't believe a word she says," he pauses, "unless it makes me sound good."

I wait.

"Three. I have three sisters."

I nod, but don't fill the silence. I'd rather hear him talk. Behind us, Alex dips Christina, quite sloppily, and Christina laughs as he pulls her back up.

I bring my gaze back to Kale's as he turns me again, his hands still warm and soft. The song changes, and even though the beat is faster, we keep slow dancing. A few other couples do the same, Christina and Alex among them. The cluster of girls dancing returns to the floor.

"So you're always working on 'college prep' stuff"—he pauses and pulls his hand and mine up to make air quotes— "but you never say what exactly that is."

I try to keep the hand he's holding relaxed. "You can never be too prepared." And then I offer, "Scholarship stuff."

Kale nods. "Do you know what you want to major in yet?"

I shake my head and step out of the way of another couple dancing. Kale leads us a few feet in the other direction to give us more room. He's still watching me. "Um, well . . ." I shrug. "Not exactly." I wait for a second, remember my dad chastising me for what I watch, what I read. Harassing me about getting my head out of the clouds.

But Kale's not my dad.

I take a chance. "I want to take all the general ed classes, and I want to consider everything, try everything, but . . ." I exhale. Kale keeps his eyes locked on mine. "History," I say. "I really like history. So maybe there's something there, or something related. Maybe anthropology or sociology or some other 'ology.'" I chuckle nervously. "I don't know, but next year is as good a time as ever to start trying to find out."

Kale smiles and looks into my eyes, like I've said something particularly interesting. Like I'm interesting. My stomach is warm and tight and I'm not sure if this is a good thing or not. My hand still in his, I feel everything. The music, Kale watching me, his hand on my back. I bite my lip.

"So, Christina can't wait to get out of Silver Valley. What about you?"

"Well, there aren't a lot of options for careers here, if you haven't noticed," Kale says. "My dad drives a truck, and my mom stays at home and takes care of my little sisters." He pauses, as if he's thinking carefully over his words. "That's all my dad ever really wanted, but it's not what I want."

His smile falters. I don't like that—I don't like it when Kale doesn't smile. But I want to know more.

"Is your dad gone a lot? Being a truck driver, on the road?"

"Yeah."

I wait to see if he says anything else. People keep dancing in my peripherals, but I don't see them. Only Kale.

"It's hard for my mom," Kale finally says. "She has to take care of everything at home. I help when I can with my sisters and take care of the yard, but it's not the same. And when he gets home, all she wants to do is spend time with him, and all he wants to do is sit in front of the TV with a beer. Or lots of them."

Kale shuffles his feet. I slow my pace to his.

"I don't want to be like that," he says. "I want to get a job that makes enough money but also lets me be at home with my family."

He looks past my head, behind us, his eyes unfocused. "So I guess what I'm saying is, I'm like anyone else who wants to get out of here. But I don't think I'm better. I'm not leaving and never coming back. My family needs me. This will always be home."

I loosen my grip on Kale's hand. *Home.* We're talking about his family, which means he's going to ask . . .

On cue, Kale says, "What about you, what about—"

I let go of Kale and back away from him. "I have to go to the bathroom," I blurt. "Sorry."

Without letting him respond, I turn, rush by Christina and Alex, and make it past the gym door and into the hallway.

"Everything okay in there?" Mr. Nelson calls from his seat in front of the cash box. "I don't need to go in there and talk to some knuckleheads, do I?"

"No, no. I just—have to use the restroom!" I dash to the bathroom before Mr. Nelson gets the chance to say anything else.

I check for feet under the stalls. None. I'm alone. My breathing starts to return to normal. What was I thinking? How could I have a regular conversation with Kale? Not when I don't have the bell to save me when I need it.

Stupid, stupid, stupid. Coming here was so stupid. I should go, apologize later and say I didn't feel well. I should walk home now before I say or do anything to mess everything up.

Twisting the faucet and letting the cold water run on my hands isn't enough. I splash my face. Wipe my black, smudgy eyelids with a paper towel.

When I open the door, Mr. Nelson's standing outside of it. And behind Mr. Nelson is a tall man wearing a sheriff's uniform. His hands rest on his sides, near the gun in his holster.

My breath catches.

"Victoria," Mr. Nelson says softly, "I need you to come with me."

"What's going on?" I ask.

Mr. Nelson takes a step toward the hallway. "In my office, Victoria. It's okay. Let's get out of the hallway."

The hallway's empty, no more freshmen making out.

I look behind me at the window in the door to the gym. Christina and Alex are still dancing. I don't see Kale.

I don't move.

"Let's just go to my office," Mr. Nelson repeats. The man with a badge leads us away from the dance and down the hall, like he knows where he's going. I drag my feet behind him.

I swallow the lump in my throat, try to keep my eyes from welling up. Mr. Nelson pats my shoulder as he steps in front of me and pulls out a set of keys to unlock his office door.

"Have a seat, Victoria," Mr. Nelson says. I sit in the wooden chair across from his desk. Mr. Nelson moves slightly to stand between the sheriff and me.

"What's going on?" I ask, my voice as high pitched as ever.

The officer's eyes crinkle, his voice softer than it was before when he answers. "Your foster mother called you in as a runaway."

How did she know? "I didn't run away," I blurt. "I just went to the dance. I was supposed to be studying, I admit it, it was stupid, but I didn't run away. I swear." I look from Mr. Nelson to the man in uniform. "This is just a misunderstanding."

Mr. Nelson looks at the man hopefully. He shakes his head.

"Your foster mother called you in as a runaway. I'm sorry to say, kid, but she doesn't want you coming back there. I have to take you in." He grabs a pair of handcuffs out of his pocket.

I stiffen. "I just wanted to be normal. To go out with

my friends, to pass as just another kid. Just one time." My words start to blend together. I say them faster and faster. "I just wanted to be like everyone else, to get to go to the dance with my friends!"

I try to steady my shaking shoulders as the officer reaches out with the cuffs. Mr. Nelson steps in front of him.

"Deputy Smith. Please. Not here, not in front of the other students." He looks at me, with pity. "Her friends."

I blink back tears from falling.

The deputy nods in agreement. "All right." He pockets the handcuffs. "After you." He nods for me to walk forward.

I hang my head as I walk out in the hallway, where Christina's waiting. She gasps when she sees me.

"What's going on? Why is a cop—do you need help?"

I shake my head, lower my eyes. Christina moves toward me. Mr. Nelson puts his long arm in front of her. "If you want to help Victoria, make sure everyone else stays in the gym where they belong."

"Okay, Mr. Nelson," Christina says slowly. And then to me, "Call me, Victoria! Call me from wherever they take you, if you can. You get one phone call, right? You can look up my parents in the phone book! We can help you!"

I look back at her as I go. A couple of sophomores appear behind her. One of their mouths falls open as she sees me with the deputy. Her friend starts saying something that I can't hear as she pulls her phone out like she's sending a text. Now, everyone will know. Everyone will know within minutes. Just as I'm about to round the corner, I see him appear behind her.

Kale.

I turn away before he gets the chance to see my face, the tears that I'm trying so desperately to hold back.

The deputy escorts me in the other direction, outside to his cop car, with Mr. Nelson behind us.

"If there's anything I can do to help, Victoria, I promise I will," Mr. Nelson says.

"Thank you," I force out. The deputy opens the door and I get into the back of the car, behind the barrier that divides the front from the back. Where the criminals sit. I'm a criminal.

Out of the school parking lot, we drive down the residential streets I walk every day. Will I ever see them again, now that Connie's kicked me out? Mindy will be so mad. I'm sure this is just what my social worker needs, another delinquent orphan. For her, it's a job. For me, it's my life. I can't go home after a long day at work.

I can't go home at all.

"You okay back there, kid?"

I shake my head no. I shake all over. Those sophomores saw what happened. And by now, I'm sure everyone knows the truth. I'm not like them. I don't have parents. Connie doesn't want me. My own father doesn't want me.

No one wants me.

"It'll be okay, kid," the deputy says, eying me from the center mirror. "I know it's hard to see it this way now, but you won't be controlled by other people forever. The system, it can't control you after you're eighteen, and then the only one you have to answer to is you. And if you screw up, it's your own ass on the line and maybe no one will save you, but you can always save yourself."

I keep shaking, staring at the back of his seat in front of me.

"This whole situation sucks, don't get me wrong," he continues. "But life sometimes sucks and you might as well learn that now. You're a good kid. Mr. Nelson told me so. You've got potential, so don't waste it."

The deputy slows the car to make a right turn, and we pass a bunch of clothing and gift shops on Main Street before stopping at one of the only red lights in town.

Some kids from school cross the street in front of us. Some juniors from my pre-calculus class. The guys in dress shirts, the girls wearing skirts and cute tops—they must have been at the dance. I slump down in my seat.

The juniors don't see me. They're still joking and laughing. Like they have nothing to worry about. This is just like any other day to them. They aren't headed to jail. They aren't inmates in the foster care system like me.

Maybe if I'd never moved to Silver Valley, Kale would be with them, telling some funny story. Rather than wondering where his date ran off to all of a sudden, only to see her escorted off the premises by a sheriff's deputy. I hang my head.

Maybe I'll never be like them, maybe I'll never be normal again after this, after going to jail. *Jail.*

Maybe that's what my future looks like, a jail cell, rather than college. I was stupid for thinking I could be like everyone else, even for one night.

The light turns green seconds after the kids reach the other end of the crosswalk. The deputy eases his foot on the gas.

Next thing I know, the car is slowing again, turning right into the parking lot of a two-story brick building with a sign out front that says Silver Valley Juvenile Detention Center.

The parking lot is empty except for one other cop car. The deputy kills the engine and gets out, unlocking the door and opening it for me.

"I'm sorry about this, kid. I wish I didn't have to do this, but your case worker couldn't come pick you up tonight, so you have to stay here."

"Mindy? She knows I'm here?"

He pushes the door open farther, resting his hand on the car door, waiting for me to get out.

"Yeah, but she's on vacation, and I'm not sure when she's back in the office. You're in here tonight, hopefully not too much longer than that, and then maybe she can find a more suitable living arrangement for you. Don't tell anybody I said this, but I've met that Connie a few times at the courthouse and she's no peach."

I nod, but I don't move.

He waits, his hand still on the door. "Come on, don't make me make you," the deputy says. "It's late, and you've had a rough night. You'll feel better when you get some sleep."

He reaches his hand out to me. I hesitate but finally grab it, edging my way out of the backseat.

"Where will I go?" I ask softly as my feet hit the pavement.

"What about my stuff? Will I go back to Connie's to pick it up before they move me?"

"That I don't know, kid."

I follow him in the direction of the building. "I'll check you in," he says. "Just make sure to be real respectful, keep your head down, and you'll be fine. It's tiny in there, and there's usually no more than just a few inmates, I mean kids."

I wince.

"Come to think of it, you're the only one so far tonight."

The deputy pats me on the back, and I continue following him through the parking lot and onto the sidewalk. Once we reach the door, he rings a doorbell. A short and plump old man answers. He scratches at one of the few white hairs on his otherwise bald head and squints at me.

"What's this one in for? Shoplifting?"

I stare down at my feet.

"Nah, just a little misunderstanding with her foster mother. She's a good kid and won't give you a hard time."

I look up at the deputy.

"Well, I guess that's it, then." He nods at me. "I don't know what'll happen in the morning or if I'll see you before your social worker picks you up, so I'll tell you one thing. Have a good life, kid. Decide now that's what you're going to do and then just do it. No excuses, no blaming, just take responsibility for your own actions and your own happiness and you'll be fine. Got it?"

I swallow the lump in my throat and nod. I reach my hand out for a shake. The deputy laughs and squeezes my hand.

"You'll be okay." He pats my shoulder. And then he walks

to his car, to drive back to school and talk to Mr. Nelson or maybe to go patrol the streets.

The bald man starts coughing heavily as he turns around. I follow him inside the building. On the inside, it looks like more of a mixed-use office and home than a jail. I wait silently in the tiny hallway while Mr. Coughing collects himself. A staircase with a rail leads up to an overlook on the right, and a hallway and a few rooms.

"Come on, then," he says, his white mustache moving up and down as he continues to cough. I follow him to the left. A beat-up rocking chair sits behind a small, wooden desk with a tiny, ancient-looking television behind it.

He talks to me as we walk. "You're lucky you live in Silver Valley and get to stay here, rather than real juvie in Carson City. And believe you me, a scared little thing like yourself doesn't want to be in a place like that."

"This isn't real juvie?"

Mr. Coughing bellows at that. "You kidding me? What's this look like? There aren't even any other kids in here tonight, and I'll give you breakfast and send you on your way as soon as your social worker gets here."

He points at one of the three closed doors on the left. "See that, that's a private room in there for you. It's no Marriot, but at least you'll get to take a shower by yourself and won't be locked up with any mini-wannabe gangbangers. Like I said, you're lucky."

I keep my face blank. I don't feel lucky.

The man's white eyebrows scrunch up and his eyes soften slightly. "I'm going to leave you alone to sleep in just a minute, but there's one thing I have to do first. I have to search you."

I step back.

"I don't want to do it anymore than you want me to," he exclaims. "Let's just make this quick. Stand with your arms outstretched and legs, too, like this."

The man's uniform stretches over his protruding belly as he reaches his arms and his legs out wide to show me.

I do what he says and grit my teeth as the man bends down and quickly pats outside my dress, the inside of my legs up until about my thighs.

I shut my eyes, holding my breath, and start counting in my head, anything to take my mind off the hands on me.

He quickly moves his hands to the outside and pats my belly, skipping over my breasts and moving over my arms and back in two swift motions.

I exhale.

"That's good enough. Okay, now off to bed with you."

He pulls a key ring out of his pocket and flips through until he finds the right one. After opening the door and flipping the lights on, he ushers me to the bed, with a thin, blue blanket and small white pillow on the top.

I stand in the doorway for a second.

Mr. Coughing frowns as he looks at my—Christina's— dress. "Hold on." He disappears down the hallway and bangs around for a minute, out of my view. He returns with a pair of shorts and a shirt, the same kind I wear for P.E. class. "We have some of these lying around. They're clean, and a whole lot more comfortable than that slinky dress for you to sleep in. Don't ya think?"

He hands me the clothes, and I take them. I'll have to return Christina's outfit to her somehow. Maybe I can mail it to her after I'm settled into whatever new placement Mindy puts me in. *Placement.* A new foster parent, a new home.

No more Jamie or Lizzie.

No more Kale or Christina.

I bet I won't even get to say goodbye, just like I couldn't with Sarah. What's the point in caring about people when I always have to leave them?

The knot in my stomach tightens. I can't think about that yet.

"Get some rest. Alarm goes off at six, then you shower and eat breakfast. Got it?"

I nod.

"Oh, and I'm Sheriff Scott, just so you know. Sleep tight."

He turns around, flicks the light switch off and shuts the door behind him, leaving me alone in the dark. A second later the lock on his side of the door clicks.

I can hear Sheriff Scott turn on the microwave in the other room. Christina and I ate some sandwiches while getting ready, but my stomach grumbles at the smell of melted cheese wafting through the door.

Once in the P.E. clothes, I sit on the bed, holding my head in my hands with my eyes closed for a few minutes, trying to block out all thought. I lie down.

The pillow's firm and lumpy under my head, the blanket light and not nearly long enough to cover all of me. I shiver and pull the blanket closer to me. I just need to go to sleep. Get this night over with, face whatever I have to face tomorrow. Christina's worried face flashes in my mind as I close my eyes. I shiver. I can almost feel Kale's hand in mine, his arm on the small of my back.

I open my eyes, stare at the beige ceiling, a spider web hanging in the corner. The dusty smell of the room—the jail cell—fills my nostrils, and the coils of the thin mattress poking my back aren't enough to keep my thoughts going to where I can't let them go.

I'm shaking into the flimsy cover, wishing Mom could wrap her arms around me. Back before everything fell apart. Back when Mom and I used to do everything together. Go grocery shopping, do laundry. She was a housewife; her job was taking care of Dad and me. And my job, the way I saw it, was to be just like her. I followed her around like a puppy. She went upstairs, I followed. She went to the kitchen, I was right behind her. She joked that I'd probably go into the bathroom with her if she let me.

I pull my legs up tight into my chest. Holding on, holding on, holding on to Mom. To her memory.

I close my eyes. I'm back with Mom, not in this jail. I can almost feel her arms around me. Almost.

The writing was on the wall that Valentine's Day. I just didn't know it. Dad got so mad about our movie marathon.

Mom. I'm with her, curled up on the couch laughing, not in jail, in the fetal position, alone alone alone. My chest is so tight, my head is throbbing. Now I'm truly falling apart. *Mom. Mom. Mom.* I chant to myself.

Staring at the spiderweb dangling down from the off-colored ceiling, I'm starting to see everything clearly.

I bury my head in the pillow. Roll myself into a ball and cry. Cry for my mother. What would she say if she saw me like this? Could she have any idea this is where I would end up after she died? I wish she were here. I would give anything to have her with me, just for one more night. If she could just hold me and tell me everything will be okay.

But wasn't that my job? To tell *her* it would be okay? To always be okay?

The walls around me, the locked door, they're closing me in like an animal.

Alone, I'm alone.

What would my life be like if Mom were alive? Would we be a happy family? Were we ever, even when I was little?

Maybe before Mom showed me what Dad wanted was more important than we wanted. Or *needed.*

Before she told me, her daughter, that it was practically her dying wish that I take care of my father.

And I see the truth now, for the first time, as I shake and cry alone in this jail cell in this town I hadn't even heard of this time last year. Dad hurt Mom, too. And she didn't see it. She didn't protect me.

Now I'm crying for the life I wish I had. For the mom I wish I had, the way I wish things could have been different.

Alone. I'm alone. Maybe I've always been.

The blanket doesn't stop the shaking. It started in my chest, but now creeps through my shoulders before overtaking the rest of me. I'm nothing, alone in a jail cell, sobbing, gasping for air. Alone and crying, until I fall asleep.

CHAPTER
ELEVEN

"*T*ime to wake up!" Suddenly, bright light assaults my closed eyelids. Near the light switch at the edge of the room, Sheriff Scott stands. He's got a mug in one hand and a towel with a bar of soap in the other.

I look around quickly, disoriented. Still here, at Silver Valley's little version of juvenile hall. I sit up in the bed, rub my sore back, and blink several times. My eyes are dry from crying.

Sheriff Scott takes a sip of his coffee. "Last night was a tough one for ya, I bet, but it's over now. So, ready to start fresh today?"

I pull the blanket closer to my chest and stammer some kind of non-intelligible response. He hands me the towel and soap, and I grab Christina's dress off the floor to change back into. "Good! Follow me."

Down the hall through one of the closed doors is a tiny bathroom, scarcely decorated, but otherwise pretty normal. Sheriff Scott pulls the blue shower curtain over and waves his hand in front of the shower.

"Well, here it is."

I shut the door behind him and get into the

shower. I can't wash off last night, the humiliation. But at least I can start over. It would have never worked out with Kale, anyway. He doesn't know anything about my past, how could he like the *real* me? And Christina, she would have just left me behind when she started her exciting new life in Washington, D.C. I might as well not get attached to people when none of it ever lasts.

I finish up, towel off, and get dressed quickly.

"Is there a hamper I can throw this towel in?" I call out to Sheriff Scott as I open the bathroom door.

But it's Mindy, not the sheriff, on the other side. Blonde hair, a little lighter. Skin, a little tanner. And she's not smiling.

"Lucky I scheduled my flight to arrive a few days early to give me a chance to rest before coming back to work." She raises an eyebrow at me.

Sheriff Scott appears in the hallway behind Mindy. "Perfect timing!"

Mindy looks at me. "You ready?"

I nod and set the towel on the bathroom counter. Mindy thanks Sheriff Scott and turns, heading for the door.

I face Sheriff Scott. "Thank you, again."

He nods, his mustache curling over his lips into a small smile. "Better not see you back here."

"You won't."

Outside, the car beeps unlocked and Mindy gets in the driver's side of her silver Ford Taurus. The State of Nevada sticker on it marks it as a Child Protective Services vehicle; I bet Mindy drives something better when she's not working. She's young-ish, maybe in her thirties. Probably thought she was going to save the world when she took this job after grad school.

Her phone dings. We both glance at it, in between us on the passenger seat.

Mindy grabs the phone and scans the message. "I'm not even *officially* back from vacation yet, but the emails keep rolling in."

She dashes a quick response, her fingers stabbing the keyboard on her smartphone, and then she tosses the phone in the center console.

I sink into the passenger's side. "I was starting to wonder if you dropped my case. Whatever happened to being mandated to visit me once a month?"

Mindy's eyes widen and her mouth falls open in seeming exasperation. "I'm a couple days late on that. I saw you a couple weeks into your placement, and it's been just over a month since then. I was going to come next week, after my time off."

I roll my eyes. "Well, I guess you don't have to now, since here we are." I wave my arm in front of us.

"I have thirty kids on my caseload." Mindy pinches the bridge of her nose and closes her eyes. "I wish I could spend more time with each of you, but honestly, Victoria, you're safe, in a home where you have food and no one is hurting you." She looks at me. "I wish I could fix everything for everyone. But that's just not the reality I live in. I'm buried in paperwork, have a million calls to make, and every day I face kids' problems that no matter how hard I try, I sometimes can't fix."

Mindy's talking fast now, her words coming out almost like she's panicked.

"We don't have enough social workers to fit the need. I have so many cases. Kids separated from their siblings, kids who are in the hospital after they were returned to their parents. Kids who need intensive therapeutic help after being hurt in the most disgusting, terrible ways."

Mindy shakes her head. "I shouldn't be telling you that." She sighs heavily. "It's just there are so many kids with so many problems, Victoria, and I see them every day, and I want to help but I can't always."

She hesitates before her lips turn into a thin line. "It doesn't help that the one vacation I've taken in three years was interrupted to pick you up from juvie."

I deadpan. "I'm so sorry for *you*."

Mindy turns her head up to look at the car roof. She sucks in a breath. "I know, Victoria, I know your life is tough. I know. But you've gotta work with me here."

My stomach sinks, and for a second I want to ease up on Mindy. But I don't. She hasn't even asked me my side about last night. She just says I have to work with her, like my behavior is what causes all my problems.

"I'm sorry this is what you had to come back to after your trip to Hawaii or wherever you were."

Mindy snorts, taking her hand off the key she just put in the ignition. "Not on a social worker and UPS driver's salary. We went to Palm Springs. It was hot, and we sat by the pool all day and relaxed."

"Sounds nice."

"You're right about that," she snaps. But then Mindy sees my expression, and her voice softens. "If you act up like this again, you will march yourself further and further away from nice things and experiences, Victoria. Lying, sneaking around, and breaking the rules just isn't an option for foster kids, even if other kids pull that kind of stuff. One of your friends does something stupid and her parents ground her, but you could get sent to lock-up or worse."

I swallow. I know what Mindy means, worse than lock-up. She means an institution, with girls doing hard time for hurting themselves or other people. Connie's told me all about places like that, and how I'm *lucky* to live in a home like hers.

Or I was.

Mindy pats my knee, before bringing her hand back to the wheel.

"It's been weeks since I've heard from you." My voice comes out small.

Mindy faces forward, staring at the empty parking lot rather than at me. "Victoria, I really am sorry. It won't happen again, I promise."

I pause for a second, fumble my hands in my lap. Now seems like a good opening to get some answers. "What's going on with Sarah, with our parents?"

Mindy lets out a long exhale. "Nothing has changed." She puts on her seatbelt and glances at her mirrors, like she's about to drive away, even though the car's not even started. "Tiffany won't refute anything your father's said. She defends him, fiercely, and says you have a problem and need help."

I look down at my hands. I don't believe it anymore, don't believe that I'm the problem. But the accusation still hurts. "If I need help so much, why doesn't she try to help me?"

Mindy hands me my seatbelt. "She thinks she has to take care of her daughter first. And I'm sure that's what she thinks she's doing, or trying to do."

I buckle my seatbelt. "And my dad?" I pause, keeping my voice even. "Has he said anything else?" I look up to meet her eye.

Mindy turns her complete attention to me. Her eyes crinkle at the edges, her mouth turns down. "Tell me what happened, Victoria. Give me your side of the story."

I close my eyes. Press my index fingernail into my thumb's cuticle until the pain shoots through it.

I could tell the truth.

For the first time, I really consider it. Letting go of the horrible secret, putting it out in the open. Seeing what happens.

An image of my father in handcuffs, in the backseat of a cop car like I was in last night, fills my head. Behind actual bars for years, not a solitary room like I had for one night. I swallow the lump in my throat, fight off the tightening of my chest. I don't want Dad to go to jail. Mom's gone, and she told me to take care of Dad, even if she shouldn't have. That was her dying wish. *I promised her.*

I adjust myself in my seat. Don't acknowledge Mindy's question. Better to change the subject.

"So, what's next?" I ask. "Did a bed open up at a group home back in Reno? Or Carson? Carson City's small, but it's a ton bigger than here. I'll take anywhere, really, as long as Connie's not there."

Mindy stares at me for a moment before answering. "No, Victoria. I talked to Connie. She's willing to give you a second chance so you can finish your senior year here."

I ball my fists and look at the jail we're still sitting in front of. The jail Connie had me thrown in for going to a stupid freaking dance.

"I can't—"

"Yes, you can." I flinch as Mindy pats my leg again before finally turning the key in the ignition. "Connie's giving you a second chance, and you're lucky to get it. Not everyone gets second chances, especially kids in the system."

Mindy pulls out of the parking lot onto the street. My breathing quickens.

I squeeze my fists tighter. "But you've only heard her side of the story. You only call her, you don't talk to me! If you did, you'd know"—I stop to breathe a few short breaths—"you'd know she doesn't give a crap about me!"

Mindy opens her mouth, but I start shouting. "Sarah—I don't understand why you won't tell me anything about her or how she's doing."

A young mom stares at me as we pull up beside her at the red light. Her baby sleeps in its car seat in back.

I inhale and exhale, lower my voice. "You never ask me if I want to see her."

Mindy's mouth is a thin line, her hands tightening around the wheel. "Your father doesn't want you involved with your stepsister, and neither does her mother." After the light turns green, Mindy rolls her window down, and then speaks louder over the breeze. "Unless charges are brought against your father and Sarah leaves his care with her mother, or she's taken into state custody, you can't do anything about that. They are her guardians and they decide who she talks to. I'm sorry, Victoria, I really am, but there's nothing I can do about that."

We pass the same crosswalk where those kids walked last night.

"And as for Connie," Mindy continues, "you know a lot less about her than you think you do, Victoria. She's willing to let you live in her house, even though she thinks you've been ungrateful and disrespectful. She's willing to let you finish high school at the same school rather than uproot your life again. She's giving you a chance, now why don't you give her one?"

I fold my arms and glare at Mindy. "Look, after what happened last night, you can't honestly tell me she's not just going to throw me out in three months when I turn eighteen anyway," I say, changing tactics. "You might as well let me go back to Reno now, put me in some group home and let me finish school!"

"Connie is not going to throw you out," Mindy says. "Not if you follow her rules and behave yourself until you graduate. This is the best thing for you, to not have to move again and disrupt your schooling more than we already have."

"You're not listening, you don't understa—"

Mindy blows air through her pursed lips, cutting me off. "You're going back to Connie's."

I shake my head. Nothing I say matters. I see that now. Mindy and Connie don't care what I want or what I think.

We park in the driveway and Mindy leads the way out. She raps on the door twice, and Connie answers it. Connie grimaces as she takes in me wearing Christina's dress, rather than the clothes I left the house in yesterday.

"Why don't you go to the dormitory, and let us talk," Mindy says to me.

I turn away from her, no goodbye, and stomp through the living room, past Connie's little brat Annie. I'll just let the adults talk about me and *what's best for me*.

In the dormitory, Jamie sits up in bed and pulls her ear buds out as I stomp in. Her eyes look bloodshot and puffy. "What happened?" she asks.

But I don't want to talk to Jamie or to anyone. If I open my mouth, instead of saying words I feel like I'll just scream. And I have my own problems to deal with anyway. I ignore Jamie, change into pajamas, and climb into my own bed. I turn my back to her.

At some point, Mindy leaves, I guess. Without saying goodbye. Like I care.

I stay in bed.

Connie calls us in for dinner, and Jamie leaves without saying anything. I yell from the dormitory that I'm not hungry. Either Connie's actually decided to allow me to stay in bed, or they've forgotten about me, so I don't talk to her or anyone else for the rest of the night.

CHAPTER
TWELVE

*L*izzie and Jamie are already sitting on the loveseat opposite Connie when I begrudgingly join them the next morning. Annie is at her grandmother's house today, so the only person we have to wait on is our horrid foster mother. Per usual, Connie's sitting on the big couch, her bare feet perched on the matching ottoman.

"'Bout time!" Connie says to me. "Sit."

Lizzie scoots over to make room for me on the edge. I sit.

"I've got news. Big, big news." Connie grins at Lizzie. "You're getting adopted!"

On Lizzie's other side, Jamie leans forward. Wearing a bulky sweatshirt, she looks smaller than usual. "The Willits changed their mind?"

Changed their mind? I thought she was supposed to move in with them next weekend.

I lean behind Lizzie and try to catch Jamie's eye, but she doesn't look at me. Her eyes are on Connie, and there's a desperation in them I haven't seen before.

Connie flushes. "No, no." She shakes her head. "Unfortunately, the Willits are sticking with what they said yesterday when they called, that they changed their mind about wanting an older child. They still want a baby."

Jamie's face crumples for a second, but then she regains composure. Her body stiffens.

Connie glances at me, and then looks back to Jamie. "Not everyone has the patience and wherewithal to handle a preteen or teenager, foster teens and all the baggage they come with especially. But be patient, and hopefully another family will come along for you someday."

Jamie sags back into the couch. "They seemed lame anyway." She crosses her arms and glares at the wall.

Lizzie's eyes haven't left Connie. "Those people want to adopt me?" she asks.

I turn to Lizzie. "What people?"

Connie snaps her head toward me. "Maybe if you weren't so caught up in your diabolical plans, lying and breaking rules, you would know."

I look from her back to Lizzie. And then to Jamie, who still won't look at me. Guilt seeps in. Maybe Connie's right. I haven't paid much attention to Jamie or Lizzie. I didn't say a word to Jamie last night, even though it looked like she'd been crying.

Connie sighs, a piece of her thin, brown hair falling into her face. "Last week her social worker came by for her monthly and told Lizzie about a couple who were interested in adopting her. They'd liked the look of her in photos and had already been approved to foster kids, with the potential to adopt." She smiles at Lizzie. "They stopped by with her social worker and met Lizzie at preschool a couple of days later, and they all hit it off." Connie glares at me. "There, now you're up to speed."

"They really want me?" Lizzie sits up straighter, her eyes alight with hope.

Connie claps her hands together. "They do, congratulations!"

Lizzie starts to cry. My eyes well up a bit—*I'm going to miss her*—but I blink quickly.

Jamie turns from the wall to stare out the window behind Connie. "May I be excused?" she mutters.

"You've got homework to do?" Connie asks.

"Tons."

"Go on, then."

Jamie doesn't look at Lizzie or me as she heads to the dormitory. She disappears into the hallway. I have to talk to her, make it right. I will, in a moment.

Still, I smile at Lizzie. "I'm really happy for you."

"All right, Lizzie," Connie interrupts. "You better go and pack, and then make sure your side of the room is spick and span, you got it?"

Lizzie nods and runs off. I start after her.

"Not so fast."

I stop, my back already turned to Connie, and hold my breath. I turn around slowly.

"Annie is at her grandma's, as you know, so now would be a good time to change her sheets and tidy up your room, too, while you're at it. We should get a new girl to take Lizzie's place in the next few days, so we'll want this whole house in top shape to welcome her."

My jaw clenches. "I have homework."

Connie raises her line-thin eyebrows. "Well, maybe you should have thought about that before you went ahead and broke the rules." Connie's voice is shrill and mocking. "I figure you should be kept busy, you know, so you don't have time to come up with any other half-witted plans to trick me."

Connie leans closer from her spot on the couch. "I tried to trust you at first. I really wanted to believe you were working hard on a school project. But I just knew something wasn't right. So I called the school, to check up on you in the library while you "studied," and you know what they told me? You're not even in health class. Honestly, at least it was a creative lie, girl. I'll give you that."

Again, I start to walk away, but Connie stops me.

"Wait," she says, her tone softening. "You clearly don't see it, yet, but there are worse things in this world than a bunch of rules."

She heaves herself up to stand and steps closer to me. Automatically, I back away.

"You just got a tiny taste of what it might be like to be in trouble with the law," Connie says, leaning over me. "Maybe it'll stick with you, if you don't want to be just another foster kid who winds up in trouble. Another statistic, ruining the chance of a better life because they don't have anyone to help or guide them. I'm trying to teach you a valuable lesson, you just don't see it yet."

I scowl. Like I'm going to thank this awful woman for throwing me in jail for the night.

"Aargh!" Connie throws her hands up in the air. "Girl, you make me crazy with that thick skull of yours! Go on, then. You've got chores to do."

After putting away several of Annie's toys, washing the sheets and making her bed, taking out the garbage, and wiping off the surfaces of her toy chests—all while Connie doesn't move a muscle as she lounges on the couch watching soap operas—I head for the girls' dormitory.

The door bumps into a trash bag full of clothes as I open it to let myself in. A few pieces of Lizzie's clothing spill onto the floor. Lizzie's on the ground to pick them up before I get the chance.

"All packed up." Lizzie pushes the clothes back in.

I bend down and tie the bag for her. "I see that."

Jamie huffs. She's lying on her bed facing the wall. "Pretty pathetic that everything she owns can fit in that one bag," she snaps. "Actually, it's pathetic she has to use a garbage bag to pack in the first place. All of it's pathetic."

Lizzie mutters something before leaving the room. The door shuts behind her, leaving me with Jamie. I sigh. "Look, I'm sorry I wouldn't talk to you yesterday. I was"—I hesitate—"a mess."

She doesn't respond.

I walk to the bed and reach up to put my hand on Jamie's

bunk. "I'm sorry about the Willits. There will be another family, I'm sure of it."

"Oh yeah, because twelve-year-old girls whose parents are tweakers are right up there on the list to get adopted with cute babies and golden retriever puppies, right?" Jamie jerks away from me into a sitting position. Her eyes are bloodshot, and the rest of her face is a mix of pale and blotchy. "Especially when those tweakers robbed a liquor store and killed a college kid walking down the street when they plowed him down in their stolen getaway car?"

My hand drops. "Jamie, I'm so sorry. I, I didn't know."

"Of course you didn't know!" Jamie spits through her tears. Shouts from Connie's soap opera blare through the door. "I didn't tell you! Why would I?"

I stare up at Jamie, her balled fists, her scowl. "Jamie, what your parents did isn't your fault. You can't blame yourself for that." I reach for her shoulder, but she shoves my hand away.

"Really, is that what you tell yourself to feel better?" she hisses. "That's why you tell all of your friends you live here? Oh, that's right. You don't. But now they all know, and you'll be a reject. Just wait until tomorrow, you'll see."

I swallow. "Is that what happened with your boyfriend? Did you break up because he found out about where you live?"

Jamie laughs harshly. "You care about me and what I have to deal with all of a sudden? You aren't too busy crying about your own daddy issues and lame problems?"

My head snaps back. Heat shoots through my body.

"Fine, Jamie," I say slowly, through gritted teeth. "Fine. Be like that. I was just trying to be your friend." I turn to walk away. I'd rather watch crap TV with Connie than stay here with Jamie.

Jamie scowls. "Friends don't keep secrets, Victoria. You should have told me you were going to the dance. I could have helped! I could have covered for you."

I whip around.

"So you could have been thrown in jail with me? So you could end up like your parents?"

The second the words leave my mouth, I wish I could take them back. It's like I see them, slowly, as they travel from me to Jamie, crushing her as the blow lands. Jamie's mouth falls open, shocked. I take a step forward, slowly, and put my hands up. "Look, Jamie. I didn't mean—"

She cuts me off. "You want to talk about my parents? *My parents*? I've heard you talk in your sleep." Jamie closes her eyes and pulls her comforter up to her chin, feigning a nightmare. "No, Daddy. Don't touch me, I said no!"

My stomach clenches as I struggle for air. One word forms in my head.

Unforgivable.

"No wonder the Willits didn't want you, Jamie. No wonder."

I turn around and walk out of the room.

"I'm really going to miss you," Lizzie says to me Monday morning. I kneel, and she closes the distance between us for a hug. Her new parents won't be here to pick her up for another couple of hours, but I'll be at school by then. Jamie left ten minutes ago.

I let Lizzie go and stand. "I'm going to miss you, too, but this doesn't have to be goodbye. Maybe I'll see you again someday," I say, to make us both feel better. Maybe when I'm in college, Lizzie's new parents will let me visit her.

Lizzie's eyes well up. I look away, so she doesn't see I'm upset, too.

Standing behind us, Connie clears her throat. "Yeah, yeah. You all love each other and are going to miss each other." Her voice breaks. She inhales and seems to force it back to normal. "But you should probably get to school before you're late." Connie clicks her tongue. "Truancy is the last thing you need, girl," she adds, glaring at me.

I put my hands on Lizzie's shoulders and squeeze. "You're going to love it there, I just know it."

Having already been patted down and searched by my foster mother, I head for the door to go to school. Freedom from Connie, but what's ahead might be worse. I wish I didn't have to find out for myself—that I could just take a nap and wake up months from now, with all of this behind me. I think about all the ways sleeping through conflicts could improve my life as I walk to school along the same route Jamie and I usually walk together. She didn't even say goodbye to Lizzie.

Or me.

CHAPTER
THIRTEEN

*T*he second I open the double doors, people stare at me. Not just a few classmates watching or whispering from their lockers, but everyone. It's like they finally see the ripped, jagged parts of me—the secrets I've been trying to hide since I first stepped foot in this place. Now they know who I really am. The curiosity, pity, and judgement of all those stares stab me over and over, like needles, each time a pair of eyes looks and then darts away.

I look ahead, keeping my peripherals open for Christina or Kale, and walk straight to my locker.

"Dude, don't. It's not cool," Alex says to Zach, a few lockers away. Alex waves to me. I look away.

After a few seconds, the usual talk about the weekend continues. Alex takes a basketball out of his locker and bounces it, heading to class. I grab my history textbook and shove my backpack inside.

Zach leans against the locker next to me, his hairy arm resting above his head. "So, they let you out of the slammer, huh? Did you have enough time in there to become anyone's girlfriend?"

I close my locker and walk right past him to history.

I'm a couple minutes early, so only a few seats are taken. Christina isn't here yet. Zach walks in seconds after I sit in my usual seat. He shoots me a twisted smile.

"No need to get your panties all in a twist." He walks by me to his seat on the left. "I was only joking."

I turn to face him. "It's not funny."

"It was funny." Zach settles in his seat. "Maybe if you had parents one of them would have taught you a sense of humor."

Christina appears, slamming her textbook on the desk in front of Zach. "Well, your parents should be ashamed of themselves because they raised a jackass for a son who has the emotional maturity of an eight-year-old and, rumor has it, the penis size to match!"

"Ms. Martinez!" Santa bellows from behind us. "My desk. Now."

Christina looks at Zach the way I'd imagine she'd stare down Voldemort before tossing her ponytail over her head and stomping to Santa's desk. Santa murmurs something I can't hear and then Christina passionately whispers something back. Santa looks at me quickly and then at Zach.

"Mr. Davis, unless you want to spend this Saturday's game riding the bench due to suspension, I suggest you keep your mouth shut."

Zach nods and grumbles some weak apology. My face

reddening, I look down at my history book and flip to the chapter we last studied.

Christina puts her hand on my shoulder and squeezes it. I slump in my seat as Taylor and Lauren walk in. They look at me quickly and then away, like they feel sorry for me, before they head for their seats.

Christina leans over to whisper in my ear. "I meant what I said about Zach's penis size," she says. "Taylor slept with him last year and told the rest of the cheer squad about it. Lauren told me."

I crack a smile. "Atta girl," Christina says. And I can sense her smile, even though I don't look up to see it.

Santa calls the class to order. "I trust you all had wonderful weekends, but now it's time for some real fun. This week we're studying the Great Depression!"

Usually, reading about people who made it through awful times strangely makes me feel better. But even the triumph of those who eventually made it through terrible poverty can't lift my spirits. So many people didn't get a happy ending back then. Maybe that's the right part of history to focus on, I was just too naïve to see it before.

Several people groan as they open their books. Thankfully, most of their attention is on Santa for the rest of the period.

I rush through the open door the second the bell rings. Christina catches up to me as I try to blend into the flurry of other students coming and going to their lockers, laughing and smiling and living their normal lives with their normal parents, normal homes.

Christina doesn't say a word to me, just walks by my side, until we reach my locker. I shove my books in without looking at her and grab a notebook. I'm not mad at Christina, but pushing things in and out of my locker makes me feel powerful, stupid as it is.

When I'm done, I turn to face Christina. Her deep brown eyes search mine. "We still have about four minutes until the second bell rings. Can I talk to you outside for a minute?"

I nod, and Christina walks slightly ahead of me, her brown boots hitting the linoleum floor just a second before my sneakers do on each step. She smells like lavender and roses, a combination probably from her shampoo and perfume. I keep my eyes on the back of her head, and not at any of the people who stare at me as we walk by them.

We escape out the double doors and onto the manicured lawn, where only the smell of wet grass awaits us. No students. No teachers. No laughing or staring at me. No pity.

Christina walks us to the center of the grass, drops her bag, and then hugs me. She squeezes and doesn't let go for several seconds. I don't move to hug her back, but I let her hug me.

She finally pulls away. "Are you okay?"

"I'm fine," I answer without thinking. Christina tilts her head at me but says nothing. "I mean, no," I blurt, tears coming all of a sudden. "No, I'm not okay."

Christina embraces me again and I cry into her shoulder. This is humiliating. This shouldn't be happening to me. This isn't what high school is supposed to be like. This shouldn't be my life. It's not fair.

"It's not fair," Christina says, as if reading my thoughts. "I'm so, so sorry. I thought maybe you were embarrassed of your mom, and that's why you were so secretive. Or even of your clothes, no offense. But foster care. I had no idea. If I had known, I wouldn't have had you come with me to that stupid dance."

Christina's eyes narrow. "I can't believe that woman. What a horrible bitch to do that to you. My mother knows her. They used to go to school together and everyone in town knows she just fosters children for the money so she doesn't have to get off of her ass and work like everyone else!"

I laugh harder than this comment warrants. Christina laughs, too.

I wipe the tears from my eyes. "It's just so embarrassing. Does everyone know?"

"So what if they do?" Christina shrugs. "You can't tell me you actually give a damn about what the hillbillies in this school think?"

I cast my eyes down. That means everyone does know.

Christina starts talking louder, faster. "I sure as hell don't care what they think. If anyone here is stupid enough to judge you for something that you didn't do, that's their problem." She squeezes my shoulders again and then looks down at her left wrist, checking the time on her oversized watch.

"We better get to class."

We start walking together, but I stop. "I just need a minute alone."

Christina nods and steps forward.

"Christina, wait!"

She turns, looking confused.

"Thanks," I say.

She nods, adjusts the straps of her bag. "That's what friends are for."

After Christina leaves, I wipe my face off with my sleeve. I close my eyes and count to ten before rushing back into the building and down the hall for pre-calculus. Kale's waiting for me in his usual seat, next to mine.

I can't fall apart again. I can't cry, not in class in front of everyone.

Especially not in front of Kale.

I'm not who he thought I was. And I don't want it to be real yet—I don't want the way he looks at me to change now that he knows the truth.

I walk right past Kale and go straight for an empty seat in the back. Kale turns to me as I sit and unload my backpack. I stare down into my open math book.

A few minutes into the lecture, something about determining the conjugate of a complex number, the guy in front of me passes me a note.

A note from Kale.

I stick the note in the crease of my textbook and tilt the book up so, if Mrs. Baker were to glance in my direction, she wouldn't catch on to what I'm doing. Her back is to the class as she writes some number set on the white board. I open the note.

Victoria,

Why didn't you sit with me? Are you okay?

Can we talk at lunch?

Kale

I look back at the board and see Kale's turned away from Mrs. Baker and is looking at me. Just looking at me.

I look down immediately.

I picture Kale and me dancing, before everything went wrong. His hand on my back. Me laughing as he brags about his amazing abs. That's who he wants, a girl he can go to dances with or take on dates . . . without her getting arrested.

He wants someone normal.

I was stupid for thinking we could be friends, maybe more than friends. He's better off without me. It's time to stop kidding myself and pretending I can be a normal girl. I can't. Not until I graduate and am on my own.

So when the bell rings, I walk quickly, passing Kale again, and I pretend not to hear him call my name.

I stop at Christina's locker just as Alex is walking away from her.

"Can we eat lunch alone? I mean, without Alex and Kale?"

"Definitely." Christina nods, her Alex smile sliding off her face. "How about we sit on the bench on the other side of the tool shed outside? Where you used to sit all the time."

"Lead the way."

At the end of the hallway, we open the other set of double doors and walk down the concrete steps. Aside from the dirt and weeds, there's not much out here except a couple of cottonwood trees, just like I remember. And the single bench, my old friend. We sweep dirt off it before sitting.

I take my PB & J out of my bag and take a bite, but don't taste the bread that slides down my throat. I set my sandwich on my lap.

"So, what happened?" Christina faces me. "After you were arrested, I mean after you left, Kale and I went to Mr. Nelson to find out what was going on, but he wouldn't tell us anything."

She tilts her head at me, her voice softening. "I was so worried. Kale, too."

I stare down at my sandwich. "I wish he wouldn't worry about me."

Christina exhales loudly. "Right, like that's going to happen until you tell us what's going on."

"Nothing—nothing's going on. Not anymore." I stare at the dirt at my feet. "I lied, but now you know the truth. My foster mother is a terrible human being who apparently takes pleasure in humiliating me, but she's not kicking me out. So that's it. End of story." I exhale, releasing the air from my lungs slowly. "Go ahead and tell Kale that, so I don't have to."

"He said you're avoiding him. Are you?"

I shove my empty lunch bag in my backpack. "What would I say to him? 'I'm in foster care, so I can't go out with you?' I can't even hang out with *you*, Christina! I'm practically in jail, for a crime I didn't commit!"

Christina goes quiet for a moment. "What crime?" she finally asks.

"It's a figure of speech," I grumble, still avoiding her eyes.

Christina stares at her feet. "I know, but still. You don't have to tell me what happened, but I'd like to know. If you want me to."

I hold my backpack in my lap, pull it tightly to my chest. "I do," I say, finally looking at her. "I just don't think I'm ready."

I manage to get through the rest of the school day avoiding Kale. He sees me in the halls; I walk quickly in the other direction. He calls my name; I pretend I can't hear him.

I walk home feeling my shoulders ease up. No awkward conversation with Kale today, maybe even tomorrow. Maybe he'll give up all together.

But at the thought, my stomach twists.

When I get inside the house, Connie inspects my bags for drugs. We don't talk. I pass Jamie, scrubbing the toilet in the bathroom with gloves on, listening to her iPod. I wonder what she did to piss Connie off. Saturday is deep-cleaning day.

I walk to the bedroom I share with Jamie only now. The sheets on Lizzie's old bed are new, her coloring stuff and backpack are gone. All traces of my former foster sister, disappeared. It's almost like she was never here to begin with. Almost.

I wonder if that's how Sarah feels about me.

I climb onto my bed, pull out a notebook and a pen. *Sarah*, I begin.

I tear the page out of the notebook and crush it in my palm. What would I say to Sarah in a letter? *I hate you for not sticking up for me? I hate you for going on with your life, without me, but I miss you anyway?*

Would Mindy even give it to her? Would my dad?

He wouldn't. I know he wouldn't.

For a second, I hear my dad's voice, like he's sitting right next to me. He's saying words he's never said. "I'm sorry, Victoria. What I did was wrong. Come home."

And I'm choking and coughing, holding my stomach, holding the pain. I crumple in on myself, sobbing.

The door to the room is open, but Jamie can't hear me with her headphones on. She doesn't care about me anyway. And why should she? My own father doesn't. He won't even admit what he did. He blamed me. He left me.

My dad had been coming into my room late at night for a few weeks. He'd sit next to my bed and rub my leg, tell me he loved me, while I lay frozen, pretending to be asleep. But he knew I was awake. He'd tell me about the problems he'd been having at work at first, and then he started telling me he was having problems with his wife, too. He said Tiffany was jealous of my mother. My dead mother. He told me they weren't having sex. Or he'd complain that she wasn't any good at it. I didn't know what to say or how to respond, so I didn't. I just listened. He told me he missed my mom. He said I looked just like her. He told me how beautiful I was.

The notebook in my hand shakes, and I drop it. My body shakes all over, and the gasping for air, the crying, is getting louder. But I can't stop. I can't I can't I can't—

Connie barges into the room, "What in God's name—"

She freezes. Shock registers on her face when she sees

me. Connie must have heard me crying but not have been prepared to see my utter loss of control, the sadness from which I've sunk into and can't imagine ever crawling out of again. She looks behind her at the open door, and then closes it and approaches me, slowly. Like I'm a wounded animal.

"I didn't want you to come live here at first," she whispers. "I don't know if Mindy ever told you that."

I keep shaking, keep crying. Why doesn't she just leave me alone?

Connie speaks louder over my sobbing. "It's not because I believed what your dad said, though. I may not be a college graduate, but I'm not an idiot." She looks around the room, as if someone is going to pop out from a corner and save her from talking to me.

I squeeze my eyes closed, block her out, block everything out. I can't do this. I can't let her see me like this. I pull the blanket closer to my face, as if it can hide me, as if I can pretend I don't exist.

"If your dad was really worried about you, if you really did what he said you did, he wouldn't send you away and let that be it. He would answer all the questions, he would take all the classes CPS asked him to, he'd get you into family counseling. He wouldn't abandon you."

I open my eyes. My face and shirt are soaked. Connie looks back at the door again. My head throbs; my throat is swollen from all the sobbing.

Connie walks around the side of the bed to me. She holds her hand out like she wants to touch me, but doesn't. Instead she keeps talking.

"Which made me think he was lying." She leans closer to me. "When the police officer asked you that first night if anything else had ever happened, and you said no—you didn't want to go forward with charges or anything like that—it just reminded me of me. It made me so mad because that's what I did. I protected the person who hurt me and suffered for it *for months* before I told my momma what had been going on. I didn't think I could stand to look at you and be reminded of that every day."

I wince as I swallow. Look up at her.

Connie sighs, closes her eyes for a moment and then opens them. "Reading your file, talking to Mindy about you, seeing you every day reminds me of what had happened to me and I hate it, but I believe you. I always have. I know you didn't do anything wrong."

Connie puts a hand down to steady herself, and then slowly sinks to the ground to sit next to my bed. She hesitates before awkwardly reaching up and putting her hand on my knee.

I feel it heavy, feel her touch. But don't move. Slow my breathing, slow my tears.

"Victoria, you can tell me what happened. You can trust me."

Trust. And like a flood, they come back. Tears, shaking, coughing. My chest squeezed, pinch tight, no air. I feel like I'm dying.

"Sshh, shh," she says, reaching her arm around my shoulders and I stiffen. She squeezes softly and then pulls her arm away.

"You don't have to say anything until you're ready. It's okay."

"Why are you doing this? You hate me," I choke out between sobs.

Connie shakes her head. "I don't hate you. I hate what seeing you reminds me of."

I breathe and hold the air and the tears in for a few seconds before letting it all go. I sit up straighter, pull my knees into my chest. "What do I remind you of?"

She closes her eyes and folds her thin lips into each other. "Me, and what my stepfather did to me when I was twelve years old."

A tiny tear trickles down Connie's cheek. I wipe my own face and take a few deeper breaths.

Pictures of what I imagine Connie would look like as a child run through my mind. Her stepdad, what he may have done to her. I close my eyes. No, I don't want to see, I don't want to think about it.

I still can't tell her. She'll believe me, she'll want me to talk about it, to tell Mindy. To tell the cops.

So my dad can call me a liar, so it can be my word against his. So I can feel the pain of everything all over again, and again, and again, as he lies more and more.

I won't tell Connie.

I won't.

Connie pulls her hand back and we both sit still, saying nothing.

CHAPTER
FOURTEEN

*C*onnie and I both look to the door as we hear Jamie stomping in the hallway. Connie wipes a tear from her eye, smooths the crinkles out of her gray sweatshirt. She stands and faces the door as Jamie opens it.

Jamie stops, taking her headphones off. "What are you doing in here?" she snaps.

Connie stares for a second before coming back to herself.

"I can be wherever I damn well please," she says. "It's my house." She walks past Jamie to the hallway, no backward glance or anything.

Jamie looks at me expectantly, not noticing or not caring that I've been crying. "What was that all about?"

"Nothing," I say coldly. Like I'd tell her the truth after what she said about my dad and my nightmares. "Nothing you care about anyway."

Jamie pauses for a second, like she might object. But then she glares at me and puts her headphones back on before walking up the ladder to her bed.

It's my turn to make dinner tonight. Chicken casserole from the box—bon appétit.

After setting Annie's plate in front of her, I sit on the other side of the table next to Jamie.

"Mom, the foster girl burned my food." Annie whines.

"Don't call her that, baby. Her name is Victoria," Connie says from the head of the table.

We lock eyes for a moment. Connie takes a sip of lemonade. "And Victoria, don't burn the casserole next time."

I stare down at my plate. "Okay, sorry."

She may have a heart in there somewhere, but there's truth to what Christina's mom said, too. Connie just doesn't want to get off her ass and do anything herself.

Still, I wonder what happened with her stepdad.

Her stepdad.

Her stepdad.

I stop breathing. The dining room and faces around me blur out of focus, my heart pounding. I hold the edge of the table in front of me.

If my dad did whatever he did to me, why wouldn't he do it to Sarah?

But then again, Dad ignored me entirely when Tiffany was around. He only lurked into my bedroom when she was asleep—and even that only started happening right before the night he sent me away. He and Tiffany had been fighting more than ever.

My mind wanders back to the big blowout at home six months ago. When things seemed to really turn for the worse.

Dad and I were in their bedroom, on their bed, watching a movie. Tiffany was out running errands, and Dad said he missed spending time with me. That's why he told me we should hang out in his room and watch a movie, rather than in the living room with Sarah. We needed time just for us, he said. He closed the door behind me.

I clutch my cup of lemonade.

That day, I sat up in his bed, snacking on a bag of potato chips as we watched the movie. He laid next to me. Close, with his hairy hand resting on my knee. We didn't say much. After a while, he slid his hand a bit higher and I froze, the chip I had been chewing losing its flavor. Heat flooded my chest and it felt as though a rock had dropped in my stomach. Dad didn't move or respond, he just kept his hand resting lightly on my thigh.

Suddenly I wanted to cry or scream or bolt from the room, but I didn't. Instead, I chomped hard on the chip, biting my tongue. A sharp pain joined a wet and warm copper taste in my mouth. I swallowed, careful not to move, and glanced at my dad, whose eyes were still locked on the TV. I wouldn't make this a big deal. I pushed the thought away, but not his hand.

Seconds passed, but it felt like hours because I was holding my breath. I couldn't focus on the movie anymore. I didn't feel right. I stared at the antique wooden dresser under the TV, my thoughts racing. It was probably just because I wasn't used to hanging out with him anymore, I told myself. Plus, he wasn't drunk. He was sloppy when he was drunk, always wanted to hug me way more than usual. Maybe I was just too sensitive. Dad always did say I read into everything too much.

Connie drawls on in the background, talking about the new girl who's going to take Lizzie's place soon.

I can hear her but I'm not here with them at the table. I'm back there on the bed with my dad.

When I finally scooted over so there was about a foot in between us, his hand rested on the bed. Neither of us said anything as we continued to watch the movie in silence. My breathing returned to normal. I was right, I had thought. There was nothing to worry about. I shouldn't make a big deal out of nothing. About halfway through the movie, Tiffany stormed in.

"What are you doing in here?" she snapped, and then as an afterthought: "And why was the door closed?"

Dad sat up in the bed. "Oh," he said, looking behind her to the door, then at me. "You must have closed it behind you, Victoria. I didn't notice."

I shake my head now, like I shook my head then. I had started to protest. "What? I di—"

Dad laughed and turned his attention back to Tiffany. "What's the big deal? What are you so bothered about? I can't spend some quality time with my daughter?"

Tiffany looked behind her and then back into the room. "Sarah's your daughter, too. She texted me. She said you two were in here. She felt left out."

I stood, ready to find Sarah. She told on us. She was always the center of attention and just once my dad wanted to spend time with just me, and that was the end of the world?

"I better go find Sarah, make sure she's not feeling left out." I snapped.

"Just hold on, Victoria," Tiffany said, calmer than before. "We're all a family. Sarah has every right to be included."

I shook my head, unbelieving. "Seriously? Like you're mother of the year? Tell me what a great mom you are to me, how you *include* me in everything. I'd love to hear all about it."

Tiffany scowled as she took a step closer to me. "You wouldn't let me, even if I tried." Her voice broke as it got louder. "You never have. How am I supposed to compete with your perfect mother? How am I supposed to compete with a dead woman?"

Dad reached for the remote and turned the TV off. He stood, his fists balled, and glared at Tiffany, lowering his voice. "Victoria, go to your room. Now."

"Gladly." I knocked against Tiffany's shoulder as I stomped into the hall. I was too angry to say another word, not even to Sarah for texting her mom about me. I heard Dad and Tiffany shouting at each other that night. I knew Tiffany would blame me. And I didn't care.

"Victoria!" Connie's yell finally breaks through my thoughts. "What on Earth? I've been calling your name and it's like you can't even hear me."

I look at Jamie next to me. Usually, she would have nudged me to let me know I was spacing out. But she didn't.

Instead, my foster sister stabs her food. I shake my head and blink several times. Force a bite down.

Sarah's fine, I tell myself. She hasn't said anything to Mindy, and Mindy asks her all the time. And she hasn't said anything to her mom, either, because Tiffany—despite her many, many flaws—would never keep Sarah in a situation like that.

Everything must be okay. I look around the dining room, at the people around me who aren't my family, who are barely more than strangers. It's not Sarah I need to worry about, it's me.

Kale is standing at my locker when I walk into school the next morning.

"Victoria, please just talk to me. I'm"—Kale takes a deep breath, his voice wavering—"I'm worried about you."

I hold the handle to my locker, biding my time. I have no idea what to say.

"Please," he whispers.

I look at the dark-navy locker, not his face or his blue polo shirt that brings out the color of his eyes. "What do you want?"

Kale puts his hands in his pockets. "I want you to talk to me. I want to know if you're okay. Why are you avoiding me?"

I open my locker, glad its door can separate me from Kale's worried face. Stare at my books and pens inside. "It's not about you, Kale. It's about me, okay?"

He walks around to the other side of me so I can see as he crosses his eyes and sticks his tongue out.

I can't help but laugh.

He laughs, too. We're both quiet for a moment.

I shut my locker and Kale takes his hands out of his pockets, fidgeting, watching me.

"We all have problems. It's nothing to be ashamed of. So, you're in foster care?" he says, all nonchalant. "You could have told me. It doesn't have to be some big secret."

The smile slides off my face. I don't say anything. He doesn't understand. He can't.

Kale shifts from one foot to the other. "I already knew," he says softly.

I snap my head at him.

"Well, actually, didn't *know*, but suspected," he adds. "Taylor said something about seeing you at church with—"

"Great." I step away from him. "So, you already knew how pathetic my life is and you thought, what? It would be fun to watch me fall apart? Why are you telling me this?"

Kale's eyes widen. "No. I just, I just didn't think it was a big deal. I mean, yes," he adds, reining me back in as I open my mouth to argue. "It is a big deal. I'm sure it's the worst. But you didn't seem to want to talk about it. I like you. Where you live shouldn't have anything to do with that."

Even though Kale means well, he doesn't understand, he *can't* understand, it's so much more than where I live. I exhale, long and heavy. Drained.

Kale scratches his head, speaking slowly, as though he's trying to choose his words carefully. "Victoria, like I said, everyone has problems. I'm not saying what you have going on doesn't matter, but you don't have to let it ruin everything else in your life. Think about how depressing it would be if we all did that. My life isn't perfect, either."

I look at our shoes like I'm talking to them, rather than

Kale. "It affects every aspect of my life, my future. It's not as black and white as you think it is."

I step back. I can't get into this. Not now, not at school. Maybe not ever.

"Look, I . . ." I hesitate, mulling over what I could possibly say that wouldn't give too much away. "I had some problems at home, and my family and I haven't worked it out. And at Connie's, at my foster mother's, it feels like I'm walking on eggshells all the time. Like I'm not wanted, like I can't just be."

Kale draws an invisible line in front of him with his shoe. His voice is low, soft. "I can't imagine anyone not wanting you around, because I think you're great."

He looks up and meets my eye. A lump forms in my throat, and I can feel my eyes beginning to water. But *I can't.*

I cross my arms. "Everything, my whole life, changed when I moved here, and I just want to be normal, to at least *feel* normal while I'm at school. To pretend like everything else isn't a mess. So I don't want to talk about it anymore, okay?"

Kale's quiet for a moment as he watches me. I can't tell what he's thinking, and I hate it. My jaw tenses.

"I have bigger problems than what I'm going to wear to a school dance or boys or dating or anything anyone in a normal family has to worry about, even messed up ones." Even yours, Kale.

Kale's face falls slightly, his frown making his usually happy-go-lucky face look almost like someone else's. We stare at each other for a long awkward moment until Kale grins. "Boys? As in plural?" His voice is light, like we hadn't been talking about something so serious. Like maybe he's trying to cheer me up. "Well, maybe if there were just one boy, like *me*, you'd have enough time for that." Kale grins at me. "I promise, I'm enough to keep even your most ravenous appetite satisfied."

I crack a smile, just for a second. I turn to face him completely.

"What do you want from this? From me? I don't think I can give you what you want."

Kale widens his eyes in exaggeration. "What do I want? Let me see. World peace. A motorcycle." When I start to interrupt, he shakes his head vigorously and raises a finger like he's just getting started. "To be the first guy named after a vegetable to walk on the moon. To get a B or better on my Spanish quiz this afternoon. A million bucks. To go on a date with you."

"I can't," I snap. "Don't you think it's hard enough as it is—"

Kale bends down as if he's about to kiss me, but then stops a couple inches away. He pulls back, his face reddening. Stammers. "I'm sorry, I don't know what I was thinking, that was stupid."

Suddenly the smell of him, a mixture of soap and hair gel, makes me smile and propels me forward. Without thinking, I lean up, touch my lips to his, feel them grin against mine.

Kale lingers for a moment.

I can feel his breath on me.

He pulls away just a couple inches. "I'd also settle for

walking you to class and carrying your books for you. Sitting next to you at lunch. Walking you home from school. Kissing you again, every so often."

My face tingles. I stare at him for a moment. Our faces are so close. Half the school could be watching behind us for all I know. But I don't think I'd care.

I look down at my book and notepad. Still smiling.

"May I?" Kale gestures to my books.

I nod and he takes them from me. And I realize that when we kissed, unexpected as it was, I liked it. I didn't flinch or recoil or want to run away. I didn't think of anything else, none of my fears or about what happened in the past. I just thought of him.

We hold hands as we walk down the hallway. "So, a motorcycle, huh?" I say, lightheaded and excited. Surprised. Full of so many feelings that I can't quite name. "I never would have guessed."

A few people stop their conversation at their lockers to look at us as we pass them.

Kale doesn't seem to notice. "Well, I gotta have a fast getaway vehicle, in case I need to spring you from jail."

I laugh. I actually laugh at this, and he does, too.

I squeeze his hand. "Good luck on that Spanish quiz."

"Ahh, luck is on my side today. *Y tú eres una muchacha bonita.*"

He kisses me on the cheek and hands me my stuff at the doorway to first period. Sitting at her desk, Christina's entire face brightens when she sees us together.

"See you later," I say as I head to my desk. Kale's eyes are alight as he watches me.

"You can count on it."

"So, do you know who your parents are?" Kale asks as he walks me home from school.

"Yes, I know my parents," I retort. "I wasn't dropped off by the stork or left on the curb outside a fire station." My face flushes, and I turn to look at him. Kale seems to hold his breath. "I'm sorry. I'm not mad," I say, much softer. "It's just frustrating that nobody really understands what foster care is." I offer a half smile. "I didn't either before I went in the system, though, so I get it."

The cool breeze blows my hair into my face. I zip my jacket up. Kale reaches over and tucks the piece of hair behind my ear, and my stomach feels warm and tingly.

We start walking again. "I'm sorry for all the questions," Kale says. "We don't have to talk about it if you don't want to."

"No," I stammer. "It's nice to talk about. I mean, no it's not, but I like that it's not a secret anymore." I sigh and kick some pebbles off the sidewalk into the street. Kale stops abruptly.

"This is my place." He points to the salmon-colored house with white trim to his right. A gate and fence about as high as my shoulders separates us from the expansive front lawn. "Do you want to come in?"

I shake my head. "I better not. I don't think my foster mom would like it. I'll just see you at school tomorrow."

"No, I want to keep walking you home, if that's okay. I just wanted you to know you're welcome any time."

I nod, so Kale takes my hand and leads me away from his house. "So, where were we? Oh, right. You weren't dropped off by the stork, which is actually too bad because that would make for a great story. I could make the front page of the newspaper with it, or write a book." He winks at me.

"You like to write?"

"Yeah, I sometimes write crime mysteries. They're short stories and I haven't shown anyone yet, even though my mom keeps bugging me to show her. I'm not gonna lie, though, they're really good."

"I'd love to read them," I say, smiling. "I mean, if you find me worthy."

Kale chuckles. "If you play your cards right. But don't change the subject." He raises his light brown eyebrows at me. "You know your parents."

I roll my eyes. "Yes, I do. My mom died of cancer and my dad, he's just not a good parent. I mean, he was." My hand twitches in Kale's, but I don't let go. "Or, I thought he was. But then he got remarried and after a while he and his wife started fighting a lot, and he started acting"—I pause, not sure how much I want to divulge—"weird."

I close my eyes for a second, take a quick breath. It feels strange talking about this to anyone, even if what I'm saying isn't the whole truth. Kale keeps walking beside me, silently. Listening.

"My stepmom didn't like how much time we spent together, and they fought about it," I finally say. "I have a stepsister, too, Sarah. But I never see her. I never see any of them."

Kale stops at a stop sign in between streets and turns to face me. "So your dad just gave you up because his wife didn't like you? He just drops you off at someone else's house like you're a dog he's returning to the pound?"

My throat tightens. Sure, that's not the whole story. But that's all I'm willing to say right now. I can't stand the anger in Kale's pale-blue eyes, though, even though it's not directed at me, so I look down. "Well, I don't think about it much. I mean, I try not to." I let go of his hand and let mine drop to my side.

Kale registers something in my face, because his voice softens. "I didn't mean to say that. I just can't believe a man could abandon his own kid that way. It's just wrong."

I shrug, halfheartedly. "Well, his loss, I guess."

"No." Kale takes my hand back in his softly. "His loss, *I know*."

I smile and look away, a little embarrassed by his sincerity. "So, your family. Your parents, married still, but your dad's gone a lot?"

Kale nods. "A good and bad thing."

I wait, and he sighs. "Christina already told you, you don't have to pretend like she didn't. She told me." He pauses a beat. "It's okay."

We start walking again, but I keep looking at him.

He looks away, frowning. "I get it—if I'm going to ask

you stuff, I shouldn't be surprised if you ask me." He looks back in the direction of his house, still holding my hand. "My dad's an alcoholic, a mean drunk, never around. And when he is, he's always yelling at my mom about how she needs to do more, clean the house, make him food whenever he wants it, be whatever he wants whenever he wants it."

Kale looks back at me and shrugs. "And she should just leave him already—we could live with my aunt and uncle, or she could kick my dad out." He shakes his head. "My mom's just scared. She hasn't worked. She got pregnant right after high school, married, had more kids, the usual small-town story. She should go back to school, and she knows it, but I don't think she will."

Kale looks into my eyes, and I hold his stare. "I don't know if my dad will ever change or if she will, but I want to go to college and get a good job. Then I can make enough money to help her leave him, if she hasn't by then."

I stare at Kale's lean frame, the way his pants hang on his narrow hips, how his shirt fits loosely. I don't know how big his dad is, but I don't want to imagine a grown man screaming at his wife and kids, or Kale trying to stop him, wanting to protect them.

Kale looks down at our hands, and no matter what he says about everyone having problems, I know he's embarrassed. I was wrong about him earlier. His problems may be different from mine, but none of us can understand what's going on in another person's life from the outside looking in. No one can really see the quiet you carry, unless you let them. I lift his hand to my lips, and then I pull him closer for a hug, and he doesn't stop me.

The next day Kale, Christina, and I sit together for lunch at one of the small gray tables along the wall—a healthy distance away from the long tables where bigger groups tend to sit, where Christina and Kale used to eat lunch with Zach, Taylor, Lauren and the rest of their jock friends. But they'd rather sit me with now, thankfully.

I trade my PB & J sandwich for Christina's tuna roll and we both give our Cokes to Kale because he says he gets hopped up on sugar and we want him to prove it.

"Ahh," Kale says gleefully as he slams down the second empty can. "Mrs. Baker will have you to thank for my behavior in class."

"I certainly hope not." Mr. Nelson's voice says from behind Kale and me. We turn around.

"I hope this young man isn't bothering you ladies," Mr. Nelson, in his normal, small-town-principal way, continues. "He can be quite the handful."

"We don't mind." I smile at Kale. I blush and then laugh at myself.

"Oh, young love," Mr. Nelson says. "You better treat this girl right, young man, because if I hear otherwise, you'll have another thing coming." Mr. Nelson grins at Kale. He starts to walk away, but before he's out of earshot says: "I guess getting put in pre-calculus isn't the worst thing that can happen."

He's right. Some things just work out for the best. And I realize I don't mind being stuck in such a small school, weird principal and all.

Christina leans back in her seat. "So, I was accepted into GW. But, it's no big deal," she quickly adds.

"It is a big deal!" Kale interjects. You've been talking about getting the hell out of here to move to D.C. and start a women's revolution since you were practically in diapers!"

Christina's smile widens. "Okay, so it might be a big deal. But I'm still holding out to hear from Georgetown." She puts her hands down on the table and leans over toward Kale, dramatically.

"What about you, Kale? I know you have a year to go until you graduate, but I also know you've thought about where you want to go."

She looks at me conspiratorially. My hands feel warm and sweaty all of a sudden.

"The usual," Kale says. "UNR, but I'll apply to TMCC, too, just in case."

Christina settles back into her seat. "Close to home," she says. "A little too close for my taste, but good for you because you'll be near your sisters. They'll miss you too much as it is." Christina pats Kale on the back.

Kale puts his arm around me. "Well, either way, no matter which school I go to, we'll still be in the same city. In a year, that is. Unless you dump me for some college boy."

My chest feels hot and tight and I don't know what to say. I quickly dodge Kale's eyes to look at Christina. "I'll miss you, Christina, but you're going to come visit us, right?"

Kale's face falls. Christina doesn't seem to notice. "Of course I will! You can't get rid of me that easy!"

Christina and I laugh, although mine is a little forced, as Alex strides up to the other side of the table and sits next to Christina. Christina tenses slightly as he scoots his chair closer to her.

"You guys coming to the game on Saturday? We're playing Virginia City and we're going to wipe the floor with them."

"Um, can't leave the house, grounded for all eternity," I say awkwardly. Alex clears his throat. "Oh, right. Sorry about that." Christina pats his hand quickly and stands, looking at me. "Want to go for a walk?"

I leave a crestfallen Kale with Alex. A few tables over, Taylor and Lauren sit eating their lunches. Lauren waves at us, and I wave back, half-heartedly. Zach walks up to them and says something I can't hear. Maybe they're talking about me, maybe Zach is making fun of me again. I look away and rush after Christina, leaving the cafeteria and heading outside. Puffs of dirt trail behind Christina as she makes her way to what's become our spot, the bench near the tool shed. We sit down.

"You're avoiding Alex already? Trouble in paradise?"

Christina leans back on the bench. "He's getting on my nerves. Yes, I like him, but I don't have to spend every waking minute with him because of it." She rolls her eyes dramatically. "I'm not one of those girls who writes guys' names in their notebooks and dreams about having their babies or anything."

I snort. "Oh, man. I was totally hoping we could do that during English class! I guess I'll just have to find something else to do. Have you ever played MASH?"

We both laugh, as Christina playfully shoves me. She doesn't ask about me and Kale, and I'm glad for it.

CHAPTER
FIFTEEN

A new girl, Samantha, moves in and takes Lizzie's old bed. Connie's got bills to pay, after all.

A couple weeks pass.

Kale refers to me as his girlfriend now.

We've kissed a few times, when he walks me home. But I feel guilty. He talks about "us" like we have a future. I nod along, not saying anything to challenge the idea, but not supporting it either. How could I commit to long distance, waiting for him to graduate? It's not like I plan on dating every guy I meet or anything, but what if we don't have time for each other and grow apart? Or worse, if the distance makes us fight on the phone all the time? What if he wants to see other girls who live in Silver Valley?

So much time will pass between now and when he's in Reno. How could he try to plan for that, when life can change so quickly? Like everything changed for me, that night with my dad.

I try to ignore these thoughts, try to act normal. I *behave myself* at home with Connie and attempt to get along with Jamie, although she hardly talks to me. She doesn't talk to anybody.

It's a brisk March afternoon, the first time since I moved here it feels warm enough to walk around without a jacket. Kale is walking me home, per usual. We pass his house, like we always do, and I still haven't accepted any of his invitations to come inside. "So, how's your family doing?" I ask. "Anything new with your sisters?"

Kale smiles. "Well, Kimmie's a toddler, so obviously she's got an exciting life. Last week, she tried to eat one of her Lego castles. My kind of girl."

We pause at the stop sign before crossing the street.

"Let's see, what else?" Kale thinks for a moment. "Last weekend, my mom said Melissa had to start helping out with chores, otherwise she'd have to get a job. My mom was kidding, but Melissa wrote up a bunch of signs advertising herself as a babysitter. We got a few phone calls about them." Kale laughs. "My mom wasn't happy."

I adjust my hand in his. "Are they going to let her do it, though? Babysit, that is."

"At first my mom wasn't down for it," Kale says, as a car drives past us. Kale walks around to the other side of me, the side near the road. "But then my dad got home last night and they talked it over and decided to let her. He said Melissa should learn responsibility and the value of money, since she spends so much of his on toys and other crap she doesn't need." Kale makes air quotes around the words. "Then again, he was pretty drunk, so maybe he'll forget he agreed to let her babysit and get mad at her when he realizes it."

"I'm sorry," I say.

Kale shrugs. "It's fine, we're all used to it."

I nod, squeeze his hand. Kale smiles at me, but it doesn't reach his eyes.

"So, where was I?" he continues. We reach the part of our walk where we both slow down because we're just a couple streets away from Connie's. "Well, last but not least, there's Alicia. Obsessed with boys." Kale looks so horrified at this that I actually laugh.

"What? No guy wants his sister dating. That's just weird." He pivots. "Any news about Sarah?"

I stiffen. "Nope. Nothing."

***

"Can I use the phone to call Mindy?" I ask Connie from the sink. I've just finished washing the after-dinner dishes.

"Why?"

I answer quickly. "I just wanted to ask her about my stepsister, make sure she's doing okay."

"Oh." Connie gets up from her seat at the table and walks to the counter nearest me. "Do you think that's a good idea?" she asks, her tone softer than before. "I know your dad"—Connie's nose lifts in disgust—"doesn't really want you two talking."

"My dad doesn't care what I want, why should I care what he does?"

Connie's lips turn upward into an almost-smile. Standing in the small kitchen with both of us in it at the same time feels strange to me. And crowded.

"Because children don't often get to choose what adults do, Victoria. And you say your dad doesn't care what you want. Does that mean you actually want to live with him?"

I shake my head and place the dishtowel on the counter. "That's not what I—" I pause, bile rising in my throat as I think of my father, what he's done to me. Now that I can face it, at least to myself, I can't stand the thought of him. "I'm just saying, if he doesn't care about my wishes, the way I want to be treated, then I don't care about his."

Connie returns to her seat at the dining room table. "Fine, fine," she says. "But there are better ways of getting what you want. Trust me, sometimes it's good not to be so obvious about your dislike for someone who has something you want, who has power over you. You get what I'm saying?"

Warmth rushes to my face. "I think so. Does that mean I can call Mindy?"

"No, not just yet, at least." Connie leans back in her seat. "It's past office hours. Mindy's at home. I'll send her an email, let her know you want to know how Sarah's doing."

"Can *you* ask her if I can talk to Sarah?"

I've asked Mindy before, but if it comes from Connie maybe Mindy will consider it. Or I could ask Christina to borrow her phone to call Sarah. It would be risky. If I get caught, or Sarah gets caught by one of our parents and they tell on me, I could get into a lot of trouble. Trouble I don't need, given that I'm supposed to be on my best behavior so Connie doesn't have me thrown in jail for breaking the rules again.

I take a deep breath, annoyed at the long list of the things

I can't control or am not allowed to do. I'll try getting to Sarah through Mindy, one last time. If this doesn't work, I'll use Christina's phone and take my chances at whatever trouble I might get into. I just need to know that Sarah is okay.

Connie clears her throat. "All right. I'll ask Mindy for you." She nods. "I promise. You can stop cleaning up now. I'll take the rest from here."

Connie stands, and I start walking to the dormitory.

"Wait." She stops me as I reach the hallway.

"Sorry," I blurt, my back toward her. "Can I *please* go to the dormitory?"

I turn to see Connie looking at me with a serious expression. "You have a birthday coming up."

Next month. My throat tightens so I just nod.

"You'll be eighteen."

I swallow. "I guess I should start looking for a place, then. Has Mindy told you about anything that might be helpful? Anything social services does to help kids who age out get on their feet?" I fold my hands in front of me, unsure what else to do with them. "I remember her mentioning something like that once, I think."

Connie puts her hand on the table and runs her finger over the wood a few times before answering. "You don't have to leave, if you don't want to," she says. "I have a form Mindy emailed me. If we both sign an agreement that you will live here voluntarily and continue to abide by the rules, you can stay here until you graduate and find a place of your own." She clears her throat. "I won't force you out. I want you to graduate high school and not worry about having a roof over your head."

I stare at Connie. "So, nothing would change then? I'd still live here and wouldn't have to pay rent or anything?"

"No rent, the state will continue your status as a ward of the court." Connie walks to the fridge. "But a few things would change."

"Like what?"

Connie grabs a diet Coke, then pauses and looks at me. "Would you like one, too?"

I shake my head no.

Connie opens her drink and takes a sip, facing me. "Well, you'd still have a curfew I'd decide on, but if you earn it by behaving yourself, you can hang out with your friends after school sometimes, go to a movie or a school dance."

"Seriously? You would let me do that?"

Connie's face softens. "You know it's partially the state's rules for this kind of home that are so strict, not mine. And the extra rules I make I do mostly to protect myself and you and the other kids." She looks down at her soda and sighs. "I've had a lot of kids come through this home—kids who've had problems, big problems—and the rules keep us all safe. But I'm not a monster. It's not like I enjoy you kids hating me all the time. I want you to have friends and a life, if you can."

I pull my hands to my face. I can't believe it, but Connie's expression hasn't changed. She's serious.

I hug her. Without meaning to, for real. She hugs back for a second and then it gets awkward and I pull away.

"Thank you," I say.

Connie laughs into her soda. "You're very welcome."

Maybe I can be almost normal. Hang out with friends, like Connie said. I could use Christina's phone to call Jess, maybe tell Jess the truth about what happened. Christina and Kale know I'm in foster care, and that hasn't changed the way they see me. Maybe Jess could come to Silver Valley and visit.

I look back at Connie, who's still smiling at me. "I, uh, I better go to the dormitory. If that's okay, that is. I have homework."

Connie nods in the direction of the hallway. "Go ahead."

Inside our room, Jamie's sitting on her bed, her knees hugged close to her chest.

I hesitate. "Something wrong?"

"What could be wrong?" Jamie says mockingly. "I'm stuck in this dump with Sasquatch out there and her awful Satan spawn. No one wants to adopt me." Her voice grows louder. "I have years and years until I age out of the system, and for what? What kind of life will I have when I finally get out? My own family, aunts and uncles, nobody wants me. *But what the hell could be wrong?*"

My stomach sinks, seeing Jamie so miserable like this. She looks smaller, her body swallowed up in that huge sweater she wears all the time. I wish we could go back to how things were before we got in that fight. But I don't know what either of us could do to make the things we said to each other okay. We can't go back in time.

"What about your grandma?" I ask. "I know she's too

old to take care of you, but at least she still visits sometimes. At least she cares."

Jamie's glare is so forceful I'm taken aback.

"I guess you wouldn't know, would you? Since you don't pay attention to anything or anyone but yourself. She's sick. For the last month, maybe longer. Maybe she hid it before. She only remembers who I am half the time now. I've got no one. Absolutely no one."

Instinctively, I pull my hand to my chest. It aches, hearing Jamie say she feels all alone. She's tried so hard to make sure I haven't felt that way since I got here, and I've let her down.

I walk over to her bunk and put my hand on the edge. "You have me. We have each other. That's something, right?"

Jamie shoves my hand away. "You've got to be kidding me!" she shouts. Tears fill Jamie's eyes as she scowls at me. "I don't have you. You're never here anymore. You're here in this stupid dormitory with me, but you're not actually with me. You're always studying or filling out paperwork or smiling about some stupid boy. You're leaving me soon, just like Lizzie. When you graduate, the first thing you'll do is get the hell out of here. You don't give a shit about me! No one does."

The door opens to our room, revealing Connie on the other side. "What on Earth is going on? I can hear you yelling and cussing, and so can the kids out in the living room with me. Jamie, unless you want your privileges taken away, you'll cut it out. Now."

Jamie whips her head to face Connie. "Privileges! What

privileges?" Jamie bellows. "You let us cook and clean for your kid and the other fosters! You let us eat the food CPS pays for when they give your fat ass a check every month! And, if I'm a *real good girl* I get the privilege of having some time to myself or better yet, watching your stupid TV shows with you? No freaking thanks. I hate this place! I hate you, and I wish you and that rotten daughter of yours were dead!"

Connie gasps. She grabs Jamie by her arm and yanks her toward the ladder on the bunk bed. Jamie grabs onto the wooden bed frame, but can't hold on as Connie drags her to the edge.

"That's enough, girl," Connie growls. "Get down and come with me. You're going to sit and wait while I call your caseworker. I may get paid, but not enough for this, you ungrateful little brat!"

Jamie lowers herself off the ladder, and Connie drags her to the door. Jamie tries to pull away from Connie but isn't strong enough.

I follow them to the living room. Jamie sits facing the dining room wall. Her shoulders shake as she cries. Our new foster sister, Samantha, watches from the couch, looking terrified. Connie snatches the phone and stabs the digits, making a call.

"You need to send someone to pick Jamie up right away," Connie says, apparently having called the after-hours number for CPS. "She's turned angry and, I fear, violent. She's a risk I can't afford to keep in the same home as my young children. Please send someone immediately."

Connie hangs up the phone. "Stay here," she says to Jamie, her voice cold and angry.

Connie walks over to Annie, who looks up from her spot on the rug in front of the TV with mild curiosity.

"Come on, baby. Let's go to your room and watch TV in there." She looks at Samantha. "You, too, honey."

Annie and Samantha follow Connie to her bedroom. Jamie stops crying. Her face goes blank.

I walk over to her. "Are you okay?"

She stands, without looking at me. "No, but I will be." She calmly walks past the bedrooms and the bathroom to the back of the house. I follow her to the laundry room, but she slams the door behind her before I can follow.

"Jamie, what are you—"

Connie opens Annie's door. "What's going on?"

"I don't know," I say. "Jamie went in there."

Connie glances at the closed laundry room door. "In there?"

I nod and Connie rushes over. She grabs the handle and starts shaking it.

"Jamie! Let us in!" She bangs on the door. Something large thumps to the ground on the other side.

Jamie?

"Jamie! Jamie!" Connie's voice breaks. "Move out of the way!" she yells at me.

I step back. Annie appears behind us, and Samantha behind her, but Connie doesn't notice.

She throws her shoulder into the door. It bangs but

doesn't open. She tries again. Connie steps back and kicks the door three times before it breaks open.

Annie starts sobbing behind me. "Mommy! Mommy!" she cries. "What's wrong?"

But Connie doesn't look back or comfort Annie, or Samantha, who appears behind her. She stares in horror at Jamie, who is hunched over on her hands and knees. Jamie's stomach surges violently as she retches over a pile of vomit on the floor. She's got white liquid and puke all over her lips and on her sweatshirt. An open bottle of bleach lies near her, its contents seeping across the tile floor.

Connie rushes forward as Jamie topples over, screaming in pain. Connie lifts Jamie's head and torso and cradles her as Jamie closes her eyes.

"Mommy!" Annie cries. Connie's tearful eyes dart up at us, as if just remembering we're here.

"Victoria, get them out of here!"

I stare at Jamie for a second, lying limp in Connie's arms, seemingly in and out of consciousness. No, she can't die. I was just talking to her.

No, she can't.

"Now!" Connie yells at me again. "And call nine-one-one!"

I grab Annie's hand. "Come on, Annie. Samantha, let's go." I lead them away from the laundry room, grabbing the phone from the receiver as I sit the girls down.

"What's your emergency?" the voice on the nine-one-one line asks me.

I pause for a second, unable to speak. "Emergency dispatch. What's your emergency?" the woman repeats.

"My foster sister drank bleach. She's unconscious. I'm afraid she's dying." I whisper the last part, so the others won't hear.

"We'll send an ambulance right away."

I tell her the address and hang up the phone slowly, almost in a daze.

When I look back, Jamie's eyes are still closed. Her sweatshirt is covered in bleach, vomit, and Connie's tears.

Samantha's crying, I realize, but I can't move. I watch Jamie, looking lifeless in Connie's arms, as Connie shakes, holding her. Suddenly, Jamie's eyes pop open and she hurls herself off Connie. She starts vomiting again onto the tile. Sobbing, retching. Thank God, she's still alive.

I stare, watching her gag, until Samantha's cries get louder, and Connie glares at me.

I try to get Annie and Samantha to watch TV in the living room, but they won't. "What's happening?" Samantha tugs at the bottom of my shirt. I'm not looking at the kids; my eyes linger on the front door. My nostrils burn where they smelled the bleach. The fine hairs on my arms stand up. I shiver and wrap my arms around myself. She's alive, she's alive, she's alive. I hope she stays that way. Please, let her stay that way.

I could take the kids outside, I should, but my feet won't take me there. I feel paralyzed, straining my ears to listen for Jamie to say something. Anything.

Outside, people don't have problems like this.

I slowly sink to the rug on the floor and put my hand on Samantha.

Sirens blare in the distance, getting louder as they come closer. Annie cries. Samantha cries. I don't.

I can't keep my hands from shaking. I can't feel them shaking, but I know they are. The vibrations rise to my chest, to my mouth, so even my teeth chatter.

We wait.

The doorbell rings, and I answer it. Two EMTs dressed in black uniforms almost like hospital scrubs stand outside. I lead them to the laundry room where Connie cradles Jamie. Foam and vomit drip from Jamie's mouth and cover her shirt. Her eyes are closed.

The woman EMT gently removes Jamie from Connie's arms and the man helps her set Jamie on the gurney.

Jamie's body starts to convulse, shaking violently all over. A sob escapes from deep within my chest. And the tears pour down.

Jamie's body goes limp as the EMTs strap her into the gurney and wheel her off to the ambulance. Pale and disoriented, Connie follows them. We walk past the kids and head outside.

The woman EMT opens the ambulance back door, and the two of them lift and pull the gurney and Jamie in. Connie climbs in and sits beside the man as he opens Jamie's eyelids and inspects her.

Connie leans over to get a better look, her lips quivering. The woman EMT starts to close the door.

"Wait," I say. I don't know for what. I just want Connie to know I'm standing here. She looks at me as if just noticing I followed her outside. Her eyes shoot to the front door where Annie and Samantha watch us, tears soaking their young, puffy faces.

"Stay here with them," Connie whispers. "Tell them it's going to be all right."

"Is it going to be all right? What's going to happen?"

Connie shakes her head. "I don't know."

We look at each other for a moment and then the man EMT clears his throat. "It's time to go. Watch yourself."

I step back from the door so he can shut it. The ambulance drives away.

Samantha calls out to me from in front of the house. "Where are they taking her?"

I walk slowly toward the girls, one foot in front of the other. Lean down to answer her question softly. "To the hospital."

"Is she going to die?"

Annie yelps and instinctively I wrap her in my arms. Jamie Jamie Jamie. Please be okay. Please.

"Everything's going to be fine," I lie. I grab Samantha and bring her into our hug. The three of us cry together for a few minutes, in the doorway outside. A door creaks open nearby.

I lift my head from between Annie and Samantha's shoulders. A few neighbors stare out their windows, others stand at their open doors. A middle-aged man from a couple houses over watches us from the edge of his lawn. "What's going on? Do you girls need some help?" he calls.

I shake my head and lead the girls inside.

Annie and Samantha settle down eventually, watching

cartoons together. Annie even shares some of her toys with Samantha as they play dolls.

Hours pass.

The phone rings.

It's across from me, just a few feet from where I sit on the loveseat, right next to Connie's spot on the couch. I let the call go to voicemail. I'm not allowed to answer or even touch the phone without being told to first.

"Victoria, it's me," Connie's voice says on the answering machine. "You can pick up."

I snatch the phone. "Is she okay?"

"She's going to be," Connie says.

I sob into the phone, letting go of all the fear, all the tightness in my chest.

Connie sighs heavily. "Thank you for watching the kids. Can I talk to my baby?"

I inhale quickly, suck back the tears. "It's your mom." Annie looks up at me from her spot on the floor.

Annie grabs the phone and clutches it to her ear. She cries, and waits, Connie apparently soothing her. She kisses Connie through the phone and says goodnight, and hands me back the phone. Samantha's watching the TV quietly, so I don't ask her if she wants to talk to Connie. But Connie does. "Can I talk to Samantha, too?"

I watch Samantha listening to whatever Connie is saying. She nods, tells Connie she's scared.

I step closer, and I can hear Connie's voice soothe Samantha. "It's going to be okay, sweetheart. I promise."

"I won't be home tonight," Connie tells me when I take

the phone back. "Are you going to be all right watching them?"

I hold the phone closer to my ear. "Yes, of course," I say, thinking that it may be illegal to leave us foster kids unattended, but not caring.

"Thank you. Goodnight, Victoria."

"Goodnight."

CHAPTER
SIXTEEN

*A*t some point, I put the girls to bed, tucking them each in. I can hear Samantha sob herself to sleep. She cries for her mother, and I sit at the edge of her mattress, rubbing her shoulders until she calms.

Back in bed, I stare at the roof of Jamie's bunk above me, unable to doze off for most of the night.

Connie comes home before sunrise. I hear the front door open, her fumbling in the living room, and rush out to meet her.

"She's okay," Connie says when I reach the living room. "She vomited so much, and the doctors need to keep her for observation for a little while longer, but she made it."

The sky is black outside the window, the room dark. I flip on the light switch. Connie blinks several times and stares down at her clothes, the same she wore yesterday. With bloodshot eyes she looks back at me. "Jamie's stabilized. Her caseworker's there with her now."

"Is she coming home?"

Connie shakes her head. "She can't come back here."

I cough, sputter, try to choke out words. "So what, you just throw her out on the street? She's only twelve!"

Connie quickly cuts me off. "I couldn't take her back, not even if I wanted to, no matter how hard I try."

I shake my head angrily. I don't say anything. I can't.

Connie walks to the fridge and opens it, grabbing a bottled water. Not knowing what else to do, I follow her, stopping by the table.

Connie drains half the bottle in one swig. She wipes her mouth with the back of her hand.

"Jamie tried to kill herself. She's a suicide risk." Connie clears her throat. "She can't stay in a home, not even one with a ton of rules and supervision like this one, until she gets treatment. I've had a girl who turned suicidal before and the best thing was getting her the help she needed."

My jaw clenches and I turn to the wall, the same one Jamie faced right before she went to the laundry room to drink that bleach. I can't stand to meet Connie's eye when she's talking about rules rather than Jamie's life and how she isn't even going to try to help her.

Connie sighs. "She has to live," she pauses, seeming to weigh her words, "in a special place, where there's staff to supervise her around-the-clock, she can get group and individual therapy, where a doctor is always there to prescribe medicine if she needs it or change the dosage. A place where she'll be safe. I can't give her that."

I whip back to her. "You mean a mental hospital?" I slam

my hand down on the table in front of me. "You're sending her to a mental hospital?"

Connie looks behind me, down the hallway to where the girls are sleeping. "I'm not doing anything." Connie pinches the bridge of her nose. "I told you, there's nothing I *can* do. Jamie made a choice when she drank that bleach." She shakes her head vigorously, keeping me silent. "I'm not saying I'm not sorry, or that I wish I hadn't done some things differently, but it is what it is, Victoria."

Connie finishes her water and tosses the bottle into the recycling bin. "I'm just happy she's okay. And I really am sorry, Lord knows, for a lot of things. Right now, though, Jamie needs a place and people to keep her safe from herself. Apparently she'd been cutting herself for months and hiding it."

My hands instinctively grasp my forearms. Jamie had been wearing her sweatshirt more often, I realize. I saw the scab on Jamie's arm. Believed her lie about how she got it.

"She's been cutting?" I whisper, more to myself than to Connie.

Connie nods solemnly. "Unfortunately, yes. Jamie was having problems in school. And then her grandma got worse and the failed adoption . . . it was all too much for her." Connie shifts her weight from foot to foot, her eyes cast down.

"That girl's got more problems than either I or her social worker knew," she continues. "Even if I did have a choice, it would be a risk having her around my children, including you. You're my responsibility, too, and I have to take care of all of you."

I clench and unclench my fists. Twice. I exhale, looking around me, but not really seeing. "So what, are you going to get another foster kid now to take Jamie's place? Is it going to be like she was never here, like with Lizzie?"

Because you *need* the money.

I clamp my mouth shut rather than scream those words at Connie.

She frowns. "It's not like Lizzie was never here, Victoria. She has a family now; that's what's supposed to happen. This is supposed to be a temporary thing—I take care of you kids until your parents have worked out a solution with social services so that it's safe for you to go home, or you get adopted, or—in your case—you turn eighteen and go out on your own."

Connie's eyebrows furrow and she watches me silently for a moment. "And no, I don't think we'll get another girl living here just yet. I think we could all use a little time to wrap our heads around what happened with Jamie first."

I swallow the arguments, the angry words I could throw at Connie, blaming her for Jamie, blaming her for so many things. I want to hate her for this, but I can't. I can hate Jamie's parents and mine and the stupid foster care system that won't let Jamie come back. I hate all of it.

But I can't hate Connie, at least not anymore.

"Fine."

Connie walks out of the kitchen to stand next to me. "I'm so sorry you kids had to see that." She sets her hand down next to mine on the table. "Victoria, are you all right? What happened was awful. And I know you love Jamie. I care for her, too, even though you probably don't see it."

I bite my lip. Bite back a retort.

"I'm fine. I mean, no I'm not, but I will be."

I will be. That's what Jamie said to me before she did it.

Connie stares at me for a second and then slowly, awkwardly, raises her hand to rest on my shoulder.

I bristle. "I'm not going to off myself anytime soon if that's what you're wondering."

Cringing, Connie takes her hand back and scowls at me. "That's all I can hope for. Are the girls still asleep?"

I step out of the way. "Yeah, Annie cried for hours before going to sleep. Samantha, too. They're scared."

Connie nods before heading to Annie's room. I glance up at the clock on the wall in the kitchen. I have to start getting ready for school.

If Jamie were here, she'd be getting ready, too.

At least she's alive, I tell myself. Even if she doesn't want to be.

Christina waves her hand in front of me after the bell dismisses us from first period. "Earth to Victoria!"

She drops her hand. "What is with you today? Are you okay?"

I hoist my backpack into position and stand. "I'm fine," I lie. I'll tell Christina about Jamie, just not here. Not in class.

Christina starts talking about something to do with the

lesson, but I'm not really listening as we walk into the hall-way. I can't stop thinking about Jamie.

I knew she was going through a hard time, but I was mad at her for what she said about my dad and me. I could have talked to her. I could have not been preoccupied by my own life and problems.

I should have tried something, anything. I should have showed her I cared somehow.

I should have.

I didn't.

I say goodbye to Christina as she heads to her locker and stand still once I get to mine. Jamie's convulsing body lingers in my head. Sarah's face comes to me, too. And un-bidden, Dad, lurking around her bedroom at night, like he did with me.

I hold onto my locker and take a few shallow breaths.

I missed everything I should have seen with Jamie. She's not the only one I could be letting down.

The hallway spins around me. I can't breathe.

The darkness starts creeping in at the edges of my vision. I close my eyes tight and let my forehead rest against the cold locker.

I force several breaths. Count to ten, and then to twenty.

Then I open my eyes, look around, focus on what I can see. Locker. Hallway. Kids walking around.

Breathe.

Breathe.

Breathe.

I catch Christina in the hallway before she heads to her last class. "Can I borrow your cell phone?"

"Of course." Christina fishes the phone out of her tote and hands it to me. She doesn't ask who I'm calling. She follows me as I walk to the side of the hallway, out of the way.

I stab each digit of the number and press Christina's phone to my ear.

It rings.

"Are you okay?" Christina whispers. I wave her off.

I spot Kale behind Christina, across the hall. He waves at us and bounds over. I turn, my back facing him.

From behind me, Christina brings Kale up to speed. "She's on the phone. Apparently, it's very important."

"Okay," Kale whispers. "I can wait."

Sarah's voicemail. Her voice cheerfully tells me she's not there right now, but leave a message and she'll call back.

I almost hang up, but an image of Jamie's mouth foaming with white puddles of bleach hits me.

"It's Victoria," I spit out. "Sarah, I need to talk to you. Please call me back at this number. It's important."

I hang up. Clutch the phone in my hand. Kale and Christina walk around either side of me.

Then the phone rings. Sarah. I almost drop the phone in my rush to pick up.

"Sarah, hi!" I say, breathless.

"Hi," she answers slowly, uncertainty in her voice.

Silence.

A couple of juniors walk through the double doors ahead of us, talking loudly. I hold the phone even closer and speak up. "Um, I'm just calling because I miss you. I borrowed a friend's phone."

"Then why didn't you call before? Why now?" Sarah's voice strengthens. She sounds angry.

I shake my head vigorously, though Sarah can't see. "Because my foster mom won't let me, and neither will my case worker. And Dad—my dad told my caseworker he wants me to leave you alone. And your mom, too."

Sarah is quiet.

"Mindy said I could call you if your dad let me," she finally says, "but he told me I shouldn't because you don't want to talk to me. He said Mindy doesn't know what she's talking about, that he knows what's best for you."

"What?" I say, loudly. Too loud. Christina puts a hand on my shoulder.

From his locker across the hallway, Zach and Lauren look at us. I turn away.

"I never, ever said that. Of course I want to talk to you!"

"Then why did you leave? Do you really hate my mom that much? Your dad said . . ." She pauses and exhales loudly in frustration. "Mindy said it was his choice. If he did some classes or something that you could come back, but my mom, she told me . . ." She stops. "I don't know what to believe."

"What did your mom say about me?" I hiss between my teeth.

Sarah goes quiet. Stupid, that was stupid. The last thing I need is to spook Sarah, to keep her from talking. I bite my lip. "That's what my dad told you?" I say, softly this time.

"That I didn't want to talk to you? Your mom and my dad won't let me."

I pause, to control myself. "I didn't get a say. Not in that, not in anything. They won't let me come home. They don't want me." My voice breaks, and I grip the phone tighter and avoid looking at Christina or Kale as I continue. "But you've been talking with Mindy, right? She's been checking in on you, making sure you're okay? What has she told you about what happened with Dad and me?"

"Mindy says if your dad followed social services' instructions of going to classes and therapy and checking in, that you could come home. But other than that, she doesn't want to talk about you." Sarah pauses before she adds, "At least not with me. She says it's her job to worry about you. She says I should leave that to the grown-ups. She always asks me questions about your dad and me. And your dad hates it when she calls and visits, so I just try to make it quick."

Christina reaches for me again, this time putting her hand on my forearm. The bell rings. Christina and Kale both stay where they are as the rest of the stragglers make their way to class.

The hallway is completely empty now, except for us. I clutch the phone closer to my ear.

"And my mom won't let me ask him about you, because he gets so mad when I do. Our parents, they said the most awful . . ." she trails off. "I don't understand. I don't know, I just don't know."

I grit my teeth, wishing I could block out all the rage I

feel. My words are barely more than a whisper. "What did they say?"

Silence.

Kale and Christina exchange a worried glance.

"Sarah, what did my dad tell you?"

I hear her exhale slowly. The cell phone shakes in my hand against my ear.

I'm not going to get anywhere with Sarah about this on the phone while she's at school. I can see that now that she's skirted around my question so many times. And that's not why I called her.

"I, I can't explain everything right now," I tell her. "I'm at school. I just—just tell me that everything is okay," I plead. "Nothing weird is happening at home, right? No one's hurting you?"

Kale's eyes widen, and Christina grabs his elbow.

"Victoria, I don't know. Your dad, he . . . he . . . I can't. He says the strangest things to me, he's always paying so much attention, complimenting me in really strange ways, and if I don't respond how he likes he gets so mad and he . . . and, I don't know why he . . ." she stutters. "I don't know."

Tears fill my eyes. That's how it started with Dad and me, him saying things I didn't understand. The attention. The boomeranging between being happy with me and angry. Me not knowing, not understanding.

Sarah sniffs, crying audibly now. "What does it matter anyway? You aren't here, you wouldn't understand."

Before I can respond, I hear an adult's voice in Sarah's background. "What are you doing in the hallway?"

"I have to go," Sarah says.

"Wait, Sarah!"

She hangs up.

CHAPTER
SEVENTEEN

*T*he first time I met Sarah was not even a year after Mom died. Dad and Tiffany had met at the grocery store—Tiffany was working as a checkout clerk—and they started dating shortly afterward. She had light-blonde hair, big teeth, and a long, thin face. She sank those pearly whites into Dad as soon as he introduced himself as a widower.

In the checkout line, while Tiffany scanned and bagged our food, they bonded over being single parents. "It's so hard. It'd be nice to have someone, an adult, to talk to every now and then," she said.

She acted surprised at my father's dinner invitation, as if she hadn't been shamelessly hinting at it. "Oh, well I'd love to. Let me just see when I can find a sitter. My daughter always comes first."

What a crock.

I was furious watching them make goo-goo eyes at each other. I stood behind my father, arms crossed, as his attention floated away from mourning my mom to the grocery woman like she was the food on the conveyer belt. My mom loved him with all her heart, she did everything for him. And here Dad was hitting on some young, single mother. It was gross.

Two months later, Dad was already head over heels in love, or so he said. The night Tiffany and Sarah came over for the first time, I hid in my room, feigning a stomachache so I wouldn't have to see them.

I heard Dad explain to Tiffany that I wasn't feeling well. I imagined her touching my father's arm from the other side of the door as I heard her say, "It's hard for all of us. It's an adjustment." I imagined she smiled sweetly or did something else ridiculous like that.

That shrill voice again. "Would it be all right if Sarah went to Victoria's room to see if she wants one of the cookies we baked? What do you think, Sarah?"

I strained to hear Sarah mumble some kind of response— maybe she wasn't that happy about meeting me, either—and when I heard her footsteps coming to my room, I bolted from my desk and jumped in bed.

Sarah knocked on the other side of the door. I closed my eyes.

"Can I come in?" she asked. Her voice sounded young and nervous.

"I'm not feeling well," I called meekly.

"Please don't make me stay out there with them," she whispered, loud enough for me to hear, but likely not reaching our parents in the kitchen. Tiffany was probably starting to make the meatloaf she'd promised to feed us.

"Fine!" I called, abandoning the pretense of being weak. "Come in."

A slim, blonde girl with bangs too big for her smallish head walked in with a plate of chocolate-chip cookies. She grinned at me as I sat up in bed. "You're not really sick, are you?"

"I'm sick of a lot of things," I said. "But nauseated? Not so much."

The little girl laughed and walked to the foot of my bed.

"Those cookies for me?"

She nodded and held the plate in front of her, offering them to me.

"You can sit if you want," I said. She sat on the edge of my bed and put the plate in between us. I grabbed a cookie, popping about half of it in my mouth.

"So, how old are you?" I asked after swallowing. Dad had told me, but I forgot.

"Ten," Sarah said. "You?

"Thirteen. You an only child?"

She nodded. I grabbed another cookie.

"Me, too," I said. "So, your mom really likes my dad?"

"Yeah." She fidgeted, thumbing the end of her pale-pink skirt. "I think they want to move in together."

I choked on a cookie. "What?"

"I heard my mom talking to him about it on the phone last night. I think that's why we came over. To see how we all get along."

Heat rushed to my face. "You know my mom's been dead for less than a year, right? My dad is still grieving."

Sarah looked down at my bedspread. "I'm sorry." She waited what seemed like a long time before speaking again. "Maybe having my mom around makes him feel better."

I tilted my head, that was true. I chewed another cookie as a new thought occurred to me. If Tiffany lived here, maybe Dad wouldn't be so much work for me. Not having to cook dinner anymore would be a plus.

I inhaled another cookie. It would be nice for my dad to stop crying so much, I thought. Or for someone else to be around to help me with him when he did.

"This whole moving in together thing might not be so bad after all," I said.

Sarah pulled a pack of playing cards out of her purse. What child has a purse? "You want to play a game?" she asked.

I sat up and folded my legs underneath me on my bed. "What kind of game?"

"Oh, anything. I only know solitaire, though. Can you teach me something?"

Across from the bed stood my bookshelf, packed with textbooks from school, an assortment of books, and a couple of board games. Mom loved to play board games. "I don't know any card games except Go Fish," I answered. "You have to know how to play that one."

"Nope, can you teach me?"

"Sure." I took the cards from her and taught her how to play during the half hour or so it took before Dad and Tiffany called us to dinner. And I thought maybe having Sarah and her mother around could be a good thing.

Back in the empty school hallway, I shake the memory off. "I need to get to Sarah."

Kale's eyebrows furrow. "That was her on the phone, your stepsister, right? Did something happen?"

Christina ducks her head closer to mine. I lean in and keep my voice down. "I don't know." I hesitate, look around. "I don't know, I don't know, I don't know."

Christina's eyes narrow. "I *know* you don't want to tell us what happened, but Kale and I are your friends, you can trust us."

My shoulders sag. Trust.

The weight of all the secrets weighs down on me. Not telling them I was in foster care didn't help anything—and they wouldn't have cared anyway. Kale's eyes are wide as he watches me. Christina puts a hand on my shoulder. Trust.

"My dad," I say, slowly, "he drinks a lot. And he's sad. And angry sometimes. And ever since my mom died I've just been trying to help him keep it together, to keep our family together. Things got better for a while after he remarried, but when he and my stepmom started fighting a lot, he started falling apart."

Kale and Christina watch me silently. Waiting. My words start coming out faster now, and I'm shaking. "The night I left home, the night I was taken away, he said some things that weren't true. He said I did some things, but I didn't. He did."

Christina whispers. "What did he do?"

I try to steady myself, but my shoulders won't stop shaking. Christina squeezes my shoulder.

That night comes back to me, hitting me with the force of a freight train. Dad pushing himself on me, his tongue shoved down my throat, his hands—

"He tried to kiss me." My voice breaks. "Not like you kiss your daughter, but—"

I can't bear the way Kale's face scrunches up in disgust. Tears fill my eyes and well over. Faster and faster. I start choking on them.

Christina steps closer to me, slowly, and puts her arm around my shoulder. I cry more, and she pulls me into a hug.

That's it. That's all I can tell them.

"I'm sorry I didn't tell you," I sob. "I couldn't. It's humiliating. It's sick. *It's wrong.* These aren't normal problems. I just want to be normal."

She strokes my hair. "Ssh, shh. Don't apologize. It's okay."

I cry into her shoulder, unable to look at her or Kale. "If something happens to Sarah, it'll be my fault."

"It won't," Christina says sharply. "It's nobody's fault but your dad's. Don't you dare blame yourself."

I feel a hand touch my back softly. Kale's.

I pull away and nod.

I quickly fill them in on how upset Sarah sounded, how she said my father had started saying strange things, and how that's exactly the process started with me. "I don't think I'm going to get answers on the phone with her."

I hate this. I hate not being able to do anything. I have to do *something*. I can't let Sarah go through what I did.

Kale steps closer to me. "If your sister needs help, can't you just call your social worker and tell her?"

I whip to face him. "Really? Because she's been so helpful so far?" I shake my head, trying to force down my misdirected anger. "She won't do anything unless Sarah specifically tells her what's happening, and she won't even tell me—she's scared, Kale! And I have to go to her to find out why, I have to convince her to talk to me, to tell Mindy about whatever's been going on, because something is."

My dad's been saying *the strangest things* to her. It's more than what she said that bothers me, it's the fear I heard in her voice, the confusion. It reminds me of how I felt, of what I knew deep down was wrong but couldn't admit. It's like the way I hid from what happened.

The way Tiffany never told anyone about her bruises. The way my mom let Dad walk all over her, and pretty much taught me to do the same.

Dad's hurt us all before. And he's not going to stop. I can't believe I couldn't see that until now.

Kale and Christina look at each other, and I can't take it. I can't take all of this standing here and doing nothing.

I swallow, then pull Mindy's business card out of my backpack.

I dial her number, put my finger up to tell Christina and Kale to wait.

And of course I get Mindy's freaking voicemail. Of course.

"Mindy," I say breathlessly. "Look, I know you're going to get mad, but I called Sarah and she's not okay. She told me my dad's been paying a lot of attention to her and saying weird things. She needs your help. You have to go over there.

To her school. Get her to tell you what's going on. Right now." I close my eyes. "*Please.*"

After hanging up, I squeeze the phone in my hands. I can't count on Mindy. She hasn't helped me, *really helped me*, so far.

"I need to get to Reno. I need to take a bus or hitchhike or do something." The words come out before I realize I even planned to say them. "But I need to go, now."

"What? You can't just go now." Christina puts her hand on my shoulder, holding me steady. "We have school and you'd be marked as a truant. You could get in serious trouble."

"Then I won't come back. I need to do this."

Kale waves his hands in front of me. "Whoa, whoa, whoa," he says. "First off, no way you're hitchhiking. That's not a good idea. And Christina's right, you can't just leave school. Can't you call Sarah back to find out what's going on first?"

"I don't think that's enough. She said I wouldn't understand because I'm not there. She's not telling me the whole story. I didn't tell anyone what was really going on either, when I was in her situation."

I hang my head.

None of us did. Not Tiffany, not Mom.

I wipe my face, smoothing my shirt down in an effort to compose myself.

Christina and Kale follow me to my locker. I open it for no reason and stare inside for a moment before coming back to myself. I slam the locker shut. The clang echoes in the quiet hallway.

"I have to see her face to face. I have to convince her that I know what she's going through and that she needs to tell someone," I finally say.

"I'll take you." Christina's eyes are locked on mine. "If you can't get through to your case worker, if she doesn't pull Sarah out of there once she gets your message, I'll drive you in the truck if you wait until the weekend. Can you just wait a couple of days?"

I hesitate, but Christina continues. "I wanted it to be a surprise, but my parents called Connie to see if she'd let you come over sometime, with actual permission. Connie gave us Mindy's phone number and she had my parents get background checks, so you could be cleared to stay the night at our house. I was going to tell you today. We just found out it's okay for you to stay over now."

I stare at her, not understanding at first.

Christina squares her shoulders. "We can plan an excuse or even tell my parents what's going on." She looks at Kale, and he nods, listening intently. "With the extra days we'll have more time to plan," she says, "so we don't do anything reckless. You have too much to lose with graduation so close. We both do."

Christina sighs, and twists the end of her ponytail. "It was supposed to be a surprise," she says again, this time with a sad smile. "I just wanted you to know I love you and my family wanted you to feel welcome in our home."

Tears—of thankfulness or fear or both, I can't tell— prickle my eyes. I inhale deeply. "Okay," I say. "We'll wait to hear from Mindy." But I'm not holding my breath. "And if she doesn't help, we'll go this weekend."

CHAPTER
EIGHTEEN

*A*t lunch, Christina and I wait in line to pick up a food tray. The buffet line is longer than usual. Several people, including Lauren and Taylor, talk and laugh loudly in front of us, like they don't have a care in the world.

I look behind me at Kale. Sitting a few tables away, he stares out the window. He must feel me watching him because he meets my gaze and winks at me.

"You can go sit with him." Christina laughs. "I'll meet you back over there after I get a sandwich."

I'm about to respond, but Christina's big, brown eyes widen. She takes a step and leans her head forward.

"Shh," Christina whispers. "Do you hear that? I think they're talking about you."

I look ahead but can't tell who she's talking about. "Who?"

Christina mouths, "Taylor."

The group of freshmen in between us blocks Christina and me from view. We move as close as we can without seeming creepy or being spotted. Taylor's facing Lauren, and Lauren's back is toward us.

Taylor opens her purse and grabs some lip gloss. She applies it and keeps talking. "I mean I basically knew something was off since the day she walked into this school," she says. "They've all got problems, those foster kids. My cousin is in the same grade as one of her foster sisters at the middle school, the one who just tried to kill herself. It's so sad, right?"

My mouth falls open. Taylor's gossiping about Jamie almost dying, like she's not even a person, as if she's just another conversation topic like the gross lunch food or who's dating whom.

Christina moves to step toward them, but I grab her shoulder. "Don't."

She looks at me incredulously, but my glare holds her in place. I don't want to make a scene and give Taylor another thing to gossip about. Christina crosses her arms and exhales loudly, but watches Taylor intently, as if she's still ready to pounce.

"I saw Victoria at church once sitting with Connie Mahoney." Taylor gives Lauren a knowing look. "She said she was volunteering. I just can't believe she kept it a secret for so long in this town." Taylor's voice becomes louder, almost like she wants people to hear her. "And what a big secret. Well, she's in foster care for a reason, you know," she says, like she's relishing this big, fat juicy piece of gossip. "One of the ladies at church told my mom that her dad kicked her out because—"

"What did my dad kick me out for, exactly?" I say loudly enough that Taylor and half the lunchroom can hear. I step out from behind the freshmen so Taylor and Lauren can see me.

Taylor snaps her mouth shut so fast it's almost comical.

"Uh, oh, um," Lauren mumbles.

Christina follows and stands beside me, glaring at Lauren. "Are you serious?"

I hold my hand up, stopping Christina again.

The lunchroom goes quiet, each head turning to see Taylor and me facing off. I drop my hand.

"You know what? No." I look at Lauren's reddening face and Taylor's look of confusion. "It's not even worth it."

I turn to Christina. "Let's go."

Taylor grabs Lauren's arm. "Whatever. You guys are being so dramatic. Come on, Lauren."

Lauren looks at Christina and then me. "I didn't mean—"

But I don't hear the rest of what she says, because we've already started walking away.

"Bitches," Christina says as she slams her hands on the empty table. "And now what am I supposed to do for lunch?" We left the line without Christina's sandwich. And I don't trust my shaking hands to reach for my food out of my bag just yet.

"What happened?" Kale asks.

"They were talking about my foster sister Jamie, and about me being in foster care. About my dad, about . . ." I trail off. I swallow the words I'm thinking and look at Christina and Kale.

"What happened to your foster sister Jamie?" Christina asks.

"It's true what Taylor was saying. Jamie tried to kill herself."

Christina inhales sharply. "Is she okay?"

I hold onto the table in front of me for a second. Kale leans his elbows in front of him and puts his chin in his hands as his eyes wrinkle in worry.

"She's okay," I tell them. "They moved her somewhere where she can get help. It's just, I should have done something. Helped her. Seen it coming. I don't know."

I put a hand to my stomach. It feels like something is squeezing it.

"I wish . . ." I pause, catching my breath. "I'm just so sorry." A tear slides down my face, and I wipe it away quickly.

"I was going to tell you, but then the thing with Sarah . . ." My shoulders are shaking. I need this conversation to go back to normal. To something within control. "I can't go off campus, but you can go grab something if you want."

"I'm good here." Kale gives Christina a look before he scoots closer to me and puts his arm around my shoulders. "And don't listen to them." He shakes his head and shoots a baffled look in the direction Taylor and Lauren are standing. "It's stupid. They're being stupid."

I exhale, calming myself.

We sit in silence for a few minutes, waiting for Lauren and Taylor to get their sandwiches and go outside, and then for the lunch line to die down. I try not to think about whatever Taylor was about to say about my dad and me. *My dad.* My stomach gurgles. I blink several times.

Alex emerges from behind Kale, using his shoulder to open the double doors that lead into the lunchroom from outside. He's holding a big box of pizza and a stack of paper plates.

He plops in the seat next to Christina. "Hey, babe. If you give me a kiss I might share Kale's and my pizza with you." He looks at Kale already eating a sacked lunch and shakes his head. "I don't know where it all goes."

Alex leans forward and kisses Christina quickly. She laughs and swats him off of her. Alex sits back and opens the box of pizza. "Mmm." He takes a small stack of paper plates from under the box and hands a plate to Kale, then to Christina and me.

If I go see Sarah, if I try to talk to her, I'll be knowingly going to Reno, closer to my father. I swallow. My stomach is squeezing. Maybe if eat, I'll feel better.

I pull my sandwich out of my bag. My mouth waters as I force myself to swallow a bite. But I set it aside, the food's not sitting well.

I grab a slice of pizza, chew without tasting. Slow bites.

Christina rages on for a few minutes about how awful Taylor is and what a backstabber Lauren has become, but only a few moments later the incident already seems like a distant memory. What does it *really* matter what people at school might know about me or what they might say, when Sarah could be in danger?

With Alex with us at lunch, there's no bringing up our

plans for getting to Sarah. Christina tosses a baby carrot from Kale's packed lunch at Alex's head as he teases her, only for him to catch it in his mouth. Kale holds my hand.

But then Jamie's nearly lifeless body flashes in my mind, followed by the image of my dad coming on to Sarah. My father looming over me. My stomach gurgles painfully again, much worse than before.

"I have to go." I cover my mouth and rush out of the cafeteria to the bathroom. I don't have time to care about all the stares I get from the people I pass as I do.

I heave myself through the first stall and fall to my knees before puking my guts out into the toilet. I grasp each side of the bowl and squeeze, coughing and squinting my watery eyes.

"Victoria!" Christina doesn't bother knocking before opening the stall and standing behind me.

She leans down and puts her hand on my right shoulder. "You okay?"

I shake my head.

"I'll go easy on the PDA with Alex from now on, seeing as how you have such a fragile stomach." Christina forces a laugh, but I can hear the worry in her voice.

I flush the toilet and push myself up.

"I'll get you a paper towel."

I follow Christina out of the stall to the dispenser in front of the mirror. She hands me one, and I wipe my mouth with it.

I splash some water on my face and rinse my mouth, before wiping my face off with my shirt.

"Gum?"

Christina digs in her tote and grabs a pack, handing me a piece. "Minty fresh."

"I'd take any flavor as long as it doesn't taste like pizza." I pop the gum in my mouth.

"Are you sick?"

I wipe at my eyes and shake my head. "Jamie. Sarah." I breathe in heavily. "It's more than that. I'm really scared of seeing my dad."

Christina takes my hand and squeezes it. "You won't. We'll make sure of it. He won't go anywhere near you."

I hold the sink in front of me.

Christina's eyes narrow, like she's trying to read my mind. "It's not your fault, you know. What he did to you."

I nod, still not convinced. "And I'm worried about Sarah, and nervous about sneaking around to see her."

Christina turns her back toward the mirror and looks straight at me. "We'll be really careful. I promise."

I nod again. Release the sink.

I can't look at myself in the mirror anymore, so I turn to face Christina. She tilts her head at me. "I think you should go home for the day."

She hoists her bag up on her shoulder. "Let me go talk to the office. I'll tell them you're puking in here and that they should call Connie."

Christina walks out of the bathroom. At least no one else was in here to witness that. Half the school saw me run in here, so they probably knew I was barfing, but at least they didn't see me cry.

Christina is back in a few minutes. "Connie's on her way."

I finish wiping my face with a paper towel. "Thank you. Tell Kale I'm sorry I can't walk home with him."

Christina waves it off.

"Can I use your phone? I want to try Sarah again."

Christina grabs her phone out of her bag and hands it to me.

"I'll text her, since she's in school," I say, as I think it through, "but I won't leave my name or anything. I'll do it in code just in case someone is checking her messages."

"What will you say?"

I shrug. "'Hey, it was good talking to you earlier. Want to continue our talk in person. I'll call you soon to set up a time to hang out.'" I'm making this up as I go, but it's working so far. "'Call me back if you need me' or something like that. Keep it casual-sounding, but she'll recognize the number. What do you think?"

"Send it."

I type the message quickly and hit send.

Outside of the bathroom, Christina hugs me and offers to stay while I wait for Connie, but I tell her I'm fine. I sit on the bench in the hallway, at the other end of the school office. I'll see Connie from the window when she gets here.

Twenty minutes later Connie's white mini-van pulls up. She parks in the handicapped space right in front and heads inside.

"You all right?"

I nod.

"Well, getta move on then." She charges into the office, and I follow her.

Becca stands behind the front desk. "Hello there, Ms. Mahoney," she greets Connie, before looking at me. "Sorry you're not feeling well, dear."

I nod.

Becca pushes a piece of paper on the desk toward Connie. "Sign here, please, and mark the date and time."

Mr. Nelson opens the door from his office behind her. "Well hello, Victoria. I hear you aren't feeling well."

"I'll be fine. I just need some rest, I think," I say, craning my head up to look at him.

He smiles at me before addressing Connie. "Ms. Mahoney, you ought to know that Victoria's been doing really well. She's got top marks in all of her classes and has been a joy for teachers, I hear. We'll be sad to lose her to TMCC in the fall."

"Oh." Connie clears her throat. I haven't told her about TMCC yet. "Well, yes. I'll miss her, too."

We all stand in awkward silence for a moment before Connie clears her throat again. "We should get going—don't want you infecting the other kids here with whatever you've got. I had the little ones go stay with my mom and her husband just in case. They're certified by the state as respite caregivers, you know. Last thing we need is three sick kids instead of just one."

I look down so Connie doesn't see the face I'm making at this whole foster-mother-of-the-year performance she's giving.

"See you soon, Victoria," Mr. Nelson says.

"Feel better!" Becca adds.

I wave and follow Connie out to the van.

"Do you think you have the flu?" Connie asks as I push an empty McDonald's bag to the side with my foot to make room for me in the front seat.

"I don't think so." I buckle my seat belt.

Connie pulls the handicap sticker off the center mirror and puts it in the cup holder in between us. I never asked her what it was for or what her handicap is. She eyes me distrustfully for a moment.

"Connie," I begin. "I called Mindy. I know you like to talk to her for me, or whatever, but I need to talk to her. She didn't answer. It went to voicemail."

Connie frowns. "What's going on?"

"I'm worried about Sarah. I know I'm not supposed to, I know you're going to be mad, but I just couldn't take it anymore. I called her. And she's scared, I can tell, and my dad's—"

I stop, take a long hard look at myself in the center mirror.

"I think my dad's hurting her. If he hasn't already, he will."

Connie's eyes widen, and she turns to me entirely. "What did she say, Victoria? What did she say your dad is doing?"

"He's making her uncomfortable. Paying too much attention to her, saying weird things."

"What kind of weird things?"

"She didn't say."

Connie lifts her eyebrows at me.

I hit the dashboard, so tired of not being taken seriously. "She's scared, okay, she's not supposed to be talking to me, remember? I just need Mindy to go to her and get her to talk. Something's going on, I know it!"

Connie lifts her arm, and it looks like she's about to reach out to me. I flinch away. Her arm falls to her side. "I believe you, Victoria. I believe you, but you know there's a process Mindy has to follow—"

"I need to know Sarah's okay. You have to understand." My eyes widen, staring into Connie's, trying to will her to help me. "After what happened to Jamie . . ." I trail off.

Connie nods. "The second we get home, I'll call Mindy again, okay? But if Sarah doesn't tell her anything, which we have no reason to believe she will, because believe you me Mindy has tried many, many times to get through to that girl, you're gonna have to let it go."

I open my mouth to argue, but Connie won't let me.

"Mindy has been calling Tiffany a few times a week to check in on her and Sarah when your dad isn't home. She's keeping an eye on the family and waiting for proof, for something definitive that would allow her to act, but right now Sarah isn't talking. She's had every opportunity to tell the authorities about anything going on at home." Connie's tone changes from soft to brusque when she sees me turn away from her, balling my fists. "You have to trust that the professionals can do their jobs and hope that Sarah will speak up if anything is wrong."

From over my shoulder, I hear Connie take a deep

breath. "I know this can't be easy," she says, "Trust me, *I know*. But you don't need any trouble right now. You're so close to graduating, getting out on your own. You can start over. That's a gift, really it is."

We've been sitting in this car not moving and getting nowhere. The sooner Connie starts driving, the sooner I can get away from her, go to my room, *the dormitory*, and start planning my trip to Reno to see Sarah.

Connie makes no effort to move. At all.

"Getting sick at school because you don't feel well is one thing, but"—she puts her hand up as though she anticipates me arguing—"no matter what you say, I hope you aren't doing it for anything else. It's a long, hard road I wouldn't wish on anyone. And you've got enough problems as it is."

I shake my head, not understanding. Connie's eyes crinkle at the edges, making the wrinkles around her mouth look more pronounced.

"It must have been something I ate."

Connie shakes her head at me. "Try again."

"It's been a hard day."

Connie sighs heavily. She pauses for a moment, and I feel like I can see the wheels turning in her head, like she's trying to decide something.

"I remember when I went to school here," Connie finally says. She looks through the window at the brick building.

I'm quiet for a moment but soon realize Connie's not budging. "Christina told me you were here at the same time as her mom," I say through gritted teeth.

Connie stares ahead at the school—though she seems

wistful, like she's really a million miles away. "Yeah, yeah I was. She was one of the few kids who were nice to me here, not that I ever thanked her for it. I was awful to her and to everyone. High school wasn't a very happy place for me." Connie fidgets in her seat. "I can't imagine it ever is for overweight girls with mamas who are the lunch lady."

I release my clenched fists. "Your mom worked here?"

Connie starts the car. "She did. And the kids were plain awful to her and to me. Called me Little Miss Piggy and called my mama Mama Sausage."

I wince. I've thought hateful things about her, even if I didn't say them. "I'm sorry," I whisper. And I am. It would be awful to be called those kinds of names, anytime, anywhere, but especially at school.

Connie puts her hands on the wheel. "I didn't want Mama to feel worse than she already did, since she left her husband years before for what he did to me. She felt so guilty, like it was her fault. So when the other kids called me names, I pretended it didn't bother me."

She reverses the car and pulls out of the parking lot.

"I started dieting—well, to be honest, it wasn't so much a diet as an eating disorder," Connie continues. "Mama didn't like that much, but she didn't understand. She was always more secure in herself than I was. She didn't let what other people thought bother her. She was always so strong, even after my dad had a heart attack and died a few years after I was born. It was just her to take care of me, and she was fine with that. At least until my stepdad came along."

Connie keeps her eyes locked on the car ahead of us,

driving slowly on the residential street. "Even though it didn't work out with him—after what he did to me, thank the Lord she kicked him out and turned him over to the police—at least she had people her age who wanted her when she was younger. She was seen as attractive by boys at school, and not just her stepdad."

Connie sighs, her voice barely loud enough for me to hear. "She knew what that felt like, and then she got remarried again, to her current husband."

Connie stops at the stop sign, near Kale's house. I wonder what she would say if I told her I had a boyfriend. I wonder if she knows Kale's parents. Would they have been nice to her like Christina's mom, or did they call her names, too?

"I guess I've never thought of you being my age, caring about kids or school or dating."

"Oh, girl, I cared a lot about that kind of thing back then. But things really turned around for me when I started losing weight junior year, and I came back after that summer even thinner." She starts coughing, and I look down at my hands until she stops. Connie keeps talking, the words pouring from her.

"Boys were noticing me. The girls didn't like the competition, so they kept taunting me—but the boys, they were a lot nicer. By then, though, I'd stopped paying attention to any of that. Because I thought I had it all worked out. I had myself a grown man."

Connie smiles, closing her eyes for an instant before looking back at the road. We're just a few streets away from her house.

"I met Bill at the community college in Yerington. I took some classes there to get ahead. He didn't know me as Little Miss Piggy. He told me I was beautiful."

Her ringless left hand slides down the wheel, her right hand still holding tight. "By mid-way through senior year I had a great big engagement ring on my finger. Mama was so happy for me. She loved Bill and all the girls were jealous, even though they'd never admit it."

"You went to college?" I stare at Connie's left hand as she reaches it back on the steering wheel, try to imagine it with a fancy diamond ring on it. Her knuckles are large and her nails short from biting them. She's never mentioned college before. I just figured she hadn't gone.

Connie smirks, but keeps her eyes on the road. She flicks on the turn signal and takes a right. "I did, until Bill and I got married that summer," she says. "He kept going to school and I got a job as a waitress, which I thought was good at the time because it kept me moving on my feet. Great exercise. And we stayed together for years and I kept myself skinny in the worst ways. I was so afraid he'd leave me, I started throwing up in the toilet after meals."

I swallow, tasting the gum and a bit of leftover pizza. I hold back the urge to gag. "That's not why . . ." I trail off. "I appreciate what you're trying to do, but really I'm fine."

Connie sighs, raising her thin eyebrows at me. "Sure you are." She shakes her head.

"What happened with you and Bill?" I keep my eyes on the truck next to us on the road as we pass it. "Why did you two break up?"

Connie frowns and taps her fingers on the wheel. "After a while I just couldn't do it anymore and the pounds kept piling on. Bill said he didn't mind at first. He had gained quite a few pounds himself, but he blamed that on my cooking, not all the damned beer he'd been drinking." She glances at me and then looks back at the road. "So he finally left me a few years ago, after Annie was born."

Connie pulls onto our street. Once we're in the driveway, she puts the car in park and turns to face me. I glance out the window as a beat-down F-150 roars to life in the driveway next to us, smoke coming out of the exhaust. "I'm so sorry, Connie, about what you went through. I really am."

Connie and I lock eyes. "Don't be. I'd rather be alone than with someone who doesn't love the real me."

She turns the car off and unbuckles her seatbelt. "And I'll be damned if I ever change for a man again. I'll eat whatever the hell I damn well please, because I want to, no matter how much weight I gain. To hell with Bill!"

Connie leans back in her seat, facing forward. "I know what you think of me. But I'm telling you, girl, I'm doing this because I want to help. I was lucky, I had my mama to love and support me through hell and back, but I know what it feels like to be unwanted. That terrible feeling is why I foster you kids."

She reaches out and pats my knee. I don't flinch or move away.

"I've lost my patience with you more than I like to admit." Connie shakes her head. "I don't want you to blame yourself for what happened to you. But I don't think you should misplace blame, either. What's happening isn't my fault. It isn't Mindy's fault. It's your father's fault."

She stops, letting that last bit sink in. "Since you couldn't control what happened to you, you might feel helpless, but you aren't. You don't need to go getting an eating disorder or marrying the first fool who pays you attention. You don't have to do what I did. You can come out of this okay, if you want it bad enough."

I take a deep breath and nod.

Without another word, I open my door and head for the house, Connie walking beside me.

That night, after still no word from Mindy, no response to the voice message Connie left her, I dream about my father. In the dream, he was wiping off a cut on my knee after I fell off my bicycle when I was little.

He put a bandage on it and then kissed the top of my knee, just like he did in real life.

"All better," he said.

I hugged him. And then I woke up.

"How do you feel this morning? Think you can stomach some breakfast?" Connie calls to me from the kitchen after I shower and leave the bathroom, dressed and ready for school. Spatula in hand, she flips a pancake.

"Breakfast?"

"Chocolate chip pancakes," Connie replies. "Grab a plate and take a seat. I'm cooking this morning."

I smile without meaning to. But then I remember Sarah.

Annie and Samantha stayed the night at Connie's parents' house, so it's just us here. We can talk.

"Have you heard back from Mindy?"

Connie nods. "She called when you were in the shower, I'm sorry. I asked her to wait, said I'd have you come out to talk to her. But she was in a rush, so she asked me to deliver the message."

My jaw clenches. Mindy, always in a rush.

"Help yourself to some milk, too." Connie points to an empty glass in front of my seat. I sit and stare at her. Waiting.

"Mindy called Tiffany. She also went to Sarah's school yesterday afternoon to talk to her. Sarah said she's fine, that nothing's going on with your dad at home."

Connie eyes me as she takes the last pancake off the griddle and puts it on a plate, before taking it over to me.

I put my head in my hands and squeeze my eyes shut to keep from crying. Nothing I do, none of it makes a difference.

Connie clears her throat. "Eat," she says softly. "Please."

After a moment, I let my head go. I spear two small pancakes roughly, pour some milk.

Connie takes four pancakes for herself and sits at the head of the table. "I'm not saying you're wrong, Victoria," she says, cutting her pancakes into squares. "And neither is Mindy. Maybe Tiffany got to Sarah first. Maybe she told her not to say anything. Or maybe Sarah's just scared." Connie sets her fork down. "Girl, you of all people know how terrifying it is to talk about something like that. You've got to. You still won't tell us what happened."

I stare at my pancakes as if I'm talking to them. "If I

tell you want happened, if I tell you my dad hurt me, would Mindy take Sarah away from him?"

Connie tilts her head at me, frowning. "Mindy would tell Tiffany your accusations, and we'd hope she'd leave with Sarah on her own, but we know that's not necessarily the case with that woman. There would be an investigation, of course, and if CPS deemed Sarah to be in danger, they'd remove her from both your father and her mother's care."

I slam my hands on the table. Connie flinches as my silverware clatters on the plate.

"So even if I said my dad hurt me, they might not take Sarah away?"

Connie's voice softens, her words come out slow. "I can't say for sure. But my guess is they can't just take a child away from her mother like that. They have to prove—"

"So it's exactly how it's always been. My word against his?"

I stand. Connie reaches for my shoulder and I yank it away.

She rises to her full height.

"Sit. Eat," Connie commands. "Victoria, I know this is frustrating. But you didn't eat dinner and you puked up your lunch yesterday. You need to eat."

I sit, kicking my feet angrily in front of me. I take a swig of milk.

Connie sits back down. We're quiet for several minutes as I seethe. Finally, I can't take the silence.

"I didn't realize you cook."

"Yeah, well, we can't eat eggs every morning, even though

you make them so well." Connie's lips stretch into a smile. I roll my eyes.

Connie's face falls. She's trying. I see that, even if I would rather be anywhere else in the world than here with her.

This settles it. I have to go to Plan B. I can still help Sarah. I can still stay the night with Christina and go to her myself.

But I can't be obvious about it, I can't set off warning bells for Connie.

"Connie, can I ask you something?"

"Ask away."

"You helped Christina's parents get approved to have me stay over with them but didn't tell me. Why?"

"It was supposed to be a surprise. You surprised?"

"Yeah!" I blurt. Even though Christina told me, I want Connie to feel good about helping, if even in a small way. Especially since I need her to let me stay the night there so my plan of meeting up with Sarah will work. "Wow, that's—that's really great. Thank you."

Connie laughs, her shoulders relaxing. "I take it you are feeling well enough to want to spend the night soon?"

I swallow. "If you'll let me, I'd like to this weekend."

"Okay," Connie says, picking up her fork again. "Ask Christina when Maria and Jorge will let you come over, and that's fine by me. Just let me know when you plan to leave and come back. And no drinking or anything else illegal, got it?"

"I promise. Thank you!"

"Yeah, yeah. Eat your pancakes."

CHAPTER
NINETEEN

*A*t school, I can't focus. Christina told me that Sarah replied to the text I sent her—*got it, thanks.* So at least she got the message and knows I'm coming to see her soon. I'll call on the day we come over. It'll be the weekend, so she'll answer. During each class, I watch the clock, waiting for school to end so Christina, Kale, and I can walk home together and make our plans. When I'm not thinking about Sarah, I'm thinking of Jamie.

Jamie's doing well in treatment, Connie told me on my way out of the house. She says I can write Jamie a letter next month if she earns her privileges to get mail at the treatment center. I'll tell her how sorry I am. I'll tell her I'll call as soon as she's allowed to take phone calls. I'll tell her I won't let her down again.

———

I get a bathroom pass to leave class early, just to be alone. After, I head to my locker, my mind wandering back to the time Sarah was trying to learn a choreographed dance from a DVD. She had to learn the moves to try out for dance team at the beginning of the school year. I heard the music playing from my bedroom and went out to see what was going on.

Sarah bopped and shimmied along to the beat in front of the flat-screen in the living room.

"Want to learn it with me?" Sarah asked as she did a spin and dropped into a squatting position, part of some elaborate move I wouldn't even begin to know how to accomplish.

I chuckled. "Not even a little bit."

She kept moving around to the beat, smiling. "Come on!"

I walked over to her, and swung my arms in the air, mimicking the dancer on the TV. "Like this?"

Sarah tried to stop herself from laughing, but she couldn't.

"Hey, I'm not *that* bad!" And then, to prove it, I tried the turning-into-the squatting move she did earlier. But I lost my footing, and toppled into Sarah, taking us both down in the process.

Behind us, Dad and Tiffany started cracking up. Apparently, they'd been watching from the kitchen.

From the ground, laughing with Sarah, I remember feeling happy. Feeling like a family as Dad and Tiffany came over to the living room and helped us up.

The bell rings. Kids start spilling into the hallway from various classrooms. "Victoria! Victoria!" I whip around to Ms. Claire's voice in the hallway. She walks out of her office and takes a few strides toward me.

"I got an email from TMCC's financial aid department," she says quietly, her red hair falling over her shoulders as she stops in front of me. "It said someone had emailed you about your award letter but hadn't heard from you. They wanted to see if you still go to school here or if you were moved to another foster home."

My chest tightens. I used to check my email every day, but I haven't at all since the dance and then what happened with Jamie. "I haven't checked my email. Um, can I do that now?"

Ms. Claire nods. "Do you want to use my computer in my office?"

I follow her through the hallway. Inside, she closes her door and motions for me to sit in her chair. "Go ahead."

I pull up the browser, then my email account and log in. At the top of my inbox, there it is—an unopened email from TMCC's financial aid department. My heart hammers as I turn back and look at Ms. Claire.

"Open it!" She gestures with both hands.

I hold my breath and click on the email. My mouth falls open.

"I've been awarded more than tuition costs." I stare at the number. "It says I'm receiving a full federal grant, to pay for all of my tuition next year, but why did they give me more money than I need for that? Is it a mistake?"

Ms. Claire leans over my shoulder. "Do you mind if I take a look?"

I nod, and she does. "It's not a mistake, Victoria. The extra money here is meant to help pay for your living expenses. The government does that sometimes for students with a great financial need, like for foster kids to help them pay for expenses while they attend school—it looks like part of that is the educational voucher program we talked about. Did you turn that paperwork in, too?"

I nod.

"Well, there you go! You have money to pay for school and then some! This is great news!"

I shake my head, dazed. This is what I wanted. This is what I wanted all along. I get to go to school, I get to move on, I get to be free.

But then warmth rushes to my face and my mouth goes dry, because I can't—I can't just forget about Jamie. About Sarah. "I should get to class now." I stand.

Ms. Claire furrows her light eyebrows. "This is good news, Victoria. I'm so happy for you."

"Thank you, thank you so much." I step toward the door. "I have to go now."

Ms. Claire watches me leave. I walk down the hall, seeing but not hearing everyone around me.

This is all almost over. I'm going to leave here in a few months and be done with foster care. Everything I wanted. Almost. But Jamie has years left to go in the system, years of loneliness, and Sarah is still with my dad. He could have been hurting her this entire time. And I hardly even thought about it before. I only thought about myself.

I feel someone beside me. "We have a take-home pre-calculus test due Monday." Kale takes my books from me. "I figure we can work on it on the car ride home, after you see Sarah."

"Already did mine," I say automatically. I blink a couple

times and focus on Kale. "I wanted to make sure everything was ready to go for this weekend, including homework. Just in case . . . You know, better to be prepared."

Kale swings an arm in front of him. "I expect that kind of can-do attitude to continue in college—you'll make the honor roll, for sure. Dean's List or whatever awards they give to smart people like you. You know, it won't be long before we're back at the same school, so I'll be able to see it for myself." He winks at me.

Not that again. I can't think about a couple years from now. I don't know if I can even get through this weekend.

"I can help you with the pre-calculus test on the way home." The words rush out of me.

Kale's face falls.

Automatically, I grab his hand. "College, yeah. Although that'll be a while for you, junior." I squeeze his hand, trying to bring our conversation back to being comfortable.

Kale presses his lips together, as if waiting for me to speak. I don't. He exhales, and the smile returns to his face. "What I lack in age, I make up for in maturity. And sex appeal."

I laugh, relieved, if only a little. We stop next to the door to my class. "I'll still be at a different school for another year by the time you start going to UNR, though. I'll be at TMCC for two years before I can transfer, so you'll be there before me." I watch a few classmates walk through the door.

"Actually, I was thinking about going to TMCC," Kale says. "Like you said, it's cheaper, and that way I can save my parents some money."

My face tenses. "I don't want you to make any educational or life decisions based on me," I say slowly, carefully.

"It was just a thought."

I turn to face him entirely, my throat tight. I'm not just protecting myself at this point, I'm protecting Kale. "Just don't, okay?"

Kale's face goes blank. He nods at the door. "I guess you better go in there. See you later."

I take my books. "See you." I take a few steps to my desk. When I look back, Kale's gone.

After class, Christina and I walk to the cafeteria together for lunch. Kale's sitting at our usual table by the window, talking to one of the guys on the cross-country team.

Kale and the guy do some kind of dude handshake before he walks away. Christina drops her bag to the ground and sits. I sit next to her and look at Kale, who's suddenly very interested in his turkey sandwich. I cast my eyes down.

Christina glances at Kale, his expression, and then at me, my guilt, and stands back up.

"I'll leave you two alone." Christina gives me a look. "See you after school, when we make our diabolical plan."

Neither of us say anything for a moment after Christina walks away.

I stare at my fingertips in my lap. "I'm sorry about earlier. It's not that . . ." I pause, and like a balloon as it deflates, I exhale. "I'm happy that we're going to live in the same city after you graduate. I'd like to think we might get the chance to have a shot at an ordinary relationship, where we can actually hang out outside of school and things can be more normal."

I stop fiddling with my fingers and intertwine them in my lap, forcing my gaze back to Kale. "I just don't want you giving up anything for me, not something that you worked hard for and deserve. You've already done so much just by standing by me through all of my drama. I don't want to cause more."

Kale shakes his head. "You don't."

I look into Kale's soft blue eyes and remember how striking they were when we first met. And how they're even more striking now that I know how kind and wonderful he is on top of being so warm and funny.

"Let me finish," I say, reaching for his hand. "We need to make our own decisions for no other reason than for what's best for ourselves, individually. Everything that happened with my dad taught me that more than anything. Love isn't selfish." I look pointedly at Kale, who went very still when I said the word *love*. "It's about doing what's best for the other person, and right now what's best for each of us is to focus on ourselves and school. And not making any rash decisions."

Kale's voice comes out higher than usual. "Love?"

I chuckle, happy that I'm the one who made him uncomfortable for once.

"Or *like*, like a lot. That is also good."

Kale and I both laugh, and my tenseness melts away. I lean in and kiss him, slow and long enough to get in trouble if a teacher sees. And I feel butterflies, warmth in my stomach. I feel like everything is right, just for a moment, even as everything else seems to be falling apart around me.

I relax my shoulders, scoot over to Kale's side of the table and lean into his shoulder.

Kale's nose brushes my hair. "I'm okay with waiting and seeing how things go. Even if it's not easy."

I look up at him. "Thanks, Kale. You're not so bad for a guy who's named after a vegetable."

Kale kisses me again, and my thoughts aren't on vegetables or Sarah or Jamie for just a moment. A moment that ends too soon.

After school, Christina meets Kale and me by my locker and we walk outside through the parking lot together. My chest is tight. Christina's boots clink on the sidewalk as she walks, just a little faster than Kale and I do. "I'll walk with you guys for a few minutes and then head back to my truck," Christina says. "I don't think we need to spend too much time plotting."

"And why is that?" Kale steps around to Christina's other side so he's next to me. "Let me guess. You have it all figured out already?"

Christina sneers at Kale but laughs. "Yes, as a matter of fact, I do have a plan. Or at least part of one. The rest, I figure, we can improvise." We turn the corner, wait for a car to pass at the stop sign, and cross the street. "I have money for gas," she says.

I swallow, realizing how dry my throat is. This is real.

I'm really going back to Reno, to see Sarah. "That's great, Christina." I cough. "Thank you."

Christina pats my back and offers me her water bottle, which I wave off.

Kale is quiet, his eyebrows furrowed. "This could be dangerous," he finally says, hesitantly. "Are you sure we shouldn't tell anyone?"

I look up to the cloudless sky, so tired of this question. "Who could we tell? Your parents would probably try to stop us from going, and social services and the police haven't done one freaking thing that makes it seem they believe a word I say anyway." I lift my hands up in the air in frustration, then drop them to my sides. "I just need to check, I just need to know she's okay."

I inhale, forcing myself to calm down, forcing myself to speak softer and to not freak out on Kale for stuff that isn't his fault.

"I let everything that was going on with Jamie get past me, because I was too worried about my own life." I stare into Kale's eyes, willing him to understand. "Sarah might be in trouble now, too. I *have* to help her."

Sarah could be in danger every minute we aren't there to help her get away from my dad.

Kale squeezes my hand.

"Look, we probably won't see my dad . . ." I trail off, then cast my eyes down. "I'm planning to meet Sarah somewhere a safe distance away. But just in case, maybe you two should drop me off for a while and come back."

Christina glares at me. "That," she says, "is the stupidest thing I've ever heard."

Kale nods. When I open my mouth to argue, he tugs my hand. "No. We're coming with you. Like you said, your dad won't be there, and even if he is, all the more reason for us to come. We aren't going to listen to you, Victoria. So there's really no point in wasting time arguing about it."

I look back and forth between them, and I know that they won't agree even if I keep trying. So finally, I nod.

Christina's voice becomes brusque, matter-of-fact. "So you'll come over first thing Saturday morning. Connie agreed to let me pick you up, so everything's good on your end, right?"

I feel the urge to cough again but fend it off. "Right. She trusts us, even though she shouldn't."

"Don't worry about that." Christina shakes her head. "Sometimes doing the right thing means breaking the rules, Victoria. This isn't like when you lied about where you were to go to a dance. This is about your stepsister's safety."

Kale stops suddenly. I try to keep walking, but he doesn't move, the weight of his body holding me in place.

"You went to jail for going to a dance," he says, grasping my hand tightly. "Jail! I don't really care if I get caught—my parents would probably just ground me or something—but it's not like that for you."

I shrug, having already thought of this. It's a risk I'm willing to take. A risk I have to take.

"Wait," Kale continues. "I know this is important." He looks at me, then at Christina and back. "We just haven't thought it through. If you went to jail last time, what would they do to you this time? Kick you out? You'll have nowhere to go."

"Don't be ridiculous." Christina narrows her eyes at Kale. "She could live with me. My family would never let her be homeless. And neither would yours."

"What?" I stammer.

Christina's eyes soften. She touches my shoulder. "Let's hope it doesn't come to that. Or at least that if you do move in, it's because you want to and not because Connie throws you out."

Thank you. The words won't come out, but I manage a weak smile for Christina.

Kale loosens his grip on my hand and exhales, apparently resigned. "Fine, so what else do we have to plan?"

"Once we get to Reno, I'll ask her to meet me somewhere nearby."

"Okay, then what?" Christina turns to the street in front of us. We're just a block away from Kale's house already.

"Then, I'll ask her what's going on with my dad, I guess. I'll ask if anything's happened. If he's, if he's been acting weird or anything." I take a deep breath. "If not, I'll tell her what he did to me. Maybe that'll get her to talk."

We all go quiet for a moment. "Either way, I'll make sure Sarah has Mindy's number and tell her that I'm moving to Reno soon."

Kale pulls my hand to bring me closer to him, to hold me. I step back. "I'm fine."

Christina says softly, "And what if your dad is acting"—she pauses—"*weird*?"

"If she says yes . . ." I'm breathing in short, quick breaths now, and I have to pause to control it. "We'll make her file a report or take her home with us. I'll get in so much trouble, I know, but I won't let him hurt her."

Christina and Kale exchange looks, like they're trying to think of a way to talk me out of doing this. "Well, do either of you have any better ideas?" I snap.

"No," Christina says slowly. "No, we don't. This is a good idea. You guys go on." She turns, slightly. "I'm going to go back to my truck."

"All right," I sigh. Sorry for yelling. Sorry for being so upset all the time. "See you tomorrow. And thanks, Christina. And Kale. Thank you both."

Christina nods, looking at Kale long enough for me to wonder how much they really want to go through with this, and then she walks away.

CHAPTER
TWENTY

I don't call Sarah again. I don't want to risk blowing our cover. But I do text her, asking questions about how she's doing, vague enough that she won't get in trouble if her mom happens to pop over her shoulder and see a message. Sarah doesn't give me much by way of answers. She just says she wants to see me face to face.

I pack the stuff I'd need for a sleepover on Friday after school, so when I wake up Saturday morning, all I have to do is shower and get dressed. In the bathroom, I look at myself in the foggy mirror.

I look the same, but I'm not the same. Still, I remember the night Dad threw me out like it's happening right now. It's so fresh, even though it's been months.

Dad, Sarah, and I stayed up watching a movie together in the living room, except Sarah fell asleep on the couch and after the movie, she went to her room. Tiffany had already gone to bed.

I said goodnight to Dad, and he tried to hug me. I dodged him, not wanting to hurt his feelings but also not wanting a hug. Not wanting him to linger, and then get angry at me when I moved away. The last few days I'd felt like I couldn't get away from him. Wherever I was, wherever I went, he was there. Watching me.

That night I heard Dad in the kitchen, fumbling in the cabinets, likely looking for some booze. I climbed in bed before turning on the desk lamp on the bedside table next to me, pulled out a biography of Alexander Hamilton, and forgot about Dad. Until I heard a knock at my door.

He usually didn't knock, and he didn't come in when he thought I was awake, at least that's what I thought. I flipped off the bedside light, hoping he'd go away after a few minutes. But Dad kept knocking. I set the book down quietly, climbed out of bed, and adjusted my shirt to make sure I was fully covered. I flicked the light switch on the wall before opening the door.

"Can I come in?" Dad slurred.

"It's late, Dad." My words came out calm, nonchalant, but my entire body tensed up. "I was asleep."

"Liar," he said with a lopsided smile. He pushed by me, pawed his hand at the switch, turning the light off, and shut the door. I turned to flip the bedside light back on but then felt him pushing himself against my back behind me. I froze.

"You're beautiful, Victoria," Dad whispered into my ear, his hand on my shoulder. "Too beautiful."

Fear coursed through me, paralyzing me, like I had forgotten how to move, how to breathe. His hands slid down my arms and gripped my waist. And then he nuzzled his face into my neck, kissing it before I jerked away. I felt like an animal in the middle of a highway the second before getting plowed down by a speeding car. I had to get away get away get away, before it was too late.

"Don't be afraid of me, Victoria." Dad's glossy eyes lingered on my lips. "I would never hurt you. I love you. All I want to do is love you."

I stepped back, backed away until my legs bumped into my bed. Trapped.

"Dad, please don't. I don't—"

Dad pushed closer to me. I could smell whiskey on his breath. A scream began to build deep within my chest, but when I opened my mouth I couldn't let it go. I couldn't do anything.

"Don't be like that, baby." He leaned closer to my face.

"Dad, stop!" I tried to shout, but he covered my mouth with his sweaty hand. He stared straight into my eyes, angry, determined, as he held my mouth and nose closed tightly. I couldn't get oxygen into my lungs. After I stopped squirming, he released my mouth and slid his hand to my neck. I sucked down gulps of air like it was water.

He leaned in close and forced his lips onto mine. His fingers wrapped around my neck, holding me still.

Dad's tongue forced my mouth open and I could taste the alcohol, warm and wet. I jerked and pulled but his fingers tightened, squeezing my neck so hard my vision started to blur and turn black around the edges.

I stopped moving completely, frozen still as Dad pushed his groin against me and moaned. I felt him against my pajamas and I wished I was dead. I wished I'd died instead of

Mom. I wished he'd kill me right then and there so I didn't have to feel him against me.

I didn't move. I didn't breathe. I didn't know how to think anymore as Dad's hand slid to my waistband, his fingers pushing my underwear aside.

I felt him reaching where I'd never been touched and I woke up out of a trance, pushed him as hard as I could, and screamed.

He shoved me so hard, my back knocked against my headboard, knocking the wind out of me. Then he threw his hand over my mouth, pinning me on the bed. He was so heavy. I couldn't see past his shoulders, his wild eyes. I clawed at his hand, his shoulder, struggled as I sank further into the bed under his weight.

And then the door opened, the light turned on and Tiffany burst in.

"What's going on here?" She stared at us in horror.

Dad jerked away from me, so quick it made my head spin.

"What the hell is wrong with you?" he screamed at me, alert all of a sudden. Not the groping, sloppy drunk he was a minute before. "Dear God, why would you do that, Victoria? I'm your father, for Christ's sake!"

I stared up at him silently, too terrified to speak. Hot tears poured down my face.

"What's going on?" Tiffany yelled at my father. "What are you doing in here?"

My father whipped around to face her. "Keep your voice down, Tiffany," he hissed through gritted teeth. "Don't wake Sarah. She doesn't need to see this."

Tiffany stared at him. "I don't understa—"

"Victoria called me in here," Dad panted, adjusting his shirt. "Pulled me in here, pulled me down on top of, dear God, I can't even believe . . ."

He looked at me in absolute disgust and my throat closed and I was choking, choking and crying and not seeing or knowing what to do.

Tiffany raised her hands to cover her mouth.

Dad's face turned grim, and I didn't recognize him. Who was this man pretending to be my father? *How could he do this?*

"I should have told you before," Dad said to Tiffany. "The things she's said, the things she's tried to do," he sputtered. "I was just trying to protect my daughter. But it's gone too far. She needs help."

My voice was raw, my throat pulsing from the sharp pain in my neck where my dad grabbed me. "Dad, why are you doing thi—"

"Stay here," he barked. "I can't stand to look at you. I need to figure this out. I thought I was protecting you, but I can't anymore."

Tiffany looked confused for an instant, then disgusted. He ushered her out of the room. She didn't even look back at me. Neither of them did.

I held my knees close to my chest and cried. Minutes passed. Neither of them came back to my room. My thoughts raced, but they were jumbled, incoherent. None of it made sense.

And then Dad and Tiffany came back, and he dragged

me outside. Threw me out in the cold. Shivering, shaking, sobbing.

Before I knew it, the police officer was there. And then Fran arrived.

Inside, Tiffany glared at me like I was the most awful, horrible person in the world, then retreated to her bedroom. Dad was lying about me. Sarah was still asleep in her bedroom. I was in a daze. None of this could be real, I thought. It isn't real. That was the last time I saw them.

And now, nearly three months later, I'm going back.

I walk back into the dormitory. My eyes linger on Jamie's old bunk. I wrote her a letter, even though she's not allowed visitors, calls or mail yet. I need her to know I still care, that I'm sorry. I apologized for how I acted and told her I love her.

Connie hasn't sent the letter yet but, when she does, I hope Jamie understands how sorry I am for abandoning her when she needed me most. How I won't make that mistake again, not with her and not with Sarah.

Christina should be here any minute. The weight in my chest grows heavier. It's almost nine a.m. I head out to the living room without asking. I haven't asked to enter or leave a room since what happened with Jamie, but Connie hasn't mentioned it.

"The room's ready for inspection."

Connie sits up a little off the couch, adjusting Annie on her lap. "Don't worry about it today. But thank you for cleaning up. You can just relax until your friend gets here."

"Do you want to check my bag?" I ask robotically. The doorbell rings.

"That must be her." Connie lifts Annie off her lap and walks to the door. I follow her.

"Hi, Connie!" Christina says, with exuberance I haven't seen her use before. "It's nice to meet you, finally. My mom said you said it's okay if I pick Victoria up myself. She said she called and checked with you."

"That she did," says Connie. "She assured me you're a safe driver."

"The safest."

Connie turns to me. "You got everything you need?"

"Yep." I hoist my backpack in front of me so she can see. Connie glances but doesn't do a full search. "All set."

"Well, all right then." Connie steps out of my way. "Behave yourselves. I'm trusting you both here."

"Of course, and thanks for that!" Christina says. "We'll see you tomorrow morning."

Connie pats my back and nudges me forward. "You two have fun."

I zip my bag quickly and follow Christina to her truck, parked on the side of the curb. Christina unlocks the passenger door for me and opens it. "After you."

"Thanks." I lift myself in, dumping my bag in the small interior area behind us. Christina walks around, hops into the driver's side.

"Okay, so I told my mom what we're doing."

I gasp. "What? Why?"

"Let me finish." Christina raises her hand to stop me

from interrupting. "Look, we don't know what could happen. We're going to be in a whole different town; someone needs to know where we are. I made my mom promise that if Connie calls, she'll cover for us. She'll tell her we went to eat or something. But I don't think Connie will call because they already talked on the phone yesterday. She trusts my mom."

I keep staring at Christina, knowing it's too late to make a difference but still trying to form some kind of argument. "You should have checked with me first."

Christina sighs, loudly. "I know you don't like my mom knowing—and she doesn't like the possibility of having to lie to another parent, or foster parent, whatever. But I told her everything and she trusts my judgment. I'm eighteen and you're almost eighteen and we are going to have to make our own decisions in college soon anyway. She trusts us, and she wants to help." Christina pats my leg. "She knew I'd go anyway, with or without her approval, because there was no way in hell I'd let you go alone."

I nod slowly. "Okay, I guess. Thank you."

I roll down the window as Christina pulls out onto the street. My chest tightens, and I take several deep breaths. "I can't believe we're actually doing this."

Christina's ponytail flips in the wind as we round the corner and head in the direction of Kale's house. Once outside, she grabs her phone. "I'll text him," she says. "I don't really want to go in there and lie to his mom. I'd feel bad."

I swallow the guilt down again.

Kale appears outside his house and heads over to us. He opens the truck door and leans in to kiss my cheek, sliding in next to me. My stomach is in knots, thinking about Sarah, thinking about Reno, and that we're driving closer to my old life. Closer to *him*.

Christina checks the map on her phone. "We'll head west for a half hour or so before changing highways. Then another forty minutes and we'll be in Carson. We have snacks here, if anyone gets hungry." She gestures to the back at a closed paper bag. "I say we head straight there."

"Yeah," I say. "Let's get this over with."

We're all quiet as Christina pulls the truck into the road. Kale plugs his phone into the cigarette lighter and puts on some music.

The road stretches before us and eventually we turn onto Highway 395. The wind whips Christina's ponytail onto my shoulder and the music blares from the speakers. With no Connie, social worker, or anyone like that around, under any other circumstances, I imagine I'd feel free.

Instead, it feels like the air is being slowly squeezed out of my chest until there's hardly any left. Dad isn't going to be there, I tell myself. It'll just be Sarah meeting me at a park nearby, without him or Tiffany knowing a thing about it. There's nothing to worry about.

We stop in Carson for a bathroom break. Each moment seems like an hour, the minutes slowly ticking by on the car's clock. My stomach's gone from twisting in knots to gurgling. Back in the pickup, I close my eyes and lean into Kale and will the time to go faster, will everything to be all right.

Eventually, Christina fidgets beside me, handing me her phone. "You should probably call Sarah."

I dial the number and hold my breath.

Sarah picks up after the fourth ring. "Hey," she says, her voice sounding uncertain.

"It's Victoria. I need to see you."

Silence. A few seconds later, Sarah breathes audibly.

"I'm just outside of Carson on the way to Reno, so we can talk in person, like you said. Do you think you can get out of the house?"

"My mom and your dad are planning to go out for lunch. I'll tell them I'd rather stay home."

I place a hand on my chest, the tightness almost over-whelming me. "You guys are still living in the same house, right?" That used to be my house with my parents. My dad and mom.

"Yeah." Sarah sounds unsure, worried even as she asks slowly, "Do you want to come over?"

"No, no," I answer quickly. "I can meet you nearby, though. How about the park?"

We agree to meet there in about a half hour before hanging up.

I give the phone to Christina. "What are you going to say to her?" Christina asks.

"I don't know." My voice falters. "I think I'll just ask her if my dad has hurt her in any way. And tell her to tell CPS he's making her uncomfortable at home at the very least."

Nobody says anything for a while after that. I direct Christina to the exit to get off the highway, the wind blowing my hair into my face as she drives. Christina pulls the truck into the park's entrance and finds a spot toward the end of the lot, nearest the picnic benches and grill. The breeze picks up. Rays of sunlight cut through the clouds as leaves from the surrounding trees flutter in the wind. The three of us get out of the truck. "She should be here soon," Kale says as we step on the grass toward the benches. "We can sit here and wait with you."

"I have to do this alone."

"Of course," Christina says. "We won't be far away. We'll just go check out the rest of the park." She reaches her phone toward me. "Here, take my cell phone, just in case."

"Wait," Kale says. Christina glares at him, and he shakes his head at her, before coming back to me. "Why can't we stay with you?"

"I need to do this alone," I repeat. "I haven't seen my stepsister since the night CPS took me away. I'll be fine."

I take Christina's phone. Kale hugs me, and I rest in his warm chest for a moment. "Call us if you need us," he says as I pull away.

Christina hugs me, too. "We won't be far."

I watch as they walk past the climbing gym and toward the shady area with trees and a running stream. Once they're out of sight, I sit on the top of the nearest table, dangling my legs over the faded blue bench. Sarah and I used to come here sometimes to get away from our parents. I put my head in my hands.

"Victoria?"

Sarah's blonde hair whips in the wind at the edge of the lawn where it meets the parking lot. She's taller than before.

I stand, my heart thumping in my chest. "Sarah!"

Sarah's pace quickens. She holds her leopard purse tighter to her body. I take in the rest of her—purple tights, a plaid skirt and fitted coat.

Sarah drops her bag on the bench and hugs me. "Are you okay?"

I nod as I pull away. "Are you?"

The wind blows Sarah's choppy bangs into her face again and she tucks them behind her ear. "I heard you got into trouble and went to juvie for a night."

I swallow. She didn't answer me. "How'd you know that?"

"Your social worker told your dad, during one of her visits. I overheard him telling my mom. He said—" Sarah stops, looking embarrassed.

The pain in my chest returns. "Why didn't you tell Mindy what Dad was saying about me wasn't true?" The words escape my lips before I realize I'm even saying them. "Why didn't you stick up for me?"

Sarah looks down and shakes her head. "I don't know. My mom," she stammers, "she said your dad was telling the truth, and she was so sure of it. And she's my mom. I—I—I'm sorry. I didn't know what to do."

Her eyes well up.

"My mom—I'm sure you're mad at her, but she feels guilty," Sarah pleads. "I can tell she does. I think she's afraid he'll leave her if she makes a big deal about it. They fight all the time. He's always screaming at her. But she won't leave, even though I've asked her to."

My stomach clenches. Part of me doesn't want to know the answer to the question I know I have to ask. "What about what you said on the phone? He's been saying weird things, like what? Has he done anything else?"

Sarah twists her hands closer to her body, and keeps talking, as if she didn't hear me. "Your dad insisted you're disturbed—that you need help, and that being around him will make it worse. But Mindy asked all these questions about him, and he told me to not trust her. And I just didn't understand any of it." She takes a deep breath and looks away. "And then he started to act . . . and it's not right, Victoria. I know it's not right what he's doing. But . . ." She hesitates and starts to cry. "I don't know what to do."

I pull her back into a hug and hold still a moment. "What is it, Sarah?" I ask her softly. "What happened? What did he do?"

Her whole body shakes against me. "I can't. I can't say it," Sarah cries into my shoulder. "I can't tell you, Victoria. I can't tell anyone."

Every fear I've had but pushed down flashes through my mind quickly.

I need to tell her what really happened to me if I have a hope of getting the truth out of her.

I hold Sarah upright so I can see her face.

"Sarah, I was too scared to tell anyone." I look at her trembling lips and wild eyes and I know she feels terrified and alone, just like I did. "I didn't do anything. He was always watching me, saying things, I just didn't know what to say or do to make it stop."

Sarah inhales sharply and snaps her eyes shut.

"I thought maybe it was in my head, or if I told someone they wouldn't believe me," I go on. "I was afraid. And then he tried to kiss me, he *did* kiss me, he put his hands on me, down my pajamas, and I'm afraid if your mom hadn't walked in he would have . . . I swear I didn't want it. But he said it was me, trying to make a pass at him or something. That there was something wrong with me, that I was sick."

Sarah's crying harder, gasping in between her sobs. I grab her shoulders. "Sarah, what happened? Did he do something to you?"

She looks at me and shakes her head, over and over, until suddenly she stops. "He does things, and I say no. But I'm so scared of him."

Heat shoots through me. I bite my lip, clench my fists, hate him. Hate him. Hate him. "We need to go." I wipe the tears off her face. "We'll take you home and you can pack a bag, but you're coming with us. I won't let him hurt you, not anymore."

She backs away from me, her shaking shoulders moving just out of my reach. "We'll talk more," I say, my hands suspended in the air toward her. "We'll figure this all out. Please just trust me, we need to get you away from there."

Sarah shakes her head. "I–I can't just leave. What about my mom? I can't leave her with him. He'll hurt her!"

My breath catches. The bruises. He's hurting Tiffany already, I bet.

And I'm shaking my head, too, forming an argument out loud as I think of it. "Sarah, she has to see, she has to believe . . . If you leave with me now, then she'll wonder why. And you can tell her, from a safe distance away." My voice strengthens. "Your mom will have no choice but to listen to you, to look into what you're saying. To *believe* you. If you're not there, she'll know you're serious."

I swallow down disgust. That we even have to think of a way to make our stories believable is sickening. But what choice do we have?

Sarah takes a deep breath, and nods, like she's thinking. She looks up at the sky, and stops crying. "They're at lunch across town. We have at least a half hour."

I take out Christina's phone and call Kale.

Kale answers after the first ring. "Is everything okay? What happened?"

"I'm fine, Kale," I say. "Sarah's coming with us back to Silver Valley. There's no time to explain. We have to go to my old house and get her stuff and go, quick, before our parents get home."

"That doesn't sound like a good—"

"We don't have time." I cut him off. "Just come now. Meet us at the truck." I hang up.

"You're sure they're at lunch?"

Sarah nods and wipes a fresh round of tears off her face. "I'm sure."

We rush to the parking lot. I hear Christina and Kale behind us as we reach the truck.

I turn around, and Christina hugs me. "Are you okay?"

"I'm fine." I let her go and nod at Sarah. "This is Sarah. Let's get her stuff. I'll explain later."

Christina and Kale share a worried glance, but I give them a look. They can't fight me on this. We pile into the truck, Sarah half sitting on my lap as she and I both lean against the closed window.

The ride to the house is short, my chest feeling heavier and tighter the closer we get. Christina parks on the street in front of the house. I start to follow Sarah out of the truck, but Kale grabs my arm, stopping me. "What if your dad comes home?"

I pull my arm back. "We just need a few minutes."

Christina unbuckles her seatbelt. "He's right, Victoria. This doesn't feel safe. At least let us come in with you."

Sarah's voice comes out shaky. "I can go by myself. I'll be right back," she says, unsteady.

"I'm going with you." I put my arm around her. "You two stay out here to keep watch."

Christina leans back into her seat, resigned. I slide out before Kale can say anything else and shut the door.

I follow Sarah up the driveway, walking behind her as she unlocks the door and goes inside. As I inhale the familiar ocean breeze air conditioner smell, my throat constricts and the hairs on my arms stand up. There's the same leather couch. The same island in the kitchen. The cabinet where my dad keeps his whiskey.

I shake my head, trying to think clearly. Sarah heads to her room, and I follow her. I can't fall apart now. There's no time.

She pulls her backpack out of the closet and dumps everything out of it onto the floor. We open drawers and grab clothes quickly, just like I did months before when Dad kicked me out. Sarah hands me her backpack, now full of clothes. "I just need to grab my contacts. They're in the bathroom."

As she rounds the hallway corner, Christina's phone buzzes in my hand.

"We're just about done, just give us a sec—"

Kale interrupts, "Victoria, there's a Prius pulling up in your driveway."

I hear a door slam and muffled voices. A voice I haven't heard in months but would recognize anywhere. "Can I help you with something?"

I hold the phone, paralyzed.

Kale hasn't hung up yet. I hear Christina answer. "Nope, just hanging out, parked on the street. It's a free country."

I drop the phone to my side. "Sarah, they're here."

Even though I'm not holding the phone to my ear, I can hear Kale whispering fiercely. "You need to get out of there. Now."

Sarah wheels around the corner, a small bag in her hand, and stares at me. I move next to her in the hallway just as the knob to the front door starts to turn, and then opens.

My father.

As he walks toward us, I see that he's wearing the same black track pants he wore that night in my room. And it's like I'm back there. I can smell the whiskey again, I can smell his cologne—I can smell him, coming closer, forcing his lips on mine. And I want to get away from here. But my feet feel as though they weigh a thousand pounds, and my body won't listen to my mind, screaming for me to run.

I can't get enough air in my lungs, even though I'm gasping for it. I can't. It's all happening again. Dad is here. He's here.

Sarah steps back, looking smaller and smaller.

"Victoria." He looks at me with sad eyes, frowning. Like I'm hurt, like he's worried or something. Like he cares.

He sees the backpack in my hands. "What are you doing?"

Sarah looks at me, her mouth open but nothing coming out.

I don't know, I don't know, I don't know. We haven't seen each other in months. Not since—

"Sarah," my dad says softly, "go to your room. I'm sorry she brought you into all of this." He reaches for Sarah's arm, but she yanks it away from him. "Don't touch me! Don't ever touch me again!" she screams.

Tiffany appears behind Dad, leaving the door open. "Just get out of here, okay! This doesn't concern you," she calls in the direction of the street. She steps around Dad and her face contorts with shock once she sees Sarah so upset. Tiffany practically lunges for her daughter.

"Are you okay, baby?"

Sarah cries and shakes in her mother's arms, one of which has black-and-blue bruises on it. And Tiffany's collarbone is bruised, too, just like that time I saw her in the bathroom.

"I knew something was wrong, honey. You acted so strange when you said you didn't want to go to lunch," Tiffany says. "You weren't where you said you'd be. You weren't supposed to be at the park, but I could see it from your phone."

They tracked her phone. They knew where she was this whole time.

"Let's go," Tiffany says. "Let your father deal with this."

"He's not my father!" Sarah pushes away from her mother. "And I'm not going anywhere without Victoria."

Dad steps closer to us. "Victoria wanted to come home and visit," he says. He blinks several times, his green eyes wide, and for a second I think he's going to cry. "She missed us, and we missed you, too."

He's looking at me, and he's sad, and he's hurting and I believe him. He's missed me. Maybe he regrets what happened. Maybe he's sorry.

I stare at him, wanting to hear him say he's sorry more than I've ever wanted anything since my mom died.

Dad continues, "Let's calm down and talk about this." He holds his hands out at his sides and takes another step closer to Sarah and Tiffany. His eyes are locked on me.

Tiffany looks at me briefly. Unsure. Then she turns back to her daughter.

"Come on, let's go to the car, Sarah." She turns halfway to me. "Victoria, I'll call your foster mother."

Sarah jerks away from her again. "Mom, why would you do that? Why would you do that to her? He's been lying this whole time. Victoria didn't do anything!"

Dad's voice turns cold, his words clipped and low. "I don't know what Victoria's told you—"

Without meaning to, I step back. All of this is wrong. How could he say that? What *I've* told Sarah, not what *he* did? He's not sorry.

I can see Dad starting to get mad, his jaw clenching and the vein in his neck bulging. Getting mad the way he did when I didn't do what he wanted, or Mom didn't do what he wanted. Before she fell in line and did what she was told.

I'm shaking my head and tasting the salt of my tears and squeezing my eyes shut but Dad's still here and he's still not telling the truth.

"He's not going to stop," I say more to myself than to anyone else. Sarah pulls away from Tiffany and backs away from both of them. Tiffany seems to track my father's movements; each time he moves closer to Sarah, Tiffany adjusts herself to stand in front of her daughter.

Dad's voice shakes. "You see, Tiffany? This is exactly what I was afraid of. Victoria's lies, her turning Sarah against me."

He looks right at me, and his green eyes are watery, like he believes every bit of the crap he's saying.

"This is why we had to send you away, Victoria."

"Y-You're lying," I stutter. "It's not true."

Tiffany reaches for Sarah, only for Sarah to slip out of her reach.

Dad takes a deep breath, and his face seems to relax. No more bulging vein. Just plain sadness. "Take her to the car and let me deal with my daughter." His voice breaks on the last word.

Tiffany's eyes dart around at each of us.

I stare at my stepmother, needing her to believe me. She needs to finally see. "He's the one—"

"Sarah," Tiffany interrupts, looking at her daughter, "we need to go."

"No!" I shout, surprising even myself, and Tiffany flinches.

A horn blares loudly from outside. Christina and Kale. They honk it twice more.

Sarah backs farther away from Tiffany. I grab Sarah's hand. "She's coming with me." I make myself sound firm, sure and strong. "She's not going to stay another minute in this house."

Sarah holds my hand tighter. "I'm leaving with them, Mom," she says. "I'm not staying here, not with him."

Tiffany's voice is barely higher than a whisper. "Why?"

My dad shakes his head and forces forward. He grabs Sarah by the arm, wrenching her away from me. "Listen to your mother," he says. I reach after Sarah, but Tiffany gets there first, shoving my dad's hand away.

"Why doesn't my daughter want to stay here?" she snaps. "Tell me right now. What's going on?"

Dad doesn't answer. His face is wracked with grief, not anger.

"Victoria, I know you must be jealous of Sarah, that's why you've concocted all of this, made up this story in your head. And now Sarah believes it, too." Dad sniffs, but I don't see any tears. "Just know I haven't forgotten about you. I've missed you so much since you left. It's natural for Sarah and me to get closer, just like you and I did after your mother died. But I always planned, when you turned eighteen, for you to come home, for us to forget everything with CPS, to forget what you did."

"What *I* did?" My hands shake. "*What I did?*"

My hands are shaking, my shoulders are shaking, the world is shaking around me.

I'm not hoping if I say or do the right thing he'll be happy. I'm not going to protect him. And I'm not pretending anymore.

"You," I push through gritted teeth. "You, *Dad,* you are the one who did this, did everything." My heart bangs against my chest, my voice growing louder. "You stared at me, watched me sleep, compared me to your wife." I glare at Tiffany, for an instant feeling the hate I felt for her, too, when she didn't help me, when she believed my dad over her own eyes that night. But this isn't about her, it's about the man I am staring at now, really seeing for the very first time.

"You kissed me," I force out. "Groped me, touched me where no father should ever, ever even think about touching his daughter. You threw me down, you tried to, tried to, tried . . . I still can't even say it! I can't even say what you would have done if Tiffany hadn't walked in!"

"That's enough!" Dad roars. He's shaking, too, and in an instant I think of how we are father and daughter, alike in this small way, shaking when we are so upset. Bile rises in my throat.

But I won't let him stop me from telling the truth, I won't let him silence me, not this time. Not ever again.

"You are the sick one, the liar. You are the one who needs help. And I went along with it, thinking you didn't mean it, you were sad and lonely. I was supposed to take care of you for Mom, but I was wrong. And so was she."

It all started before, when Dad controlled Mom, when she showed me it was her job to make him happy, and then it was mine. When she trained me to put up with it.

I glare at my father. "You were supposed to take care of me, but you didn't. And now look at you. I'm gone but you're the same." I slash my arm across the air in front of me. "You tossed me aside like nothing happened, like I was nothing, and moved right along to Sarah. Didn't you, didn't you, Dad?"

"No."

I turn to see Tiffany, tears spilling down her cheeks. "No," she repeats, more to herself, I think, than to any of us.

Tiffany looks at my father. Her face crumbles, like she sees what her husband is, what she couldn't face that night she walked in on him attacking me.

Sarah's voices comes out louder, stronger. "He told me he'd hurt you, Mom, if I told you the truth, and that it would be no use since you'd never leave him. And that no one would believe me."

Like a switch has flipped, Tiffany springs to action. "We're leaving," she says to Sarah. And then to me, "I don't know what's going on. I–I don't know," she stutters. "Just come with me, come with Sarah and me. We'll figure this out." She reaches for my hand, and I let her take it.

Dad's eyes dart between Tiffany and me, his nostrils flaring. "You can't leave. You can't leave me."

Tiffany recoils, a look of sheer disgust on her face. Dad lunges for her. Tiffany shoves him off, but he snatches at her other wrist, ripping it from me and twisting it behind her back.

"Dad, no!" I shout.

"Get off of her!" Sarah shrieks.

I hear the doors to the truck slam loudly. Kale and Christina run through the open door, whirling by my dad. Relief rushes through me as they flank me on both sides.

"We've called the cops!" Kale holds the phone in my dad's face. "Domestic dispute, they're going to be here any second!"

Tiffany yanks her wrist back, and Dad glowers at all of us, his teeth gritted and hands clenched. Tiffany stands up straighter, her voice rough. "Get away from us."

Something fills my dad's eyes as they land back on me. Not love, or sadness, or a trace of the twisted desire he once had. He's furious. Because still, after all this time, he blames me for the way that he is. Just like he blamed Mom for his jealousy over our relationship, and like he probably blamed Tiffany for when he hurt her.

"Are you happy now, Victoria?" he says, his eyes welling. "Is this what you wanted?"

A shock of sympathy hits me. Dad is the same depressed man, the same person who needed me, needed my help.

No.

He sent me away for something he did wrong. And he

lied about it. He turned my entire life upside down. And yet, he's not sorry.

My memory flashes to him kissing my knee better when I scraped it, to us crying together when Mom died. It was us against the world. Back then, I thought that's how it would always be.

My chin quivers.

I look at my father, my dad. Daddy.

And then I remember him pushing me away from him, screaming at me that I was sick. Lying to everyone. The slam of the door as he closed it on me, left me with Fran. Left me.

"We're leaving." I say. "I didn't do this. You did."

Dad stumbles backward again, until he's just in front of the door. I fight back the tears. I won't waste any more on him. "I'm not afraid of you anymore. I'm going to tell the police what happened. And I bet Tiffany and Sarah will, too."

Dad's green eyes blink quickly, like he's dazed. "I thought you loved me." His face crumples, every bit as lost as when Mom died. "You can't mean any of this."

Then he looks at Tiffany. "You can't believe what she's saying?"

I don't say anything. None of us do.

Because it isn't just me in my room with my dad, when I was all alone, when I worried it was my fault what he did to me. It's me, Sarah, and Tiffany—together, not his victims anymore—and Christina and Kale.

We hold onto each other, standing strong on one side this time. My dad's on his own. He can't hurt me. He can't hurt Sarah. We won't let him.

My father stumbles back onto the door frame. He regains his footing, turns and heads to the Prius. We all watch silently as he drives away.

CHAPTER
TWENTY-ONE

One week later

"*I* suppose since we finished the lesson early today, it won't kill us to have some small talk," Santa says, standing in front of the whiteboard in history class Monday morning. "How was everyone's weekend? Any car chases? Did you save any damsels in distress—or did any damsels save you from distress?" He winks at Christina.

Christina grins at me—we didn't do anything this weekend but binge-watch Netflix and eat ice cream at her house. She fakes a yawn in Santa's direction.

Santa places a hand on his belly and leans back dramatically. "Oh, you're such a boring bunch. I can't wait to get rid of all of you when you go off to college or join the circus or whatever you have in mind." He smiles at me.

Out of the corner of my eye, I see Taylor's hand shoot up from her desk behind me.

"Yes?" Santa asks her.

"Lauren and I just got accepted to Berkeley."

She nudges Lauren beside her. Alex gives a blushing Lauren a high-five. "Whoot, whoot!"

Christina nods in Lauren's direction and they smile awkwardly at each other. I catch Lauren's eye and start clapping with the rest of the class.

"Well, that's just wonderful news," Santa says. "Congratulations! Don't forget us when you're rich and famous!"

Taylor beams at the applause. Lauren looks down at her desk, fighting a smile, and murmurs, "Thanks."

"And I thought Taylor would stay here forever, causing drama and popping out babies," Christina whispers in my ear. "You think you know someone."

I keep clapping. Taylor is Taylor, but at least she'll be moving to California and not Reno.

The classroom phone rings. "Behave yourselves for just a moment, we wouldn't want anyone to think we're learning in here." Santa walks over to pick up the phone.

"So, you're not concerned about long distance for you and Alex?" I whisper to Christina, watching Alex and Zach chat with Lauren and Taylor out of the corner of my eye.

Santa nods into the receiver. "Yes, yes. Of course."

"No," Christina whispers back. "I decided I'm ending things with him. I don't want to bring any relationship baggage with me to D.C."

My eyes pop, although I shouldn't really be surprised. Christina continues, "It's not like Alex and I were madly in love, and I'm going to need to focus at Georgetown."

Her acceptance letter came in the mail last Saturday,

when we were gone. Her mom gave it to her when we got back from Reno after we called Connie and Christina and Kale's parents to tell them we had to go to the police station to file a report.

Santa hangs up the phone. "Ms. Parker, your presence is requested in the principal's office."

"Oooh," the class collectively says.

Christina lifts an eyebrow at me, and I shrug. "What fresh hell could this be?" I whisper to her.

I grab my bag and head out the door, hearing each step I take on the linoleum ring in my ears. I pass my blue locker, the same locker Kale used to hover by when I first moved here. I look at the door to the girl's bathroom, where I vomited because I was so worried about what would happen if I came face to face with my dad.

I pass by the bench I sat and waited for Connie on, the gym where we had the dance, and the hallway I walked out of with the sheriff's deputy to get arrested. Across the hallway is Ms. Claire's guidance counselor office, where we talked about my future and I started to believe it all could really happen.

Last time I was here, I had no way of knowing I'd come face to face with my dad again, that he'd storm off when the truth came out. Between Tiffany filing a domestic violence report for the bruises my dad gave her and Sarah and I telling the police about what he did to us—for weeks he had been doing the same kinds of things to Sarah that he did to me and threatening her to keep her from telling—that was enough to get my dad locked up for a couple of nights.

He's out on bail, staying in a hotel room or somewhere, since Tiffany kicked him out of the house. If the district attorney takes him to trial for charges of sexual assault on a minor, I might be asked to testify.

My throat tightens. I keep walking until I reach Becca at her position at the front desk.

"Principal Nelson wants to see me?"

"Yes, dear," Becca says. "Not to worry. You're not in any trouble."

Mr. Nelson walks out of his office. "Come on in, Victoria." He opens the door wider, ushering me in with him. "Have a seat."

I sit in the single chair across from his desk and cross my legs. And then uncross them.

Mr. Nelson clears his throat. "I heard you had"—he pauses for a beat—"an *eventful* weekend recently."

I sit up in my chair. "How'd you know about that?"

Mr. Nelson tilts his head, raising his bushy eyebrows at me.

I stifle a nervous laugh. "Right, small town. Got it."

Mr. Nelson clears his throat again and picks a pencil off his cluttered-as-usual desk. He taps the eraser end on the wood in front of him. "Yes. Word travels fast, although not so fast that I'm not a week behind on hearing the news." He sighs. "I take it since you're still attending school, everything is all right between you and your foster mother? You're here, after all, and not in juvenile hall."

Mr. Nelson stops tapping the pencil and looks at me.

"I'm fine. Everything's okay with Connie. I'm not in any trouble."

Mr. Nelson exhales, and sets the pencil down. "Good, I'm glad to hear it. There would be no justice in seeing one of our best students hauled off by the police, not once, but twice in one semester."

He cracks a smile and stands, and I do, too. "You know," I say. "Connie's not *all* bad. Once you get to know her."

Mr. Nelson's eyes widen in surprise for a second, before he grins. "Sometimes people have a way of surprising you. Don't they?"

I nod and turn halfway to open the door, but pause, with my hand on the doorknob. "Thanks, Mr. Nelson. For everything."

The bell rings. Seconds later I hear the sounds of students shuffling to and from class.

Mr. Nelson clears his throat. "Now, now. Don't go getting all sappy on me, Victoria." He chuckles. "We still have a couple months until you graduate and get the heck out of Dodge. But I'll be expecting you to keep in touch with us back here in the middle of nowhere. You think you can manage that?"

I nod vigorously.

"Yes, yes, I can."

Outside Becca's front-desk station, Kale and Christina are waiting for me.

"So, what happened?" Kale asks. "Everything okay?"

We start walking to the hallway. "Mr. Nelson just wanted to check in on me. He heard about what happened in Reno."

"That was nice of him," Christina says. We head for Christina's locker.

"So, your birthday's coming up soon." Kale grabs my hand. "You'll be eighteen, so we can do something fun without having to be all secret agent about it."

Christina opens her locker, puts a book away. "Something fun, like what?" She raises an eyebrow at Kale. "Cow tipping?"

"I was actually thinking you both could come over to my house and binge-watch *Sherlock* before watching me play video games. All while telling me how amazing I am," Kale says with a grin, before taking a big step away from Christina.

She smacks his shoulder. I laugh, getting out of Christina's way. "All right, all right," I say. "I think I can come up with something to do for my own birthday!"

Christina adjusts the strap of her bag on her shoulder. "What do you have in mind?" The hallway is thinning out, the second bell about to ring.

"Something boring, something low-key," I say. "I could definitely use a little less excitement in my life for the foreseeable future."

Kale chuckles. "Boring—what we all strive to be."

"Honestly, it doesn't matter what we do," I say, "as long as we're together."

Christina and Kale keep walking down the hallway, but I reach for Kale's arm, stopping him.

"Can we talk for a minute?"

Christina looks over her shoulder at us. "See you at lunch."

As she rounds the corner, I gesture for Kale to follow me outside the double doors, toward the bench.

We sit quietly for a moment. I scratch my head, not sure where to start.

I look into Kale's blue eyes and watch the way the light shines on his face, making his freckles more noticeable. I take his hand in mine.

"Kale, through everything, my keeping secrets, lying, getting so mad all the time, I still sometimes can't believe you've stood by me."

Kale interrupts. "Victoria, not this again. It's not like I'm doing you some big favor or something. I like you, a lot, I want to—"

"Let me finish," I say, and my mouth turns up on one side. Kale chuckles.

"You've been great, and I just want you to know how much it's meant to me, having you . . ." I hesitate, run my thumb against his. "Just having you with me through all of this." I look up into Kale's eyes as I feel mine beginning to water.

Kale stares back at me. After a moment, his eyes are looking a little misty, too.

The wind blows one of my curls into my face, and Kale tucks it behind my ear.

"I'd follow you anywhere," he says. "Except TMCC, because, you know, I'll be at UNR. But in between playing Frisbee on the quad and beer pong in the dorms, I think I can pencil you into my schedule. Next year, that is. As you like to remind me, I'm still merely a junior, after all."

I laugh, shaking my head at him.

"You better make time for me," I say, and Kale's eyes widen slightly. Because I'm telling him I'm planning on there being an *us* in a couple of years when he gets to college. Or at least hoping there will be. "That is, if you don't get sick of having your college girlfriend coming back to visit you in Silver Valley by then."

Kale's grin lights up his entire face. He kisses me. I smile against his lips. When we break apart, rising to head to class, I'm already counting the minutes until the end of the period when I can kiss him again.

CHAPTER
TWENTY-TWO

"*Y*ou ready?" Connie asks me a few weeks later, buckling herself into the driver's seat of her mini-van.

"As I'll ever be." I settle in for the drive to Reno, to see Tiffany and Sarah at their house. They invited me to dinner for a late birthday celebration. I'm eighteen now, an adult. And still living with Connie.

It's not so bad now that I'm eighteen and there aren't as many rules. I can stay the night at Christina's house, talk on the phone—I even called Jess and told her what happened. Turns out my dad lied to her, too. He told her I'd run away to be with my secret boyfriend. Jess didn't believe it, of course, and she asked her parents to find out what really happened. But they wouldn't intervene. Jess promised she never lost hope, though, and she prayed for me to be safe and to come home soon.

Connie and I drive through Silver Valley, the little town that I hated so much when I moved here. We pass the crosswalk where the juniors from my school were walking and laughing while I slunk down in the backseat of a cop car. We drive by the two-story brick building with a sign out front that says Silver Valley Juvenile Detention Center, where I spent one of the worst nights of my life, second only to the night Dad assaulted me.

Connie glances at me. "You're sure you're okay with having dinner at that house? With all those memories?"

I swallow. Dad won't be there, obviously, but Tiffany will be: the woman who didn't believe me, who helped my father kick me out of their lives. What happened to me and Sarah happened right under her nose. And she said she was sorry, and she feels terrible, but that doesn't undo what happened.

"I want to see Sarah," I say. "And I want to get some of my stuff out of my room."

I unclench my fists, close my eyes, take a breath and look back at Connie. She flips her turn signal on, then pulls onto the freeway.

Even if my father doesn't go to jail forever—last I heard, he's still out on bail—he blames me. Dad won't be there to see me graduate from high school in a couple of months, or send me off to college.

I look up to stop my eyes from watering. Connie glances at me but doesn't say anything. I wish I could hate him. I thought I would, but I can't forget all the good times we had too, with Mom. I blink a few times. I knew this wouldn't be easy.

But I'm done with him.

Connie sighs. "It's okay to be angry, you know."

"I know," I say. "And I am." I roll the window up so she can hear me better. Connie looks back to the road.

"But my dad lied to Tiffany, too," I go on. "She thought I wanted them to break up, that I hated her." I close my eyes and fight to keep my voice steady. "I know she should have given me a chance to tell her my side of the story. But we all could have done things differently."

I stare out the window and watch the dry, vast hills as we pass them. "If Sarah can forgive me for not pressing charges when I should have in the first place, I"—I pause, and try to push away the tightness I feel in my gut—"I can forgive Tiffany for believing my dad and helping him keep me away."

I turn back to Connie. Her eyebrows furrow. "It's not your fault. What happened to Sarah, Victoria, it's not your fault."

I nod, wanting so badly to believe her. We both gaze ahead. The closer we get to Reno, the more small cars replace trucks on the road.

"I'm sorry I didn't tell you where I was going. I'm sorry you're under investigation." After it all went down, Connie told Mindy she gave me permission to visit Sarah, even though I wasn't allowed. I don't think Mindy actually believes her—she probably guessed Connie was trying to keep me out of trouble—but rules are rules and now, Connie and her home are under investigation by CPS.

Connie shakes her head. "Oh, come on, girl. Part of me wishes you would have asked me first, but I wouldn't have let you go, so I understand." She exhales. "What are they going to do, anyhow? Take my foster parent license? Not likely. They might just make me change the way I run my house, which I'm sure you wouldn't mind one bit."

I try not to let Connie see me smile. She laughs.

If Jamie could see us now.

"Thank you, Connie," I say, twisting my hands in my lap, "and not just for that. For going to bat for me to talk to Jamie on the phone. I know she wasn't supposed to get phone calls yet, until later in her treatment, but it meant so much to me."

Connie's face turns serious as she nods. She still feels guilty about Jamie. We both do.

I think back to my call with Jamie a few days ago. She was so surprised to hear from me.

"Victoria!" She breathed audibly into the phone. "I didn't think you'd call, not yet anyway. Especially after what I said about your dad. I'm so sorry."

"No," I interrupted. "You have nothing to be sorry for. I'm the one who's sorry. I'm sorry I was so cruel to you, I didn't know—" I stopped myself. "It doesn't matter that I didn't know what you were going through. I should have seen you were struggling. I should have listened better. Been there for you."

Jamie had gone quiet for a moment. Her voice was full of emotion when she answered. "Thank you, Victoria."

We sat in silence, both of us probably crying. I was, at least. Until Jamie filled me in about life at the treatment center. About reading and reflection time, group therapy, individual therapy, art therapy.

"Sounds like a lot of therapy," I said with a laugh.

Jamie laughed, too. "Yeah, you should try it sometime. It really helps."

I chuckled. She might have a point. "Maybe I'll look into it after I'm away at school."

"I'm understanding so much more," Jamie said, "about so many things. About how the way I think and feel about myself isn't true. It's just lies I started to believe after other people didn't treat me well."

That might make two of us. But things were getting better for Jamie, it sounded like, and for me, too. We were both ready for a fresh start.

"You'll come see me, when I'm allowed visitors, won't you?" Jamie sounded nervous, her voice high pitched.

"Of course, Jamie. Nothing in the world could stop me."

I lean my head against the van window. So much has happened this year. It's still hard to wrap my head around it sometimes. Connie clears her throat, bringing me out of my head, back into the now with her.

"Victoria," she says. "There's something I need to say."

I turn to face Connie, watch her seem to struggle to find the words.

"You may not know this, but it's not easy for me when . . ." She shakes her head, clears her throat and starts again. "The way I do things, it's to teach you kids discipline, but it's also for me. It's also so I can protect myself from becoming too close to you kids. It's hard for me sometimes when you leave. I couldn't keep doing this if my heart breaks open each time, even though sometimes I can't help it."

Connie smiles sheepishly, pats my leg and then quickly puts her hand back on the wheel. She chuckles. "Oh, well. So things will change a little bit, but that isn't necessarily a bad thing. Maybe when you come back and visit, after you graduate, you'll think my place isn't half bad!"

Connie stares straight ahead at the road. After a moment she steals a side-glance at me.

"When I come visit?" I say belatedly.

"Oh, come on, girl. You'd better. I'll be wanting to hear all about your college adventures."

She turns off the freeway exit and looks back at me, waiting for an answer.

"Yeah, I'll come visit you," I say. My voice gets stronger. "I'll come back to Silver Valley."

"Good," Connie says. "I'll even cook dinner!" She laughs, and I do, too.

"That," I say happily, "I would like to see."

AFTER

*M*indy's sitting on the couch inside my old house when Tiffany opens the door to let me in.

My body tenses. Last time I was here with Fran, the other social worker, things didn't go so well for me.

I shake my head. *They did*, I just didn't see it as good back then. But getting away from my father was the best thing for me. I have to remember that.

Behind the open door, Tiffany smiles at me meekly. "So good to see you, Victoria. Come in."

I turn to Connie's van running in the driveway and wave. She begins to pull the car out, heading to a diner nearby to get some food and wait for me so she can take me home.

Home. That's where I feel home is, back in Silver Valley with Connie. Not in this house, with Tiffany and Sarah.

"Where's Sarah?" I look around Tiffany to see Mindy sitting on the couch alone. "She's supposed to have dinner with us, right?"

Tiffany extends a hand out for me to join them in the living room. "She is. She's in her room right now. She'll come out after we have the chance to talk with Mindy."

I walk toward Mindy. I'm not sure why, but I have the sense that she wants to hug me. I sit next to her before she gets the chance. Tiffany sits on the other couch.

Mindy pulls a folder out of her purse and hands it to me. "This packet has the contact information for several nonprofits that provide resources for former foster children after they age out of the system." Mindy flips the folder open, pointing to the first page. "The first nonprofit on the list can help you get additional funding for housing, if you need it, and the second can help you get school supplies, counseling services, and further career training."

I flip through the first few pages in the packet to see a couple other documents that have information on budgeting and life skills. "Thanks."

Mindy looks around the living room for a moment, before tilting her head in my direction. "I know Connie covered for you. I'm sure she didn't give you permission to come here to speak to Sarah."

Tiffany sits up in her seat. "I don't think that's necessary."

"I'm not saying you're in trouble," Mindy blurts. "Connie is, but she's an adult and she made a choice and knows the consequences." Mindy raises her eyebrows at me. "If she *is* covering for you, I think that says a lot about her character, wouldn't you say?"

I stare at Mindy without answering. I lift the packet up. "Well, thanks for dropping this off."

Mindy's face flushes. "Victoria, I know you and I haven't always seen eye to eye, and I wish you would have trusted me enough to tell me the truth about your father."

Tiffany sighs audibly. I smile at her, without meaning to.

"But I understand why you didn't," Mindy continues. She looks from me to Tiffany and back. "The way I saw it was that you were safe at Connie's, so I focused my efforts on what was happening in this home with your father still in it, wanting to get the truth out of Sarah and Tiffany and make sure they were okay. But I wish it wasn't at your expense, and I'm sorry for that."

Mindy and Tiffany share a meaningful glance.

I nod, but don't say anything. A long, awkward silence fills the room.

Mindy stands. "I guess I better be going then. I have a few more monthly visits I have to make tonight still."

I stand, too, and exhale, relieved that Mindy's leaving. I know it's not her fault that so much has happened, but it's hard to separate her from the pain that still hasn't gone away, lodged deep and heavy in my gut. That feeling that I should be ashamed for something I didn't do, the feeling that no one would help me, even if I told.

Mindy and I stare at each other for a second before Tiffany heads to the door and opens it. "Thank you, Mindy," Tiffany says. "I really do appreciate what you've done for us."

Mindy adjusts the collar on her shirt. "Of course."

She calls to me from outside. "I'll see you at your high school graduation."

After Tiffany shuts the door, I follow her back to the couch and sit across from her. Tiffany's eyes are pleading. "I'm sorry, too, Victoria. I'm sorry I didn't see, I didn't *want* to see, what was happening under my own roof. That I didn't protect you." Her eyes well up. "I didn't protect Sarah even after you'd gone."

My throat tightens. I'm not going to tell her it's okay. It's not okay. It never will be.

"Your father, he has a way with people, a way to get what he wants, to trick people into believing every lie he says, about others, about themselves, even if you can see differently with your own eyes."

Tiffany wraps her arms around herself. I know she's talking about her situation now, the way my dad hit her, the way he made her think no one else could love her. She told me all about it that night we filed police reports on Dad.

"If I had asked you for your side of the story, if I had believed you instead of him, you could have come home. I could have saved my daughter from, from . . ."

Tiffany's sobbing uncontrollably now. Surprisingly, I have the urge to move next to her, to soothe her, to tell her everything is going to be okay. Instead, I fold my hands in my lap. That's not my job, to comfort my parents, to make their problems my own. My dad made that my job when my mom died, and even before that Mom made it my job to take care of Dad once she was gone, but it shouldn't have been. And it's not my job now, here with Tiffany.

Tiffany sniffs loudly and wipes her eyes. She gives me a small, watery smile. "I'm so glad you're here, Sarah and I both are." She inhales deeply. "Sarah!" Tiffany calls, lifting her head toward the hallway. "You can come out now."

As the door opens, I turn to see my stepsister walking toward me. Not all bounce like she was before everything happened, but the same big bangs, same kooky kind of outfit—striped black and purple dress, green tights this time.

I move toward Sarah, and we hug each other tightly.

Tiffany stands. "I'll put the casserole in the oven to reheat it."

She heads to the kitchen, leaving Sarah and me to talk.

"You okay?" Sarah asks. I wipe at my face, making sure the tears are gone.

"Are you?"

Neither of us answer.

"I'm doing better," Sarah finally says. "I'm still having nightmares, like the ones you told me you have, except they're of things that didn't happen, things that maybe your dad might have done if we hadn't turned him in."

I close my eyes. Dad had been watching and complimenting Sarah, touching her whenever he got the chance. A hand on her knee. Brushing up against her chest when he walked by. He'd pat her butt after he'd linger in on hugs and bury his face in her neck and smell her hair. He'd tell her how beautiful she was. When Sarah asked him to stop it, when she threatened to tell, he told her Tiffany wouldn't believe her. She hadn't believed he would do anything like that to me, he said, after all. And he threatened to hurt her mom. Sarah was terrified of him. Too terrified to say anything to anyone about what was going on.

Sarah told the police that just days before I called her from school Dad had kissed her, too. He tried to force himself on her the way he had with me, when Tiffany was asleep. But Sarah had reached across her bed and grabbed the remote control, turning the TV on as loud as it could go and waking Tiffany up. Dad ran to the kitchen, of course, and pretended like he was in there the whole time when Tiffany came out to see what was going on. Sarah locked her door every night after that and spent as much time at a friend's house as she could after school. The locked doors had kept her safe until I showed up the next week.

"Maybe the dreams will stop," I finally say, staring into Sarah's sad eyes, "eventually."

I still have nightmares, too. But Sarah knows that.

"You could come home, you know. Both my mom and I want you to."

This isn't home anymore.

I shake my head. "I've got a good life in Silver Valley. Friends. School. Things are going well with Connie now. I want to stay."

Sarah looks down at her feet. I can tell she's hurt by this.

"But I can come back here on the weekends sometimes, or a few holidays, once I'm living in Reno going to school. How about that?"

Sarah brightens. She wants me around, even after I left her here to fend for herself with Dad.

I force myself to stare at my stepsister now, not down at my hands or feet. To not let the sounds of Tiffany setting the table in the dining room distract me or let anything keep me from saying what needs to be said.

"Sarah, I'm so sorry. If I had told the truth, none of this would have happened to you."

Sarah blinks several times. "You don't really think that, do you? It was your dad, he's the one—"

"But if I—"

"You didn't leave, Victoria, you were kicked out." Sarah shakes her head at me. "And my mom was here. You didn't leave me alone. I was too scared to tell on your dad, too, remember?"

My bottom lip quivers. How can I believe Sarah, when I know she just wants me to feel better?

Sarah leans closer to me, and for once, I can't look away. Even though in this moment it hurts to stare at her, to stare my guilt in the face.

"It's not your fault."

I swallow the lump in my throat, and nod. Blink several times.

I wrap Sarah in a hug. "Thank you," I breathe.

"Dinner's ready!" Tiffany calls from the dining room.

Sarah and I release each other. I push Sarah's massively long bangs out of her eyes.

"I'm glad you're here," she says. "I've missed you. And honestly, no one else can understand what I'm going through now but you."

I take a long, deep breath and let it out slowly.

"Me, too," I say, meaning it with every part of me. "Me, too."

AUTHOR'S NOTE

$\mathcal{G}$rowing up, before and during my time in foster care, I didn't have a book to read like *The Quiet You Carry*. I didn't even know what foster care was, really, until I was in the system. It seemed no one around me could understand what I was going through. I felt so alone.

The Quiet You Carry is fiction. It isn't based on my life or the life of anyone I know, but it is partially inspired by circumstances I've experienced or have seen in the lives of others. Victoria isn't me, I often tell people, but her emotions are real.

According to the Adoption and Foster Care Analysis and Reporting System, in 2016 (the most recent year research was available as of this writing), there were 437,465 children in the United States foster care system.

The foster care system operates differently in each state, each county, and each city. And even under the strictest guidelines, the most rigid rules and regulations, things don't always go according to plan. This story does not necessarily reflect every situation. Victoria's story is one story. *The Quiet You Carry* isn't meant to serve as a one-size-fits-all narrative about what it's like to be in foster care. I hope to see many, many more books with foster kid protagonists because there are so many different experiences.

Reader, no matter what you're going through or have gone through, I hope you realize you aren't alone. You are not the thing that has or continues to hurt you. You matter. You are worthy of love. You are more than enough. If you are a current or former foster youth looking for community, I encourage you to check out the resources on the following pages.

I can't thank you enough for reading *The Quiet You Carry* and coming along on this journey with me. Sharing this story with you is my dream come true.

ACKNOWLEDGMENTS

$\mathcal{I}$ have so many people to thank, friends and family members who encouraged me, teachers who believed in me, and people I hardly even knew who at one point or another helped me with my writing in some way! I would thank everyone by name if had the pages, but I hope you know if you are one of the people who helped me in some "small" way—and I highly doubt it was small even if you think it was—I truly, from the bottom of my heart thank you. *The Quiet You Carry* wouldn't be sitting in your hands now without that kindness.

Hugs and endless gratitude go out to my superstar agents, Elizabeth Harding and Sarah Gerton. Elizabeth, when you first offered to represent me I didn't believe it— and I mean this literally. I thought you were just being nice because there was no way you would think my writing was good enough to represent me! Your editorial guidance has taught me so much. Thank you for never giving up on this book, and thank you for believing in me. Sarah, I don't even know where to start with you! Thank you for your amazing editorial and creative wisdom, for talking me off the ledge so many times when I thought I should give up, and for so much more. I'm honored to consider you a dear friend.

Special thanks to Olivia Simkins, Kerry Cullen, Stuart Waterman, and the rest of the fabulous team past and present at Curtis Brown, Ltd. You are rock stars!

My editor Kelsy Thompson went above and beyond my wildest dreams of what working with an editor would be like. Kelsy, your notes were always insightful and so spot-on; I could tell from the beginning that you really got Victoria's story, and every note you gave brought me closer to uncovering the heart of the book. Thank you, Kelsy! You are one-of-a-kind! Also, a big thank you to Mari Kesselring, Megan Naidl, Jake Nordby, Sonnet Fitzgerald, and the rest of the incredible team at Flux. You made my dreams come true!

The biggest possible thank you to Nikki Grimes, my mentor and friend who believed in this book before I wrote a single word of it! Thank you, Nikki, for seeing something in me years ago and guiding me from that moment on—showing me what it really means to be a writer. The in-person critiques, the emails offering suggestions, the writing and life advice—I honestly can't believe I am so lucky to have you in my corner.

Making sure Victoria's story stayed true to the realities of the foster care system wouldn't have been possible without the help of Leigh Esau, Cheryl Alexander, and Molly Blanchette. Thank you so much for answering my foster care questions. I'm also indebted to my foster care fairy godmother, Rhonda Sciortino. Not only did you change my life, Rhonda, when you introduced me to Nikki Grimes years ago, but you've continued to be an inspiration showing me and countless other former foster youth that we can succeed because of what we've been through.

Many thanks to Kay Ellen Armstrong, for not only being my lawyer when I was in foster care and then giving me my first real job in college, but for also continuing to support my writing. Kay, you are awesome! And thank you to Kim Dale, my former Court Appointed Special Advocate, for continuing to be my cheerleader throughout the years as well.

Additionally, I'm thankful for the English and journalism teachers who made me feel my writing ability was special, including but not limited to Richard Scott (7th grade) Jen Willden (8th grade) Karen Kreyeski and Chris Prater (high school), along with Dr. David Ryfe (college). Thank you to every teacher who believed in me. It made all the difference in the world!

So much love and gratitude go to my writing bestie Autumn Krause, who not only gave me thoughtful comments on this book many, many times, but who also came up with the title! Autumn, I love you so much! You are so special to me. Thanks so much, Bethany, for being so kind to set us up! Thank you to my critique partner Kathleen Chappell who has also helped me kick this book into shape time and time again, along with Nicole Green.

Thank you to the friends who have supported my dreams through hours of endless listening to me cry (I mean talk!) about them. Thank you, thank you, thank you: Carolyn Bolton, Katie Watson, Rachel Breithaupt, Laura Maher, Hannah Rael, Holly Cheek, Jason Wilkins, Angel Pacheco, Devlin Durkin, Amy Albano, Michael Tachco, Matt Lewis, Erin DeLullo, Christina Sargeant, Michael Moriatis, Karen Hammond Daniels, Alison Gaulden, Steve Galbreath, Joe Brewer, and so many more! My heartfelt appreciation to Dana DiSalvo, Dr. Sandra Hoffman, and Sharon Reynolds as well.

Special thanks to Kerrin Newberry and Jordan Ecarma for being the initial two people to read my first attempt at a novel and not running in the other direction! Thank you to authors Corie Skolnick and Andrew Klavan for reading some of my early fiction and encouraging me to keep going.

High fives to the Class of 2K19 for all of your support and marketing help, as well as to the Novel Nineteens. It's been a wild ride and I'm glad we could share it together! I also owe a debt to SCBWI; I wouldn't be writing these acknowledgments if not for everything I've learned from the conferences and meet ups.

I'm so thankful for the love and support of my family. My grandma, Maria Del Carmen Almanza, was the first person I can remember who took me to a library, fostering my love of stories. Grandma, you have been the one person who has stuck by me my entire life. I have never, ever doubted you would do anything for me, that you love me that much. You have always been my biggest fan. I am so, so lucky to have you. Thank you, Abuela!

Thank you to my sister Rachelle Grey for being the family member I geek out over YA with, and for knowing what it's like to fall in love with a story.

My mom, Barbara Burton Bushey, is my hero. Mom, though you were my teacher in high school and hardly knew me, you took me in from foster care and adopted David and me. You have loved and supported me when people who share my blood did not. You, along with my sisters and co., have taught me the meaning of family. I hope I make you proud!

I am grateful to the rest of the family for making fun of me and keeping me humble, along with encouraging me, of course! For this, I thank my sisters—Sumer, Raschel, and Sara—and their families. My heartfelt appreciation to Jim for seeing me as a successful careerwoman even when I felt like a failure. Special thanks to my brother-in-law Kevin for all those late-night talks telling me that my writing was important and worth fighting for. Shout out to my nephew Kale for inspiring me with his name!

I also want to thank my other mom, Roxanne Almanza, for making me feel like I was special and helping me believe I could do anything I set my mind to—she called me her little star, and I believed her! Though my mom isn't with us on Earth, she is in our hearts. I want to acknowledge my little brother David, who we lost much too soon, as well. I am still so grateful for the time we did have. Growing up in foster care, we always had each other, and David made sure I knew that. He was my protector. I wish he were here to see this book. I miss him every day.

Thank you to the Kallman/Barthelmess/May clans for all the love and for helping me feel like I truly belonged. Carol, thank you for trying to understand this writing business; even though it doesn't make sense, you still listened to me talk about it a lot! Don, thank you for always bragging about me on social media. DeeDee, thanks for the encouragement and for the rosé all day! Sue and Tom, your family has supported my writing and me in ways I could never have imagined, and I am so, so grateful for you. Hugs to the whole family, including the Gs.

I am the most grateful to my husband, Robby, who has believed in and supported me in heroic ways since day one. Robby, you may laugh at some of my silly habits by calling me a "creative type," but I know it is said with love. To be able to work on *The Quiet You Carry* with your support, even when that meant leaving jobs or losing income, has made the deep emotional work I had to do for this novel possible. Robby, being loved by you has irrevocably changed me for the better. You have my entire heart. And thank you for taking care of our fur baby Corgus when I was on deadline and had less time for him!

And last, but not at all the least, I am thankful to God, who has been with me through every struggle, who has picked me up each time I've fallen or have been kicked down, and who has loved me whole.

ABOUT THE AUTHOR

*N*ikki Barthelmess is a journalist published everywhere from lifestyle blogs to survivalist magazines. She entered foster care in Nevada at twelve and spent the next six years living in six different towns. During this time, Nikki found solace in books, her journal, and the teachers who encouraged her as a writer. A graduate of the University of Nevada, Reno, Nikki lives in Los Angeles with her husband and her pride-and-joy corgi pup. *The Quiet You Carry* is her debut novel.

You can find her on Twitter (@nikkigrey_), Instagram (@nikkibarthelmess), and her website, nikkibarthelmess.com.

RESOURCES

CURRENT AND FORMER FOSTER YOUTH

Court Appointed Special Advocates (CASA) volunteers are appointed by judges to represent a foster child's best interest in court. CASAs do this by getting to know the child or children they are assigned to represent, as well as the people in their lives who are also pertinent to the case (relatives, parents, foster parents, teachers, medical professionals, attorneys, social workers, etc.). CASAs inform judges and other decision makers of what they believe would be the best permanent home for the kids they represent, and what they think the children need in general. For those in foster care, consider requesting an advocate.
www.casaforchildren.org

Foster Care to Success offers tuition assistance, education and job training, as well as other support to college-bound former foster youth.
www.fc2success.org

FosterClub is a peer support network for foster youth that leads the efforts of young people from care as they become educated about their rights and empowered to make positive change.
www.fosterclub.com

Foster Care Alumni of America connects alumni in local chapters to work together, with the aim of improving the lives of current and former foster youth.
fostercarealumni.org

U.S. Department of Health & Human Services aims to enhance and protect the well-being of all Americans though providing health and human services.
www.hhs.gov

DOMESTIC VIOLENCE

The National Domestic Violence Hotline
1-800-799-7233
1-800-787-3224 (TTY)
www.thehotline.org

National Sexual Assault Telephone Hotline
1-800-656-HOPE (4673)
www.rainn.org

SUICIDE

Crisis Text Line
Text HOME to 741741 anytime, from anywhere in the U.S., to talk about any type of crisis.
www.crisistextline.org

National Suicide Prevention Hotline
1-800-273-8255
suicidepreventionlifeline.org

**FOR A TEACHER'S GUIDE TO
THE QUIET YOU CARRY, VISIT
NIKKIBARTHELMESS.COM.**